b

Death Notice

Death Notice

A Pete Brady Mystery

M. S. Karl

St. Martin's Press
New York

Library of Congress Cataloging-in-Publication Data

Karl, M. S.
    Death notice / M.S. Karl.
        p.   cm.
    ISBN 0-312-03811-9
    I. Title.
    PS3561.A6144D4   1990   89-24093
    813'.54—dc20   CIP

First Edition

10   9   8   7   6   5   4   3   2   1

This is for my daughter Summer, with love.

Prologue

THE old man heard the gate shut behind him and stood staring into the darkness. The taxi waited, door open and motor running, and for an instant, the man felt panic at the thought of the long road that would take him through the clay hills and away from three decades of his life, back to a world that was only a memory. The last twenty-nine years had been hell, his own private hell, but it was at least a hell he knew and understood. The routine of rising, working, meals, lock-down, and lights-out; the harsh snores, the screams at odd hours of the night, the random searches: He had adjusted, to the extent that anyone could *ever* adjust to a life that was less than human, and now he was leaving it all behind.

The cabby honked impatiently and the old man lifted his shabby suitcase and slid into the backseat beside the man who was already there.

"I'll take your money now, you don't mind," the driver said. "It ain't exactly my idea of a vacation to deadhead it up to Angola in the middle of the night. Be nice if they'd let you guys out in the daytime."

"You think *that* ain't a vacation, you ought to try *living* there for five years," the first man said, handing over his money. The cabby counted it and waited while the older man produced his share of the fare; but if he was expecting to hear the length of the older man's stay, he was disappointed. Instead, the man turned his face to the window to stare for a last time at the guard shack and hospital building that hid the sprawling prison farm from the road. He was leaving much of himself inside the fence, for twenty-nine years had leached away his vital juices, rendering him a walking automaton. He had come here young and angry and he was leaving old and wasted.

The cab turned around and started forward along the narrow road, and he looked out. It was just after midnight, the time that prisoners were released, and all he could see passing were shadows, but he knew what was out there. On the right, hidden by the trees, was the river, a mile-wide torrent that had drowned more than one escapee, and on the left were the Tunica Hills, a washboard of bluffs and streambeds that wore a man out before he'd gone two miles, leaving him to collapse and wait for the bloodhounds. Ahead stretched twenty miles of winding narrow blacktop, where squint-eyed farmers and prison employees watched every vehicle that passed and reached inside their doors for their shotguns when they saw a stranger.

The first time he had taken this road, he had not noticed the scenery. It had whipped by in a blur of green, his eyes seeing it all but not registering, as he fought to convince himself that it was a dream and that he would wake up and find none of it had really happened; that the guards in the front of the bus, the bars on the windows, the handcuffs and leg irons were all products of his imagination. They were not part of a dream, however, and slowly, day by agonizing day, he had been brutalized and battered into the realization that this was real, this was his life, and any life he had once had outside the sticky-hot cane fields had evaporated like the morning mist.

Yet now, incredibly, he was going back. But to what? There was no way to restore what was lost; no way to recapture the years of his youth; no way to have what other men had enjoyed— a home, family, the smiles of children and grandchildren. He shut his eyes and tried to still the trembling that wanted to take over. *God, why had it all happened?*

When he opened his eyes again, they had reached the main highway. They came to Hardwood and then St. Francisville, silent but for a few cars. Then, minutes later, they passed the nuclear plant and came down across the bridge into East Feliciana Parish.

Baton Rouge. That was the end of the line. Baton Rouge was where he would get off and spend his first hours of freedom; but by noon, he would be traveling again. And this time, he would not stop until he reached home. Then, and only then, would he find out what twenty-nine years had been worth.

Death Notice

1

PETER Brady did not go fishing with murder in mind. He'd had enough of murder in the past few years, first as ace crime reporter for the New Orleans *Times-Picayune,* and then, during the last year, as editor of the Troy Parish *Weekly Express,* when his hope for a tranquil life in the pinewoods of north Louisiana had been shattered by the killing of a prominent citizen. He'd been lucky. He'd managed not only to solve the crime but had come to terms with himself. Now, reeling in slowly from his position in the bow of Emmett's skiff, the only murder he contemplated was that of a particularly wily bass over by the shoreline, one who had already cost him an expensive lure by dragging it under a fallen log.

Emmett Larson, in the stern, popped the top of a beer can, watching the younger man's bait come up out of the water.

"He's playing with you. Might as well give up today," he commented.

Brady stowed his rod under the seat of the boat. He saw the old editor lift the beer to his lips, and then he relaxed. How long had it taken before he could watch someone else drink without feeling pangs of envy? Well, that was behind him now. He raised his own can of ginger ale and sipped. Actually, it had gotten to where it tasted pretty good.

Emmett lifted the stringer and eyed the mess of bass approvingly. "Not bad, if I do say so." He hoisted the fish into the boat and began to secure his line.

Brady looked over at the fallen log. The bass was like some of his news sources, he reflected: a lot of courting, a lot of back and forth. . . . Well, by God, he'd managed to bring most of *them* in and he'd get the bass, too.

"Kelly coming in tonight?" Emmett asked suddenly, pretending to fiddle with his tackle.

"I think so," Brady said, trying not to sound too enthusiastic. He still had trouble accepting the idea that Emmett approved of his relationship with the older man's daughter.

"Girl's got no business on those roads at night," Emmett grumbled. "Three hours to get here from Baton Rouge and every drunk in the state's on those highways on Saturday night."

"She said she had some last-minute work to finish up," Brady explained. "Something about a term project."

"And that's another thing," Emmett declared. "I thought you two were going to get married, she was going to help you get the *Express* back on its feet. But inside of six months, she runs off to Baton Rouge to get a master's degree in journalism at LSU. What kind of sense does that make?"

Brady sighed. He had to admit he had not been entirely in favor of Kelly's decision. "She did help, Emmett. But she felt as if she could contribute more if she got her degree," he said lamely.

Emmett snorted. "People down there at that school don't know how to run a newspaper. All they do is *teach*. And this commuting on weekends." He squinted. "I guess she's going to stay at your place?"

Brady swallowed. "Well . . ."

"It's okay. Not my business. Nobody else's, either. Even in Troy, things've changed in the last ten years." He shook his head again. "But I want you to talk sense to her, all right?"

Brady nodded. How could he explain about Kelly's innate independence? About the need to sort things out after she'd returned from the north and a failed marriage last year and things between them had moved so swiftly? "I'll do what I can," he mumbled.

Emmett grunted and started the motor. He guided them through a maze of cypress stumps to the mud landing and together they hauled the aluminum boat up onto the shore and hoisted it onto Emmett's trailer.

The two men got into the battered pickup and Emmett started them forward over the rough dirt road to the highway. It was late afternoon and the June shadows had already begun to lengthen, and the first mosquitoes were venturing out from the fetid puddles beside the trail.

Emmett drove without speaking and Brady lapsed into his own reverie, excited at the thought that even now Kelly was probably on her way. He closed his eyes and did not open them again until the squeal of the brakes and Emmett's oath slammed him awake and he realized they were back in Troy.

It was the same Troy—narrow, little streets, train track through the center of town, new courthouse slumbering in the golden evening, and yet something, indefinably, had changed.

He looked from Emmett, frozen behind the wheel, to the people on the sidewalk and then back to Emmett again.

"Emmett, what's wrong? What happened?"

The old editor licked his lips and then eased his foot up off the brakes, a glassy look in his eyes. Brady glanced back through the outside mirror; a couple of people on the sidewalk were staring, not at the truck but at something on the courthouse lawn. However, when Brady looked, all he saw was an old man sitting on a bench in the sun.

The truck turned the corner and two blocks later pulled up in front of the wooden frame house where Emmett lived.

"Emmett . . ." Brady began, but the other shook his head, as if to discourage a fly. Then he slowly opened the door, got out, and walked around to the boat. He found his ice chest, reached inside, and took out a beer.

"Holy Christ," he muttered. "It's true. I never thought it would happen, but it did." He swallowed half the can in one gulp and wiped his mouth with his arm.

"What are you talking about?" Brady demanded. "What's going on?"

Emmett downed the rest of the can and crumpled it in his fingers. "Back there," he growled. "In front of the courthouse, big as life."

Brady waited and Emmett shook his head again. "After nearly thirty years, they let him go. He's back. *Cory Wilde is back!*"

3

* * *

Brady sat alone in his living room, a Pete Fountain record on the turntable. In a few minutes, he would put the bass in to bake and after that, he would toss the salad. But the anticipation of Kelly's imminent arrival had been dulled by Emmett's strange reaction. The older man had refused his offer to help unload the boat and had gone inside with hardly another word, leaving Brady to drive home with the stringer of fish. Brady had cleaned the bass at once, using the time to try to make sense of Emmett's reaction.

Cory Wilde. Where had he heard that name? Of course. Cory Wilde was the man against whom the town had signed a petition; the convict who was appearing before the parole board. He had killed someone in Troy almost thirty years before and had been in Angola ever since. Weeks ago, when his name had been proposed for release, Judge Honeycutt had gathered signatures to send to Baton Rouge, and Sheriff Matt Garitty had gone to the parole hearing to present the town's views. Unexpectedly, the parole had been granted, and Brady had run a short item about it in the last issue of the *Express;* but, whatever the resentment felt by the townspeople, no one had ever expected to see him back here. Yet, whatever had happened had happened nearly three decades ago. Cory Wilde must be an old man now. Why should he strike such fear into Emmett Larson, and cause gaping among the people in the street? Well, there might be a human-interest angle there somewhere, and, since the murder was almost thirty years in the past, there was no danger of getting involved in a current investigation, which was something Brady had forsworn after Kelly had nearly lost her life last year and half the town had quit speaking to him for exposing a particularly loved member of the community as a murderer.

His thoughts were interrupted by the harsh sound of the telephone and he roused himself to answer it.

"Brady?" It was Kelly's voice, and he went on immediate alert.

"Kelly, are you all right? Where are you?"

"I'm fine, silly. But I'm still in Baton Rouge. I wanted to tell you I can't get away."

4

"Oh." He felt all the excitement leak out of him like air from a punctured balloon. "You mean you won't be coming."

"I can't. I have this damned thing due *Monday.* And I still have twenty pages to go. Please don't hate me."

"No, of course not." Inwardly, he cursed the summer session with its rigid schedules and demands. A hundred and sixty miles. It might as well be the moon!

"Brady, are you all right?"

He cleared his throat. "Yeah. Sure. You do your project and finish things up. Maybe I can run down next weekend."

"That would be great. I'm meeting some super people. There's a Jeff Baxley, who teaches one of my classes. He says he knows you."

"Baxley? Sure." A picture of Baxley's perfectly coiffured blond hair and sky-blue eyes came to mind and Brady bit his tongue to keep from saying anything. The bastard probably worked out with weights. He started to tell her that her professor had been bounced from the Shreveport *Times* before an undiscriminating faculty had picked him up, but he decided against it. "Good old Baxley," he said.

"Is anything happening in Ye Old Towne?" Kelly asked lightheartedly. "Pop's fine?"

"Yeah. Everybody's just fine." He hesitated and then took the plunge: "By the way, you ever heard of a man named Cory Wilde?"

There was a momentary hesitation. "Cory Wilde, Cory Wilde. Where have I heard that name?"

"How about *parole,* as in parole board?"

"Oh, sure. Now I remember. Dad mentioned him, I think. It was a famous murder case. Before I was born."

"But not before *I* was," Brady muttered sardonically.

"So what about him?" Kelly asked.

"Nothing, except he's back."

"Back? You mean in *Troy?*"

"That's right. And a lot of people seem pretty surprised."

"Sure. Dad said he was a pretty bad character. But he must be old by now."

"Not too old to stop cars."

5

"Well, Brady, it sounds like a story to me."

"I was afraid you'd say that." He shifted the phone from one shoulder to the other. "Look, do me a favor, as long as you're going to be spending all that time down there. Check with the local paper and the parole board and see if you can find out why they went against the locals and let Cory Wilde out. And then find why in the hell they'd allow him to come back to the place where the crime was committed. That's just about unheard of."

"Done. Anything else?"

"Yeah. Finish that damned project and get back up here. That's a message from your father, but it comes from me, too."

"You aren't jealous again, are you?"

"No, it's a little more biological than that."

"I know," she purred. "Me, too. Well, hold off. It'll be all the better."

"Sure."

When he'd hung up the phone, he wandered into the kitchen and then realized he was no longer hungry. He put the fish into the freezer and went back to the living room. For once, jazz music did nothing for him. He needed an outlet for the energy he'd stored up waiting for Kelly. With a sigh, he turned off the stereo, locked his door, and walked up the street to the newspaper office.

It took him half an hour of rummaging through the dusty files that served as the newspaper morgue, but finally he found it. And as he read it, his stomach turned.

How the hell could they *ever* have released Cory Wilde?

2

LOCAL GIRL VANISHES, screamed the headline. For the third time, Brady ran his eyes over the front-page story for June 4, 1959.

The facts seemed simple enough: On Saturday, May 30, at seven-thirty P.M., fifteen-year-old Alice Ann Potter had been picked up at her home by her girlfriend and two boys. The foursome had been seen at the Dairy Queen by a number of other teenagers and everything seemed normal. After a soda, they and several other carloads of young people had headed for the drive-in theater on Highway 84. At some point in the double feature, Alice Ann had gotten into an argument with her date, a sixteen-year-old named Bosley Cox, over comments he made about the rock idol starring in the movie. Alice Ann had left the car, slamming the door loudly enough to attract the attention of the occupants of the vehicle beside them. The ticket salesman had seen her walk out the gate. Since it was less than half a mile to the center of town and she seemed in possession of her faculties, he thought little of it. Somewhere on that half-mile stretch, however, Alice Ann Potter had disappeared.

A full-scale search had been mounted, using inmates from the parish prison to comb the ditches and the byways, and Sheriff Thomas had sent fliers to the neighboring parishes. The Cox boy had been questioned several times, but since he could account for his whereabouts for the rest of the night and over the next day, he was released.

7

Brady sighed and put aside the brittle newspaper, already knowing what he would find in the next issue.

GIRL FOUND MURDERED, read the banner. Once more, the facts seemed straightforward. An anonymous phone call had directed the searchers toward a small parcel of private land adjoining the national forest. Bloodhounds had been brought in and within two hours, the girl's body had been found in a shallow grave. A medical examination showed she had been raped and strangled. Local authorities would say nothing more at this point than that they were pursuing certain leads, but a side-bar editorial by Emmett Larson deplored the crime and hinted that the local authorities had someone in mind.

It was the following week's issue that announced the arrest of Cory Wilde.

ARREST IN MURDER, the headlines cried. This time, Brady read the story word for word, to be sure he missed nothing:

> Parish authorities yesterday announced the arrest of Cory Wilde, a resident of Ward Five, for the murder of Alice Ann Potter. Wilde, thirty-one, was arrested by Sheriff Alva Thomas on a warrant issued by Judge Troy on the basis of an eyewitness report. Wilde was taken to the parish prison under heavy guard. This newspaper has learned that Wilde's wife was out of town visiting relatives in Winn Parish the night the crime allegedly occurred. Readers will remember that it was on Wilde's land that the body was discovered last week. It is to be hoped that with this arrest, this terrible tragedy can be put to rest.

Brady stuck the yellowed pages back in the folder, reflecting on Emmett's tendency to editorialize. It was common practice on small-town weeklies, and he wondered whether perhaps he didn't bore people with his own spare, big-city style.

He replaced the folders in the file, started to close the drawer, and then stopped. Something was bothering him and all at once he realized what it was: It was not so much the fact that Cory Wilde was free and in Troy, but that he was still *alive*. In 1959, the criminal code had mandated the death penalty not only for first-degree murder but also for aggravated rape. Curious, Brady pulled open the next file drawer and skimmed through the folders until he saw a headline on the case: WILDE CONVICTED.

He withdrew the issue and moved from the dim morgue back to his desk in the big room that served as the main office.

A local jury convicted Cory Wilde of second-degree murder in the death of fifteen-year-old Alice Ann Potter. Wilde will be sentenced on August 24.

And that, surprisingly, was all. Then Brady's eyes touched the side-bar editorial and he saw that Emmett Larson had had a great deal more to say.

SAD MISCARRIAGE, the bold print pronounced, and underneath, an angry Emmett had demonstrated the acerbic style that had left the newspaper almost readerless by the time Brady had bought him out.

A learned jury of gallipots and embalmers, led by a specialist in the tonsorial art, and confused by an inept and incompetent prosecutor, have given a clear message to evildoers in Troy Parish. And the message is this: The life of a young girl is not worth the life of an adult, even when the young girl has suffered the cruelest barbarities imaginable by the mind of demented men. The last person to be executed in this parish was Cornelius Green, a Negro who had raped a white woman, and yet even Cornelius Green, in his perverted cruelty, saw fit to allow his victim to live. It can only be hoped that at the next election, voters will remember District Attorney Honeycutt's pusilanimous presentation of this case and will replace him with someone not afraid to exact society's full measure of retribution on the lawless.

Honeycutt. Arden Honeycutt. Of course. It had to be. Brady smiled grimly, going back to get the next week's issue. The voters had evidently not heeded Emmett's advice. Arden Honeycutt was now district judge and had been for some years.

KILLER METED LIFE TERM, read the heading.

Judge Creswell Troy on Monday sentenced convicted killer Cory Wilde to a life term in the Louisiana State Penitentiary at Angola. Asked if he had anything to say, the adjudged murderer screamed threats against everyone connected with his conviction, including this newspaper. Though Wilde escaped death in the electric chair through a conviction for murder in the second degree, it may at least afford the citizenry some satisfaction to know that he will spend the remainder of his natural life at hard labor in a place that, according to what this newspaper understands, may be as bad as that region to which he might have been expected to go had society exacted the ultimate penalty.

So Wilde had made threats. That accounted for Emmett's reaction. It seemed strange that the old publisher would recognize someone after almost thirty years, but, then, Cory Wilde's parole application had put him in everyone's mind; had stirred up a lingering sense of unease; and had led a concerned citizenry to oppose his release.

And yet he *had* been released. And not only had he returned to Troy but he had been sitting on a bench on the courthouse lawn in broad daylight of a Saturday afternoon, as if defying the town to do anything about it.

No wonder people had stared.

Brady put the ancient newspaper back in the cabinet, closed the office, and started home, a sense of foreboding hovering over him like a cloud. It was a hot night, distant lightning flickering on the horizon; maybe a night like the one on which Alice Ann Potter had been murdered.

Without thinking, he found himself on the highway, where a thin stream of cars came and went to and from the center of town. One passed him with loud pipes thundering and he caught a fragment of rock music and laughter.

In 1959, the songs had been different, cars had fins, and drugs had not yet made their ugly way onto the scene. Had things really changed that much? He passed the Dairy Queen, where a clutch of cars filled the available spaces. There were still only so many places to go in a town the size of Troy, he thought: one of the fast-food establishments; parking on some lonely road; the movies. . . .

He kept walking, looking away as the headlights of oncoming traffic struck his face. It was early yet, just dark at nine o'clock. In 1959, it would have been eight, though—no daylight saving. He came to the crossroads, where two highways split. At the intersection was an all-night convenience store, its gas pumps a garish yellow in the bright lights. A car had pulled up at one of the islands and a man was filling his tank.

The establishment was new; in Alice Ann's time, there would have been a boy in grease-streaked overalls to pump the gas. Score another one for change, he told himself, taking the left fork. This road was quieter, leading east, toward Jonesville. He passed the motel, where a scatter of cars on the gravel proclaimed the presence of a few timber prospectors and landsmen for oil companies.

Suddenly, Brady stopped. The motel. Was that where Cory Wilde was staying? But surely with sentiment so high, they wouldn't give him a room. He started to go in, ask the desk clerk a few questions, but restrained himself. There was no sense stirring things up. There were other ways to find out.

He kept going, the darkness deepening as he left the town behind. Now the ozone smell of the pinewoods was all around him and a faint breeze ruffled the grass beside the road, but even the breeze was not enough to dispel the heat that seemed to hang over everything.

Then, ahead of him, he saw it, a white blur jutting up on the left side of the road, like a cliff in a dark ocean. As he drew closer, the shape came into focus: It was an outdoor motion-picture screen, its white surface hanging in strips, like skin peeling from some prehistoric creature. The board fence gaped with holes, like an almost toothless mouth, and the concession shack was dark. He walked onto the gravel and through the gate, to stand in the empty parking area. Pale moonlight painted the arena a gauzy white, the abandoned speaker terminals thrusting up like so many periscopes from a quiet sea.

For a moment, Brady closed his eyes, remembering other drive-ins from his youth—the high school dates, the girls from West Jefferson High, in Metairie, and, later, a Newcomb girl who insisted on scary movies as an accompaniment to making love.

11

What about Alice Ann? he wondered. Did she have some similar neurosis, or was her leaving the car the adolescent fit of pique that it appeared? He tried to imagine the deserted lot filled with cars, a ten-foot-tall drama acting itself out upon the screen.

She had closed the car door loudly enough for the people in the next space to hear, and had marched out across the gravel and through the gate to the highway. Brady turned to trace her imagined path with his eyes and followed it, as if he were walking behind her ghostly image.

She had gone up the lonely highway, probably walking quickly, in anger. Had she expected to hear the sound of tires on gravel, proof that the others were coming after her to pick her up? No matter: It was 1959, Troy was a quiet town, and girls were not kidnapped from main highways within shouting distance of the city limits.

Except that Alice Ann was. Somewhere along this very stretch, a vehicle had pulled over and Cory Wilde had pulled her inside. Or had he just opened the door, called her name, and offered her a ride?

Had she gone willingly? Had she accepted so that when the others came after her, as she hoped they would, they would find her gone and would worry?

He passed the corporate-limits sign and saw the first house, on the right. It had been fairly early. Lights would have been on. People in the houses, watching their black and white TVs, would have heard screams. Or would they? Cars and heavily loaded lumber trucks roared down the highway at all hours, their brakes squealing. Cars filled with teenagers screamed past, the occupants yelling and laughing. His foot kicked something and he looked down. It was an empty liquor bottle. Troy was dry, and had been then, but there was always a way to get the stuff. Had Cory Wilde been drunk that night, and lonely because his wife was away?

Brady went home, ate a bacon sandwich, and went to bed, but he did not sleep well. Throughout his dreams, he kept seeing a lonely road and a young girl walking, and when she turned around to look into the glare of approaching headlights, she always had the face of Kelly Maguire.

12

3

THE next day, shortly after noon, when he guessed the family would be home from church, he called his friend Matt Garitty. It was Mitzi, the sheriff's petite vivacious wife, who answered the phone.

"He's in the backyard, cooking burgers," she said. "Why don't you come over and bring Kelly with you."

"Kelly didn't make it this weekend," Brady explained, trying to hide the chagrin.

"Then you can eat hers," Mitzi proclaimed. "You've been looking a little skinny lately, anyway."

After only a single polite demur, which she easily overruled, Brady thanked her and drove over. It was one of the newer subdivisions, backed up against the pine forest, with spacious lawns and modernistic houses that mimicked Swiss chalets. As he opened his door in the driveway, he smelled the pungent scent of hickory smoke from the backyard. Mitzi appeared at the side of the house, a red bandanna around her blond hair, and embraced him. "The great chef is in the back, imparting his secrets to the next generation."

Brady followed her into the backyard, where clouds of blue-gray smoke welled up from a brick barbecue, almost hiding the figures of the man and boy on the other side. He heard a mumbled oath and then the popping sounds of water being sprinkled on the fire as another cloud billowed up from the grate like an offering to heaven.

"Are you sure it isn't the Wizard of Oz?" Brady asked in a voice loud enough for his host to hear.

Matt Garitty stepped out from behind the pit, his forehead peppered with droplets of sweat. His eleven-year-old son, Scotty, ran to Brady, pointing at the grill. "Dad's teaching me to barbecue, but the fire got too hot."

"A mere technical difficulty," the sheriff declared, wiping a hand on his jeans and then offering it to Brady. The lawman was big, with a country air that provided instant rapport with his constituents, but Brady had learned that the rustic manner hid an astute mind.

Brady was handed a ginger ale by a smiling Mitzi, whom he knew must have gone out to the convenience store immediately after he'd called. They exchanged pleasantries and he watched Garitty pronounce the beef patties done. Mitzi and Scott went into the house for the relishes and the sheriff turned to the editor.

"So what really brings you over besides my award-winning barbecue sauce? No. Let me see if I can guess: How about Cory Wilde?"

"Bingo," said Brady. "You must be clairvoyant."

"Yup. And blind, too, if I couldn't see the bastard sitting on the bench on the courthouse lawn all yesterday afternoon. He wasn't there five minutes before I started getting calls." He shrugged. "Well, what was I supposed to do? He wasn't breaking any law. The courthouse lawn is public property. And it really isn't my jurisdiction."

"Three good reasons, I'd agree," Brady said as Mitzi and the younger Garitty reappeared.

"It's not like I don't have enough to do with regular business," the sheriff declared, waiting for the others to fix their hamburgers. "Three country stores broken into in the past three weeks and Boy Jenks is driving around in a brand-new Ford pickup truck."

"Boy Jenks?"

"The leader of the Jenks clan," Mitzi said wryly. "They live out near Lairdsburg. Not exactly the parish's finest."

"You think he's involved, then?" Brady asked, biting into his burger.

Garitty chuckled and held up a hand. "Nothing is for publication, okay? All I said was the man has a new pickup and he never had more than two one-dollar bills to rub together before in

14

his life, and one of *them* was probably counterfeit. There are lots of people who think I ought to be looking in his direction, namely our esteemed police chief, Ned Triplett, who's still smarting since I beat him out in the election last year."

"He's not too happy with me, either," Brady mused. "I think the endorsement stung."

The sheriff laughed. "I'm sure it did. And I have to admit, if it hadn't been for you, I might not have pulled it off. I don't think the law-abiding good folk around here would have wanted a sheriff who couldn't solve the murders of some of the town's most prominent citizens, even if they weren't the best-liked people." Garitty sipped at a Pepsi. "But people's memories are short. Right now, all they want is to find out who's hitting these groceries and Ned's making sure the heat stays on. So if anybody comes around asking why an ex-convict is sitting on the courthouse bench, I'm just going to have to let that be *his* problem."

"You can see how reelection affected him," Mitzi teased. "He just doesn't care anymore."

"I can tell," Brady said, smiling. "But I thought I might at least get some particulars about the case and why the man is out. I understand there was public sentiment against his parole. Doesn't the governor usually take that into account?"

"The governor doesn't sign paroles, as you know. Not that he can't twist arms, since the board members are appointed," the sheriff said. "But why should he worry in *any* case? This governor has over three years left for everybody to forget about it. And the judge was the one who spearheaded the protest. You may remember that he wasn't exactly on the governor's campaign committee. In fact, I don't think the gov got more than twenty percent of the vote in this parish."

"But Pete's right," Mitzi said. "It still doesn't make sense. If Wilde was a bank robber or burglar . . . but somebody who killed a fifteen-year-old girl? In this case he *should* have twisted some arms. And to have let him come back here, to this parish . . ."

"I have a letter from the governor in my desk," her husband drawled. "It came Friday, one day ahead of Cory Wilde. I believe the rationale was that the prisons are overcrowded; that the crime had been second-degree; and that everybody from the warden to the prison cook had recommended Cory Wilde as a model prisoner. He also cited something about the recidivism rate for murderers being less than that for many other types of criminals. As for Cory's coming back here, I've got to admit it's pretty unusual. I called the parole people and the best I can make of it is that there was a slip-up and the usual stipulation just wasn't added somehow, because they didn't think he'd have the gall. Chairman of the parole board's out of town, so what can you do? I called the governor and *he*'s at a convention in California."

"Well, *I*'m not going to vote for him next time," Mitzi declared. "A fifteen-year-old girl . . ."

"You didn't vote for him *last* time," Garitty said. "As far as the crime itself, Pete, well, I was only about eleven years old at the time. All I remember was trying to squeeze into the courtroom during the trial and having old man McGraw, the bailiff, throw me out. Said there were things a young boy didn't need to hear."

"And he was probably right," Mitzi put in primly, rising to make another hamburger for Scott, who was tiring of the conversation.

"But you must have reviewed the files in connection with the parole application," Brady persisted.

"I looked them over. But in twenty-nine years, a lot of things change. Cory's wife died a year after he went to Angola. Half the jurors, including the foreman, are dead. The man who defended Cory Wilde is dead. Sheriff Thomas is dead. Old Judge Troy is dead."

"But former District Attorney Arden Honeycutt is very much alive."

"True enough."

"Does it strike you as strange that the jury only went for second-degree?"

"Without reading the transcripts, all I can say is that stranger things happen every day. Who the hell can predict a jury?"

"I would have thought some people would have considered it evidence of Honeycutt's incompetence."

"I'm sure some of them did. But you know how things are. The next big case probably wiped it all out. And, after all, they *did* put Cory away for what was supposed to be a life term."

16

"After he'd threatened everybody connected with the business."

"Well, there's no denying some people remember that. But he's an old man. And a model prisoner. And until he starts making more threats, there's not a damned thing anybody can do."

"How about another hamburger, Pete?" offered Mitzi.

"How could I resist?" He watched her prepare a bun. "Oh, Matt, just one other thing, and then we can talk baseball."

Garitty leaned back, grinning. "Now we get to the knockout punch. And I know what it's going to be. But shoot."

Brady shook his head. "You're ahead of me every step. All I wanted to know was where a man without any friends stays in a town this size."

Garitty laughed. "I knew it. Well, I asked myself the same question yesterday after I started getting the calls during the ball game."

"And?"

"Seems like he's rented a house over on Elm, not far from where *you* live. Found a nice spinster lady who doesn't care what people think."

"A spinster lady?" Little alarms went off in Brady's head.

"The same." Garitty smiled. "Penelope Martingale. I think you did a little feature on her a couple of months ago? Something about the town's resident psychic?"

"Oh, Jesus," Brady said.

"Do you want onions?" Mitzi asked sweetly.

When the ball game was over, the Atlanta Braves having pounded a hapless San Diego team into submission, Brady left a satisfied Matt Garitty and headed home. Somewhere along the way, however, his nagging curiosity got the better of him and he took a street that led away from town and into the country. After a half mile, the street became a potholed road and lawns gave way to pastures. Here and there, lonely mailboxes proclaimed a farmhouse set well back from the highway. In another mile, the El road, as it was called, made a sudden turn left, connecting with the main north-south highway, but half a mile before that, Brady slowed for a familiar mailbox painted a garish shade of purple and swathed in a garland of holly leaves.

He slowed, intending only to drive past, when he saw the figure in the driveway, hands on hips, staring at him. From the pink silk blouse to the blue flowing gypsy skirt, it was classic Penelope, and he applied his brakes, regretting his urge to drive out this way. He pulled into the driveway and stopped. Penelope smiled like an indulgent parent who had just caught her child at the cookie jar, and watched him get out. In her mid-forties, she was tall and well proportioned, with graying braids under a red bandanna, and lively blue eyes.

"I hope you didn't intend to drive past," she said as he approached. "That would have been an unforgivable breach of friendship."

"Penelope, how could I do such a thing?" Brady asked, taking her hand.

"Easily," she said. "I know you. Better in some ways than you do yourself. I knew you were coming, for example. That's why I was outside waiting. And yet I'll bet you didn't know yourself that you'd end up here, now did you? Confess: It was a sudden whim, an urge. Most people aren't in touch enough to know that such a thing has meaning on the spiritual level. I had hopes for you, Peter, when you first came here. Your aura was dim, but there was an essential energy there. You were thwarted in your spiritual growth, guilty about the murder of that man in New Orleans, your informant for that story that won you the Pulitzer Prize. And alcohol hadn't done you any good. But after you met Kelly, your aura began to glow again. Now, though . . ." She shook her head. "I think you're letting your left brain stifle your better impulses." Suddenly, her eyes darted to the weeds beside the driveway and she strode forward, ignoring her visitor.

"Chester? So there you are. I've been looking all over for you. You bad boy." She stooped and came up with a half-grown brindled cat. "This is Chester. Chester Arthur. He's the reincarnation of the late president, you know. That's why I try to keep him inside, because I'd hate for him to get mashed in the road, but he ran right past me a few minutes ago. Of course, I can't *punish* him. I mean, you don't *do* that with a president. You can only *impeach* them. But I certainly can show my displeasure. You bad kitty." She bore the gangly feline in, Brady following down the drive and up the steps of the frame house.

She opened the screen door, released the cat, and closed the door behind Brady. The room in which he found himself had not changed since he'd done his article a few months before: A huge Persian rug covered the board floor, while on one wall hung an astrological chart. One end of the room, with windows on three sides, had been converted into a miniature greenhouse, with all manner of plants overflowing from hanging baskets and flowerpots. A Ouija board rested on the coffee table, beside Shirley MacLaine's latest offering, but there was another item—a piece of paper—that Penelope hastily gathered up and thrust away into the folds of her blouse, though not before Brady had had a chance to see that it was a computer printout. She obviously thought it inconsistent with the image she sought to convey.

"So what brings you this way after such an unpardonable lapse?" Penelope asked, sweeping her skirt from under her and taking a seat in an ancient stuffed chair. She closed her eyes and put a hand to her face. "No. Wait. I already know." She lowered her hand. "But first I need to fix you some herbal tea. Your aura's flickering a little. I have a feeling you're getting sick."

"Penelope . . ." But he recognized the protest was in vain and five minutes later, she was placing a steaming cup of unidentified liquid before him.

"Drink that before it gets cold," Penelope ordered. "It won't drain out the poisons if you wait."

Brady obediently lifted the cup and tentatively sipped the contents. The concoction was not bad, he had to admit, a trifle minty with an astringent aftertaste.

"Finish the cup," Penelope ordered.

"Thank you."

"Now," she declared, "about Cory Wilde."

Brady smiled. "All right, Penelope, I'm impressed and amazed."

"No, you're not. Your left brain is telling you that I knew that there was only one reason for you to come out here, admit it."

"Guilty."

She shook her head in mock disgust. "You see? You'll never

19

achieve your full spiritual potential until you abandon that kind of thinking and start to accept the promptings of your spirit guardians."

"What can I say? But, whatever the case, you're right: I'm here about Cory Wilde. Though I'm not sure why. I should have known you'd rent him a place to stay."

"You mean because I'm the only person in town crazy enough to do it. That's all right, I'm not offended, Peter. I know what people in town think about me. Your piece in the paper was about the only time in the last twenty years that anybody's ever treated me seriously, like a human being. And yet, admit it, even you consider me pretty weird."

"Different, certainly," Brady equivocated.

"How tactful. But you don't have to be." She sighed and stretched her long arms out in front of her, the gold jewelry flashing in the dim light from the hanging lamp overhead. "I've sometimes wished I could *be* like the rest of them. Two cars, a dog, a husband, two point three children, church on Sunday, PTA during the week. But what the hell? I *can't*." She opened her hands, palms up, almost as if supplicating. "I haven't been able to contemplate a normal life since I had my first visitation, when I was just graduated from high school. Without it, I might have married . . ." She chuckled. "Thank God I didn't. Poor man." She stared up at the ceiling, her expression wistful. "I often wonder why the spirits chose me."

"Who else is so charming and yet has such a hard head for business?"

Penelope shook her head sadly and removed the printout from her bodice. "It's no good to try to hide anything from you, you scoundrel. Well, the spirits can't do *everything*. They can only provide a direction, a strategy as to when to buy and sell. But they certainly don't lower themselves to the mundane business of account keeping."

It was Brady's turn to smile; he was one of the few people who had seen the desktop computer and printer in the converted bedroom off the hall.

"So was renting to Cory Wilde just a matter of dollars and cents?" he asked.

"Well, of course, you know it would be highly unethical for

20

me to discuss my relationship with a business client, especially since you *are* in the business of publishing, but I think I can say that my decision to rent to Mr. Wilde was the result of the same process as exists in most of my decision making."

"In English, Penelope."

She brushed her hair with a hand. "Meaning, No-Do-Tah-Wah told me that it was a good thing to do."

"Your spirit guide."

"Yes."

"And did he say why?"

"No-Do-Tah-Wah does not always give his reasons, but I have learned never to disregard his advice."

"Does No-Do-Tah-Wah harbor resentments against the people in Troy Parish?"

"He regards them as hypocrites and fools, with a few notable exceptions . . ." She leaned over to pat the editor's arm. "Shallow for the most part, and materialistic to a disgusting degree. Not to mention racially bigoted. He does not forget that their ancestors are the ones who wiped out his people. He died of measles brought in by white men, you know. But *resentment?* No-Do-Tah-Wah exists on a far higher plane than that."

"I'm very glad to hear it," Brady said laconically. "I thought it might just be an attempt to get back at them and stir them up a little for the way they'd treated you."

"How vulgar." She shook her head. "No, Peter, I did it for the same reason I do most things: I felt it was right, and this was confirmed by a Higher Authority. Besides, why should anyone care? The man has paid for his crime."

"Some people think he hasn't paid enough."

"That's because they have no concept of reincarnation. But he didn't strike me as a bad person."

Brady finished his tea and rose. "Well. It's getting on toward evening. If your spirit guide comes up with anything, let me know."

"You're being facetious, Peter." She walked with him to the door. "If you start feeling worse, come back and I'll give you some herbal medicine. Promise."

"Promise," Brady said, crossing his fingers behind his back.

It was six when he reached home. He pulled out a TV dinner, but even before he had finished, his eyes wanted to close. He dragged himself to bed and slept dreamlessly.

The next morning he awoke with a sore throat and a runny nose. He defrosted some waffle squares and had two cups of coffee, but nothing tasted right. He was already half an hour late when the jangling of his phone made him mutter an oath.

"Mr. Brady?" It was the voice of Mrs. Rickenbacker, the bookkeeper, and, as usual, she was flustered. "Mr. Brady, you have to come right now."

Brady sniffed and cleared his throat. "I was on my way out," he said resignedly. "I assume the building isn't on fire."

"Mr. Brady, please hurry."

He hung up and went out to his car, not feeling like a morning walk today. Sometimes—quite often, in fact—he regretted keeping Mrs. Rickenbacker on. Every deviation from normal was a crisis and she managed to absent herself at the most inconvenient times; But he had inherited her from Emmett and she seemed to be a part of the place.

He parked in the tiny lot in front of the one-story brick building and went in through the doorway, closing the glass door behind him. What he saw was a Mrs. Rickenbacker petrified by terror.

It took him only half an instant to grasp that the cause of her alarm was the man standing before her desk, an envelope in his hand.

"Mr. Brady, oh, thank the Lord. This is something you should . . . I mean, I'm just the bookkeeper, like I tried to explain . . ." Her explanations seemed as much directed at the man in front of her as at her employer, and Brady turned his attention to the man with the envelope.

There was, at least on the surface, nothing remarkable about him. Perhaps sixty, he wore a pair of dark slacks, a short-sleeved checkered shirt, and his shoes were polished to a high gloss. He was thin, about medium height, and his back was slightly bowed. All in all, he seemed an unlikely source for Mrs. Rickenbacker's terror.

"All right," Brady said wearily, coming around the desk.

"I'll handle it." In all likelihood, he told himself as the grateful bookkeeper scurried away to her desk in the corner, the man was complaining because a name had been spelled wrong or an advertisement had been garbled. Then he looked up into the visitor's eyes and something in him sounded a warning.

Behind the rimless bifocals, the man's gray eyes were dead.

"What can I do for you?" Brady asked, pointing to a chair on the other side of the desk and taking a seat himself. "Is there some kind of problem?"

"Not that I know of," the man rasped in a near whisper. Then he handed the envelope across the desk to the editor and when he spoke again, his voice was almost too soft for Brady to hear.

"My name is Cory Wilde and I want to run a notice."

4

BRADY stared up into the dead eyes, trying not to let his surprise show. He reached out slowly, took the envelope, and removed the contents. It was a single sheet of lined notebook paper and printed in large letters was a simple message:

CORY WILDE WISHES TO ANNOUNCE HIS RETURN AND THAT HE WILL BE LIVING AT 623 ELM, TROY, LOUISIANA.

Below it, signed neatly, was the name CORY WILDE.

Nonplussed, Brady looked from the paper to the man in front of him and then back at the paper.

"Is this all?"

"Should there be more?" Wilde asked in the same near whisper.

The editor breathed out, aware of his bookkeeper's eyes on him from her corner desk.

"Mr. Wilde, it's none of my business, but I have the feeling everybody already knows you're back."

"Will you print it?" the old man asked. He reached into his pocket and withdrew some bills. "I can pay."

"I'm not questioning that. I'm just wondering about the purpose."

Cory Wilde's lips twitched in a smile. "Let's just say I want to make it official." He leaned forward. "You do *print* announcements, don't you?"

"We print 'em," Brady said, capitulating. He reached for the pad and copied the message word for word. "Read it over and sign at the bottom if I've got it right." He swiveled in his chair. "Mrs. Rickenbacker, write Mr. Wilde a receipt for ten dollars, please."

The old man read slowly, his lips moving, and then nodded in satisfaction. He picked up the pen and traced his name, then counted out a five-dollar bill and five ones. Mrs. Rickenbacker, disapproval stamped on her features, scribbled a receipt and pointedly handed it to Brady, doing her best to ignore the other man.

"Here's your receipt," Brady said. "The announcement will run in the next issue."

Wilde dipped his head in acknowledgment. "I'm obliged," he rasped, then turned and walked out.

Mrs. Rickenbacker made a great stir rustling papers and Brady turned to face her.

"All right, Mrs. R., so you don't approve. But what was I supposed to do? This *is* the official journal of the parish. As long as something isn't libelous, obscene, or threatening, I feel a certain obligation to run it. What are we supposed to do, just carry the announcements of people we approve of? That would severely limit our political reporting."

"It's not my place to question you," the bookkeeper said primly, turning back to her books. "But a lot of people are going to be upset."

"I'm sure they are, Mrs. R." Brady placed the ten dollars in the cash box and rose. "Now, if you don't mind, I think I'll go over to the drugstore and get some medicine for this cold."

He went up the street, along the courthouse square, but the bench was empty. Crawling slowly down the street, though, its chrome trimmings reflecting the morning sunlight, was a new gray pickup with red trim, a rebel-flag plate on the front bumper and a whip antenna vibrating in the warm morning air. The driver, a grizzled man in his fifties, glared out at Brady from behind aviator glasses as Brady crossed in front of him, and then he gunned the engine ominously. Brady stopped on the opposite sidewalk, in front of the drugstore, and turned around, but the pickup was halfway down the street.

"Old man Jenks," a voice said from behind him. Sam Berry, the young pharmacist, was holding the door open, shaking his head, a good-natured smile on his boyish face. "Don't let him scare you, Mr. Brady, he's all bluff. Ten to one, the dealer'll repossess that truck inside of two months. If Jenks hasn't wrecked it first."

Brady returned the smile and went inside, grateful for the air conditioning. Sam slid behind the counter, his white coat flapping open.

"Now what can I do for you?"

"My throat," Brady said, touching his neck. "And I need something to dry me out without putting me to sleep."

Sam nodded, his face grave. "It's going around," he opined, reaching for a popular cold remedy. "Try this. Lots of people say it works for them."

Brady nodded his thanks. "I'll give it a shot." He reached for his wallet as Sam put the purchase in a paper bag.

"By the way," Sam asked. "What do you think about the Cory Wilde business?"

Brady handed him a bill and shrugged. "What's there to say? I guess I can understand people being upset."

"Upset's not the word," Sam said, leaning toward him as if the walls might hear. "Bo Potter's talking about running him out of town."

"You mean the football coach?"

25

"That's him. Alice Ann was his sister. He was only ten or so when it happened. He's some hot."

"Still, Cory Wilde's a free man. What can Bo do?"

Sam shook his blond head. "Mr. Brady, this isn't the big city, like New Orleans. People around here, well, they tend to take more things on themselves, if you know what I mean. The judge's wife, Miss Grace, was in here. She's a teacher, you know. Says Bo's stirring everybody up out at the school."

"What does she say about the judge?"

"Nothing. You know, the judge isn't one to say much. He does his talking in court. The only time I've ever seen him excited was at the racetrack."

"Admirable," Brady said dryly. "Well, I hope it works out."

He left the drugstore, the little bell over the door ringing behind him. As he crossed back toward his office, he reflected that the next issue of the *Express* was not going to do anything for Bo Potter's frame of mine.

Brady plodded through the rest of the day, grateful when Ripley Dillon, his part-timer, came in. Ripley was putting himself through nearby Fletcher College by selling *Express* ads for a fifty-percent commission, but he never objected to a break, and so Brady sent him off to cover a police jury meeting. When Mrs. Rickenbacker left at one o'clock, complaining of a headache, Brady let her go, just as glad to be by himself.

He fought the urge to go to the files and read more about the Cory Wilde case. However, there was a newspaper to get out, calls to be taken, an offended PTA president to mollify over an erroneous meeting date that had crept into the last issue.

Once, he had gotten personally involved in his work. He had been the best damned crime reporter on the *Picayune*. But that had ended when his source had been murdered for talking to him. Brady had gotten a Pulitzer for the series, but that hardly made up for the feeling of emptiness. He had come to Troy with a determination never again to let himself become involved, and Cory Wilde was not going to make him change his mind.

At four o'clock, Ripley returned, mumbling about the boredom of the last two hours.

"I'll write this up and have it for you by Wednesday, if that's okay," Ripley promised.

Brady nodded. "That's fine. I'll see you tomorrow."

Dillon shook his head. "You'd better go home, too, Mr. Brady. You look terrible."

"I'm about to," Brady said.

He waited until his assistant was in the parking lot before he heaved himself up. He went to the doorway into the morgue room, glanced over at the filing cabinets, and then forced himself away. He pulled the shade down over the front door and shut off the window air conditioner. He had just turned off the computer when the phone rang, filling the room with its harsh jangle.

Brady stared down at the offending instrument. He ought to let it go. After all, there was an answering machine. After four rings, it would take over.

The phone rang again.

And again.

Brady picked it up.

"Express."

"Peter Brady?" a harsh voice asked, and Brady had the sense that it was being disguised.

"Speaking. Who is this?"

"Never mind. Just listen. About that man, Cory Wilde, the killer. I just wanted you to know: There's gonna be trouble."

Then the line went dead.

Brady went home and tried to put thoughts of Cory Wilde out of his head. He took another dose of the cold remedy and headed for the kitchen, not really hungry and yet feeling he should eat.

But, damn it, it would be nice to know who had called him and why. Had someone found out about Cory Wilde's visit to him? Mrs. Rickenbacker was not the silent type and he knew that by now news of Cory's advertisement had probably reached half the town.

Yet, the call had not been a threat against Brady. It was unclear whether it was a threat at all; and why direct it to the newspaper rather than the local authorities?

Brady opened a can of tomato soup, accompanied it with a grilled cheese sandwich, and then turned on the television. Half-way through the news, he found himself thinking once more about the strange man with the dead eyes. Muttering an imprecation, he switched off the set, picked up his pad and pencil, and locked his door behind him.

Elm was one street over, a quiet tree-lined little street with frame houses dating from the thirties. Here and there, as he passed, he caught a glimpse of a television screen through an open front door and smelled the aroma of food frying. It was still daylight and children played in driveways, their laughter hanging in the warm summer air.

He came to a corner and crossed over and all at once noticed the change.

In this block, the silence almost shouted. There were no children outside, and the doors of the houses were closed. Even the cars he passed seemed to have their windows rolled up, and he knew that if he tried any of the door handles, he would find the vehicles locked.

He was only halfway to the next cross street when he saw the reason: Cory Wilde was sitting on his front porch, a dim figure in a white shirt, rocking slowly backward and forward, like the pendulum of an ancient clock keeping the count of the seconds.

Brady went up the sidewalk, stopping at the base of the red brick pillars.

"Mr. Wilde," he said.

"Mr. Newspaper Editor," the old man replied in his strange whisper, still rocking. "Did you come to give back my money or are you just passing the time?"

"Just call it a visit," Brady said.

Wilde nodded. "Come on up then." He nodded at an empty rocker. "Sit."

Brady went up the steps and took a seat in the empty chair.

"You don't figure this will ruin your reputation, do you?" Wilde asked, half-jokingly. "In ten minutes, everybody in the parish'll know you were here."

"You aren't afraid of exposing yourself like this?" Brady asked.

"Afraid?" Wilde laughed silently. "That's a hell of an idea."

Brady started rocking, slowly, letting silence take over. Silence made people nervous, made them talk to break the quiet.

More than one interviewee had blurted out a crucial fact when the silence had become too awkward.

So Brady rocked; but after about ten minutes, he concluded that the technique was not going to work with Cory Wilde. Maybe Cory Wilde was used to silence. Or maybe he had forgotten that Brady was there. The editor was about to get up and make his departure when the old man spoke.

"You haven't asked me why I came back."

"No," Brady said. "But I'm willing to listen if you want to tell me."

Wilde nodded. "You ever been to Angola, Mr. Brady?"

The reporter flinched, not wanting to call up the memory. "Once, a long time ago," he said. "When I was working on the *Picayune*."

"An execution, was it?" Wilde shook his head. "Bad. But maybe not so bad as spending your life there. At least with the chair, it's over quick. When you're in for life, there's no quick ending. Unless you're lucky. Somebody stabs you in the shower. A guard shoots you trying to escape. I've seen men jump in the river knowing they didn't have a chance. They just wanted a way out." He rocked some more, the dead eyes staring at something beyond the street. "When I went there, they still had the cane fields. You ever cut cane, Mr. Editor? Up at four, eat some grits, fall in line, walk a mile to the fields, all the guards on horseback, of course. Get there at six, with the sun just up. They hand out the cane knives. You start down your row . . ." He coughed. "They've got snakes in those canebrakes. Big ones. Ever seen a man bit by a canebrake rattler? Isn't pretty."

He rocked back and forth and Brady waited. The old man started speaking again: "Heat. By eleven o'clock, it's ninety-five degrees and your clothes are sticking to your body. Lifting that cane knife is like picking up a sack of lead. And there's always a guard behind you, ready to jab you in the back with a gun barrel if you slow down too much. Men died in those cane fields, and some cut off fingers, or toes, or hacked into their tendons so they wouldn't have to go back." He blew out and gave his head a little shake, as if to dispel the memory. "'Course, they don't have the cane fields anymore. Changed all that a few years after I got there. Now it's the bean fields, the cattle, the mattress factory, and the sign shop. I guess it's better. But it's not like home." Wilde stomped a foot down on the wooden floor of the porch. "*This* is home, Mr. Editor. This is where I was born, where I met my wife. I spent almost thirty years away. But now I'm back and I want everybody to know I'm not leaving again."

Brady nodded. "I suppose that's normal. On the other hand, there are a lot of people who wouldn't feel comfortable coming back where they aren't wanted."

"Probably. But I'm not one of them. No, sir," Cory Wilde affirmed, rocking forward, "this is where I belong. Nobody's going to chase me away."

"Putting a notice in the paper, though, is almost like a dare."

"They can take it any way they like."

Brady watched the old man rock backward and forward, his face set, and he thought about the closed doors and the lawns without children, and suddenly it all came clear.

"You *want* them to be upset, don't you? You want people in Troy to remember it all and suffer."

Wilde smiled grimly, his eyes still far away. "I suffered," he declared. "Suffering's a part of life."

"Alice Ann Potter suffered," Brady said quietly.

The rocker moved backward and forward and then Wilde said in a voice almost too low to be heard, "Yes. But for her it was over quick."

"She was fifteen," Brady persisted. "Nobody deserves to die that young, for no reason."

"People don't *deserve* anything," Wilde said tonelessly. "Any good that befalls man is only through God's grace. Otherwise, expect tribulation. Isn't that what they teach?"

"Mr. Wilde, aren't you *sorry*?"

Wilde's head swiveled slowly toward the editor and he stopped rocking.

"Sorry? I used to be. But sorry doesn't change anything, not anything at all. So somewhere between the cane fields and the long nights after lock-down, I stopped being sorry." He turned back to face the street and started rocking again. "It's kind of nice out here, isn't it? Kind of quiet and peaceful."

Brady rose. "Good night, Mr. Wilde."

* * *

Back home, the editor popped open a can of ginger ale, as if to
wash away the bad taste in his mouth. The swelling in his throat
was worse and he felt like he was getting a fever. Then the telephone rang and he recognized Penelope's voice.

"I had a premonition. You aren't feeling well, are you?"

"Well . . ."

"I didn't think so. Your voice sounds terrible. I have to go
out in a few minutes. I'm going to drop something by. I've been
giving it to Mr. Wilde, for his throat problem."

"His throat?"

"In prison, some kind of illness. You've heard the way he
talks. This is guaranteed to cure. Of course, it works better if
you're attuned to the higher planes, but . . ."

Brady started to answer but he was distracted by a sudden
pounding on the door. "Penelope, I have to go. Thanks."

He hung up and went to the door, wondering who it might
be. He opened the door and started. It was Matt Garitty.

"Matt. Is everything all right?"

He stepped back to allow the lawman in, but the sheriff
shook his head. "Things are definitely *not* all right. You got a few
minutes? I thought you might want to take a ride."

Brady shut the door behind him, tried to thrust his physical
discomfort out of his mind, and climbed into the unmarked white
sedan. Garitty waited until they reached the highway. Then he
turned on the red flasher atop the dash and pressed down on the
accelerator.

"So what's up?" Brady rasped, touching his swollen neck.

"Got a call from the patrol supervisor," the sheriff explained.
"Wreck down on Highway Twenty-seven, near Lairdsburg.
Sounds pretty bad."

They were outside town now, whipping around cars and log
trucks as dusk closed around them.

Brady hunkered back against the seat, listening to the
crackle of the radio.

"Central, this is Troy Three. Fire truck is at this ten–twenty
now. Has Troy One been notified? Over."

31

Garitty lifted his microphone. "Central, this is Troy One. ETA is five minutes. Over."

"Troy One, Central. Roger."

They turned right off the main highway and onto a narrow blacktop, winding up into the piny hills.

"This isn't just any wreck," Brady observed. "What makes it special?"

They went around a corner and the sheriff hit his brakes. Ahead, a sheriff's car blocked the road, and Brady saw an ambulance and a fire truck. Garitty slid off to the side of the blacktop and the two men got out. A young deputy came forward shaking his head.

"Got the fire out, Sheriff, but it was too late. Won't be any way to get him out until the wreck cools."

Brady followed a grim-faced sheriff through the cars and past the fire engine, where firemen were hosing down the remains of a gasoline spill.

It was just beyond the fire truck that Brady saw the cause of the commotion; and even after his years as a reporter, the sight made him flinch. A mangled and burned mass of metal lay coiled about an oak tree, only charred rubber tires attesting that once this had been a vehicle. Brady looked back over his shoulder and then once more at the sickening lump of steel. The driver had evidently been speeding, failed to make the curve, and kept going. Then his eye struck something in the grass. He bent over and picked it up. It was a rebel-flag license. He stared back at the wreck, suddenly recognizing details, such as a vestige of chrome exhaust, and a blackened wire that once must have been an antenna.

"Matt, I know this truck. It belonged to—"

"To Boynton Jenks," Garitty confirmed. "That's right. And when this mess cools off, I expect we'll find what's left of him inside the cab."

An image flashed into Brady's mind of the surly unshaven face that had glared at him that morning in front of the courthouse. He stepped away from the emergency crew and lowered his voice: "Matt, does this have something to do with those burglaries?"

"I'd like to think so," the sheriff said. "It would solve a lot of problems. But there's another possibility, and that's why I brought you."

"Oh?" Brady felt a tingling. "And what's that?" he asked.

The sheriff leaned back against his car and fixed the newsman with a thoughtful eye.

"You didn't read about the trial? Twenty-nine years ago, Boy Jenks was the chief witness against Cory Wilde."

5

"WHAT?"

The sheriff smiled at Brady's surprise. "That's right. I went back this morning and pulled the old trial transcript. Boy Jenks swore that he saw Cory Wilde pick up Alice Ann Potter that night about a quarter of a mile from the drive-in."

Fragments of the old news stories flashed through Brady's mind. A secret witness . . . of course. Boy Jenks.

"And you think there may be a connection?" Brady asked.

Garitty shrugged. "Dunno." He reached into his car and took out a long flashlight. With Brady behind him, he walked over to the wreck and then back up the rubble-strewn road in the direction from which the death vehicle had come. Then he walked over to the deputy who had greeted him and put a hand on the younger man's shoulder. "You were right, Eli. Remind me to give you a raise. Or at least a day off."

Eli, a skinny man in his early twenties with a freckled face, smiled. "Thanks, Sheriff. I didn't know if it was important, but . . ."

"It's important," Garitty confirmed.

"Okay," Brady demanded. "What did I miss?"

"Ever see a wreck before a wreck?" the sheriff asked, leading him back the way they had come.

Brady frowned, wishing his physical condition would allow him to focus his mind. Then, staring down at the dark blacktop in the puddle of the sheriff's light, he suddenly understood.

"By God," he exclaimed. "You're right." He turned, looking back at the wreck, and then forward again, at the curve. "There's debris on the highway from before he left the road."

"Score one for the *Express*," Garitty said. "It looks like the tree only finished the job."

"Which means he either hit somebody or . . ."

"Something else happened to his truck," the sheriff confirmed. "Now, between you, me, and the other ten thousand citizens of this parish, Boy was known to take a drink every so often, and the autopsy ought to show if there was alcohol or some other substance in his blood, even as charred up as he is. But these skid marks aren't in the opposite lane and there aren't any I can see from a second vehicle." Garitty folded his arms and gazed back in the direction of the wreck, now lit by the garish red lights of the emergency vehicles. "So whatever hit him must have come out of the blue."

Brady turned his back on the death scene, suddenly wanting to shut it out of his mind. He had come here to get *away* from this, damn it, so why did it keep seeking him out?

He felt the sheriff's hand on his shoulder. "You know, you can't *really* get away from it, Pete, if that's what you were thinking. It's what you are and what you're good at. I saw that when you figured out the MacBride case. I brought you out here because I figured I might need you again."

Brady started to protest and then stopped. He and Garitty had been through this before: the obligations of the press, its independence as a separate entity. And he had found that what sounded good in the city did not always work in a country town.

"I don't know what I can do," he said weakly.

"I don't, either, right now. But that fellow, Cory Wilde: You spent a while rocking on his porch this evening. No, I wasn't spying. I got a couple of phone calls from concerned neighbors. I'm convinced the man's up to something. And if you manage to put it together, I'd like to know."

Brady nodded and opened the car door. "Right now the only thing I feel like putting together is some aspirin and water."

When he reached home, Brady found his screen door slightly ajar, a paper bag inserted between the screen and the main door. He picked it up and a piece of paper fluttered to the ground. He retrieved it and read: *Peter: One tablespoonful in one cup of boiling water, before bed. Go straight to bed afterward. Pen.*

Brady managed a smile and opened his door. His throat was almost swollen closed now; clearly, the nostrum he had purchased at the drugstore hadn't worked. He sniffed the concoction from Penelope's paper bag and drew back, his head swimming. What the hell had she given him? He started to call her but thought better of it. He was in no mood to hear about spirits and planes of existence. Well, he was headed for bed, and most homegrown remedies were relatively harmless. He followed her instructions, adding a spoonful of the dried herbs to a cup of water, heated in the microwave. He stirred in the medicine, watching the water turn a muddy brown.

Boy Jenks had been the main witness against Cory Wilde. Now Jenks was dead. But Wilde had been rocking on his porch while Jenks was dying. . . .

Brady tried to make sense of the two facts and then gave up. He felt too rotten to think just now. He lifted the cup and sipped.

The taste was bitter but the warmth felt good on his inflamed tissues. He took another swallow.

Well, Pen, he said to himself, testing his neck with a hand, not yet.

He started to put the cup back on the counter and watched, fascinated, as it slowly descended from his disembodied hand, finally touching the Formica surface with a crack like a shattering glacier. A stray drop of liquid sailed away from the counter, caught the light, and spun a rainbow web across his vision as it descended like a tiny silver ball, to fragment on the vinyl floor.

A sense of wonderment spread over him. Like voices from far away, thoughts connected in his mind: *The herbs. Penelope's damned herbs.* He stumbled toward the doorway, caught the frame, and watched the colors of night vibrate with the music from his stereo.

The phone. He had to call someone. Emmett. Emmett could help. . . . He lurched toward the instrument, a man waist-high in water. The music laughed at him and he saw that the telephone was glowing, like a radioactive stone. He drew his hand back and then forced himself to reach forward. This time, the receiver squirmed out of his grasp, its body drawing into a coil, a forked tongue spitting from a diamond head.

Brady shrieked and felt the floor coming up at him.

He didn't fall, however. He flew. Below him, the forests and swamps shot past at breathtaking speed. He laughed into the night: Why did he need a car when he could fly? He sucked in the fresh night air and saw lights ahead and knew he was approaching the city. He had never been to Kelly's apartment, but somehow he knew which one it would be. It was just off campus, in a section of newer apartments, and he dove downward, zeroing in on a second-floor doorway. He pressed his face against the big picture window, reveling in the sensation and the knowledge that he had broken the bonds of physical existence. He took a deep breath and pushed through the window, feeling the glass part like water around him, and all of a sudden he was in the apartment himself.

He felt it as soon as the darkness closed around him. She was here, inside, but something was terribly wrong.

"Kelly . . ." The name echoed in his mind but he knew that no word came out. Instead, the only sound was coming from the next room, the bedroom. He tiptoed across the rug and slowly pushed open the door.

A soft light from a window painted a stripe across the naked bodies on the bed and he turned away, suddenly nauseous. The atmosphere was suffocating and he needed fresh air. He staggered toward the door, reached out, and opened it.

He jumped back in shock. There, facing him in the entrance, was Ozzie. *Ozzie . . .*

He turned to run, then caught himself. How could he run from Ozzie? Ozzie had died because of him. Ozzie had given him the material that had produced a Pulitzer story. But people had learned of it and Brady had found Ozzie floating faceupward in the swamp, his throat slit.

"Ozzie . . ." Brady reached out and Ozzie tried to say something, but his mouth wouldn't work, and as Brady strained, trying to understand, Ozzie pointed apologetically to the gash in his neck and gave a little shrug, like a man who had lost his larynx in an operation. He turned to leave and Brady ran after him. The frantic Brady crashed through the railing without realizing and saw the ground rushing up.

He would be dead in a second and yet that second was an eternity; and it was during that eternity that he saw the old man across the courtyard, smiling at him, as he rocked slowly backward and forward on the balcony, as if he had all the time in the world.

When Brady awoke, his head was clear and the swelling in his throat was gone. He blinked in the morning sunlight and swung himself out of bed. The clock read seven. He had a full hour to fix breakfast, dress, and walk the three blocks to his office.

He showered, shaved, dressed, and went into the kitchen. The paper bag with Penelope's herbs was on the counter where he'd left it, beside the glass. He smelled the glass and made a face. He washed it out and then placed it in the drainer. He put the paper bag under the sink and fried some eggs. Then, realizing he was hungrier than usual, he added four pieces of bacon and made some toast.

When he stepped out into the morning sunlight, he realized he felt good, more energetic than he had for weeks. Glimmers of grotesque dreams still clung to his mind like cobwebs, but he swept them back. He unlocked the office, took his seat at the rear desk, and sat down to think.

Whatever Penelope had given him had contained a powerful psychedelic. It was not an experience he would want to go through again, he told himself, and yet, through some mechanism, it had rid him of his cold. He started to call Penelope but decided against it. What was he going to say? Your medicine was too strong but it did the job?

Instead, he went to the morgue files and pulled the folder with the issue on the Cory Wilde trial. This time, he read it closely. Matt Garitty was right: The evidence was there. Boynton Jenks had been the chief witness, and the only eyewitness, to Cory Wilde's contact with the dead girl.

Mrs. Rickenbacker slouched in at eight-thirty, avoiding Brady's gaze and going directly to her desk. She had, Brady realized, probably been on the phone all night, exchanging gossip, and now was afraid he would confront her; but nothing was further from his mind. Ten minutes later, a breathless Ripley arrived, his face slightly flushed.

"Mr. Brady, I heard about the accident last night. I thought I could run over to the courthouse and throw together a story . . ."

Brady smiled and put a hand on the young man's shoulders. "Sorry, Ripley. Next time. I'll take this one myself."

"But it's only a car accident . . ."

Brady nodded sympathetically and promised him the next opportunity. Then he walked over to the courthouse. The deputy in the sheriff's office greeted him and held open the swinging gate as he threaded his way past the desks to Garitty's inner sanctum.

The sheriff put down a thick bound volume and shoved his chair back from his desk.

"I was wondering how long it would take for you to get over here. Here it is." He thumped the volume he had been reading.

"What?"

"The original trial transcript. I was glancing over it. I got it out of the clerk's office. I figured you'd be wanting to look at the thing."

"Matt, you're a mind reader."

"Not as much as I'd like to be."

"I don't guess you have any further information?"

The sheriff's brows rose. "At eight-thirty in the morning? You must've stayed up late watching 'Quincy' reruns. The wreck's hardly cooled and as for what's left of Boy Jenks, well . . ." He made a little face.

"I understand." Brady picked up the big book. "Thanks, Matt. I'll bring this back as soon as I finish it."

"Please do. The judge has the only other copy. I guess there's another one in the LSU Law School, but I'd hate to have to try to lay my hands on it."

Brady thanked him and went back out, down the courthouse steps. Suddenly, something he had completely forgotten sprang forward into his memory: the warning on the phone, shortly before he had gone to visit Cory. Somehow, in the excitement of the wreck, the incident had slipped his mind. It might just have been some local troublemaker, venting his spleen, but, on the other hand, there was no disregarding the fact that a man had died shortly thereafter.

When he got back to the office, Ripley had left on his advertising rounds, and Mrs. Rickenbacker had laid a prim little pile of message slips on his desk.

"Some people aren't very happy," she pronounced with satisfaction as he sat down. He ran through them. Most were names he knew only slightly, but one did ring a bell. Bo Potter, coach at the high school, and brother of the murdered Alice Ann.

He returned the calls, saving Potter's for last. The reactions he got varied from querulous to blistering, and two people said they were canceling their subscriptions. He was still staring at Potter's number when he heard the front door open.

"You can go for a break, Mrs. R.," said Emmett's voice.

An odor of cigarette smoke preceded the older man as he stumped over to where Brady sat, and then, laying his fisherman's hat on the desk, he took a chair. The door closed as the relieved bookkeeper scampered out, leaving the two men alone.

"Damn, boy," said Emmett, running a hand through his short, oddly golden hair. "You're fixing to get yourself in a worse mess than I *ever* did, and *I* had almost everybody in town on my ass."

"Mrs. R." Brady sighed.

Emmett nodded, taking out his cigarette. "Yep." He lit up and puffed. "Case of divided loyalty. She worked for me for so long, she kind of feels she still does."

"And so, in keeping with her sense of duty, she felt like she had to call and tell you about Cory Wilde's ad."

"About his death notice," Emmett said, staring the younger man in the eye, "That's what it is, you know. Because it's gonna cause somebody to get killed, if it hasn't already."

"I guess *you* wouldn't have agreed to run it."

"Me? He wouldn't have asked. But if he had, I'd have kicked him out on his butt. I may be a member of the Fourth Estate and all that crap, but I'm also a member of this town. And I don't have any use for that man."

"You made that pretty clear in your column at the time."

"Damn right. He was just lucky he didn't get the chair, which was what he deserved."

"Why didn't he? You pointed out in your column that there were people who got it for less."

"Good question," the old editor agreed. "I attended the trial. And there was nothing wrong with the state's case. Of course, Wilde claimed he was innocent. Said he wasn't anywhere around, that he was by himself, at home. His wife was away. You see, Cory had a hell of a temper. Whenever he and his old lady had a disagreement, it usually ended up with a fight and she'd take off for the relatives, over in Winn Parish. That wasn't the sort of thing they could enter at the trial, but everybody knew about Cory's temper. So he couldn't prove he was by himself and the state had a witness, even if he wasn't the parish's most upright citizen. There wasn't any reason for him to lie. And the body was found on land that Cory Wilde owned, not a quarter of a mile from his house."

Brady tapped the table with his pencil. "Why would he bury her on his own land?"

Emmett snorted. "Why not? Best way to make sure nobody would find her. It was a couple of acres off the beaten track. Only reason she was found was because they got an anonymous call to look for her there." Emmett shook his head angrily. "I'm telling you, what he did to that little girl was vicious and unforgivable."

"Which makes second-degree sound all the more unrealistic, at least for thirty years ago."

"I know, I know. And I fault Arden Honeycutt, there. After a solid case, and a strong cross-examination of Wilde, who took the stand, he gave a summation that was pure Milquetoast. Old Judge Troy didn't help much, either. The charge he read the jury only confused everybody, made it sound like anything short of mass murder was second-degree."

"Who was Wilde's lawyer?" the younger man asked.

"Fellow named Epstein, Dave Epstein. From the only Jewish family in town. Not a bad fellow, but he had a whiny voice and a little mustache, and thick glasses, and . . ." Emmett shrugged. "Just didn't have much rapport with the jury, if you get my meaning; bunch of good old boys . . . the foreman was the town

40

barber, Gil Simmons . . . and here the defense was using two-bit words. But Cory didn't have any money and Epstein was the one the judge appointed, and he did his best, and when it was over, he was as surprised as anybody else. He felt like he'd won."

"Where is he now?" Brady asked.

Emmett blew out a cloud of smoke. "Shady Acres, in the Epstein family plot. Heart attack, about twenty years back."

"Great. Look, Emmett, you said some pretty harsh things about Cory Wilde in your column, and he made some threats. You must be a little worried now that he's loose."

Emmett stared at the wall and put his hands behind his head. "Well, I've got to admit it was a shock seeing him on the courthouse bench the other day. I mean, there's no reason the man should ever have been let loose. But as far as him taking revenge . . ."

"Boy Jenks is dead."

"Yeah, I heard. But the only surprise there is that it didn't happen years before. Ten to one, when the autopsy results come back, they'll show Boy was blind drunk."

"Maybe so," Brady said. "In the meantime, I haven't got any choice but to run Cory Wilde's announcement."

Emmett shoved himself up and threw his butt down on the cement floor. "Okay. Can't say I didn't try. Let me know when you get ready to lay out the last issue. I'll write a restrospective."

"You're a real comic, Emmett."

"Naw, I'm not," Emmett growled. "I just think sometimes you have to use common sense." The old publisher stumped out and Brady heaved a sigh. Thanks to Emmett, Mrs. Rickenbacker would probably spend the next hour at the beauty parlor, gabbing with the other ladies. He might as well make use of the time. So he moved over to the computer and knocked out a story on the Jenks accident, leaving out speculation, and printed out a copy. He scanned the result, correcting a few typos, and then printed out a clean copy.

The door opened and Ripley breezed in, droplets of sweat on his face. He went to the refrigerator in the morgue room and got out a can of Gatorade, which he drained at a gulp.

"Hot out there," he proclaimed. "And dry. Lots of the places that used to invite me in for a Coke were too busy today, if you get my meaning. Mr. B., that ad from Cory Wilde is about to do us in."

"And hurting your commissions," Brady put in.

"I didn't say that, but . . ."

"But you're a gentleman." He got up. "Look, I have to make some rounds myself. Do you have time to sit here a while before you go to your afternoon classes?"

"Sure. And if anything comes up, I'll call Mrs. R. I know where she hides out."

"Good man." Brady left, taking the transcript with him. He checked Bo Potter's number. It was the high school, which meant Potter was working today for some reason, during the normal summer vacation. He thrust the message slip into his pocket and drove out through the center of town to the new high school just outside the city limits. It was a low modern building with a dome-roofed gym attached via a breezeway, and the football field and track in the rear, against the pinewoods. The editor found a place in the almost-deserted lot and walked across the asphalt to the main entrance.

The halls were dark and smelled of wax. The only noise was the sound of a copy machine, drifting toward him from the open door of the main office. He went in and the sound stopped. A moment later, a woman came out of one of the side rooms, her hand unconsciously reaching up to reassure herself that her gray hair was still in place.

"Oh, Mr. Brady," she said, squinting slightly from behind her bifocals. "How are you today?"

"Mrs. Honeycutt," Brady said, recognizing the judge's wife. "I'm fine. But don't you get a vacation?"

The older woman flushed slightly and looked away. "Well, I just have some catching up to do. I . . ." She looked up. "Was there something I could help you with?"

"Coach Potter called me. Is he still here?"

"Coach Potter? Oh, dear . . ." She clasped her hands together. She was a thin woman, who, Brady seemed to recall, taught math, and, for the past year, had served as a substitute assistant principal. "I suppose he's upset about—" She cut herself off. "Well, it isn't my business. Come back to my office; I'll call and see if he's still on the grounds. He was teaching a remedial

42

science class for seniors who failed last year, but I don't know if he left or not."

He went through the gate and followed her back to one of the offices.

"You'll have to excuse the mess," she said, reaching for the microphone of the PA system. "I've been sorting out student records."

Brady smiled, his eyes scanning a desk so cluttered with folders that the only other object visible was a small double frame with family photos. In the frame, Brady saw, was a considerably younger judge, smiling in a way that Brady had never seen him beam in the flesh, and the publisher wondered whether it was before or after the Wilde case. In the picture opposite was a handsome young man in an army uniform, the son who had died in the service. It was one of the quiet kinds of tragedies that affect families, coloring all subsequent experience, and Brady wondered idly how it must be to deal with young people now, ever reminded of one whose life had been snuffed out.

"Coach Potter, please report to the office when you have a chance," Mrs. Honeycutt intoned. She looked up from the mike. "I think he was down in the science lab, at the end of the building. You might meet him if you walked down that way," she suggested.

"Thank you." Brady started out, then halted. "Mrs. Honeycutt, you remember the Potter murder, don't you?"

The teacher stiffened and her hand formed a fist at her side.

"That was a long time ago," she said in a near whisper. "There are some things you'd rather forget. I . . . I wish this man, this Cory Wilde, had never come back to stir it all up."

"A lot of people seem to feel that way," Brady agreed. "And it's understandable. The man made a number of threats . . ."

"Arden isn't afraid of his threats," she said coolly. "Now, is there anything else, Mr. Brady?"

"No. Thank you, Mrs. Honeycutt."

Brady walked out into the hallway, turning over in his mind the woman's reaction. He came around a corner and before he had a chance to look up, hands were grabbing him, slamming him against the wall, and the breath went out of him in a rush.

Instinctively, he realized he had just met Bo Potter.

43

6

"YOU son of a bitch, I oughta kill you," snarled the man holding Brady by the throat. He was six inches taller than the newsman and outweighed him by fifty pounds. Brady eyed one post-sized bicep and decided tact was preferable to physical resistance.

"I can't talk if you hold my throat," Brady said.

"Maybe you talk too much," the mountain declared. "And maybe you talk to the wrong people."

"If you'll let go of me, I'll talk to *you*," Brady promised. "That's what I came for, to hear your feelings."

"My feelings?" the coach demanded, then suddenly dropped his arm, letting Brady straighten his collar and take a deep breath. "What the hell do you know about my feelings?"

He had a square jaw, a boot-camp haircut, and a scar just under the right eye.

"Why don't you tell me?" Brady asked.

The big man squinted at him, and then shrugged. He pointed down the hallway and Brady followed him into the deserted teachers' lounge. Potter went to the soft-drink machine, inserted two quarters, and took out a diet cola.

"They didn't have any call at all to let that murdering bastard out," Potter said bitterly. "No call at all."

"Why do you think they did?" Brady asked, taking a seat in one of the chairs.

Potter shook his head. "How the hell should I know? Bleed-

44

ing-heart governor, I reckon. Rehabilitation. I'll tell you about rehabilitation."

"Do you remember the trial?" Brady asked.

Potter swigged from the bottle. "Sure I remember it. I was eleven years old. Alice Ann was fifteen. There were two others between us. They've moved away. Better to forget it all. But not me. I'm damned if I'll forget." He fixed Brady with a baleful eye. "Word's out you're going to print some kind of threat from him."

"No threat," Brady said calmly. "An announcement. I wouldn't print a threat. But if a man wants to print a notice of his existence, I can't very well refuse him."

"Everybody knows the bastard exists. Why does he want to rub it in?"

"I don't know." Brady shifted slightly in his seat, wording his next statement carefully: "Everybody seems pretty sure Cory Wilde killed your sister."

"He was convicted," snorted Bo. "What else is there to say? He was convinced by a jury. The only problem was, he didn't get the chair."

"The chief witness doesn't seem to have been the parish's favorite citizen. I wonder why they believed him?"

Bo set down the empty bottle. "Oh, I see what you're doing. Trying to throw doubt, acting like a damn defense lawyer. You want to put *us* on trial."

"Nope." The newsman tried to keep his voice level. "Just trying to get at what happened."

"I'll tell you what happened," Bo declared, rising. "Cory Wilde killed my sister and yesterday he killed the man who testified against him, and he's not going to get a chance to kill anybody else." He moved to within inches of the publisher's face. "And anybody that helps him is going to have me to deal with."

Brady caught a movement from the corner of his eye and was relieved to see Mrs. Honeycutt in the doorway.

"Coach, one of the students is looking for you," she said.

Potter's shoulders sagged and he moved away, nodding. "Right. I was on my way."

As he made his way out past the woman, he seemed to Brady to have shrunk slightly, a tired man with only anger keeping him in motion.

Brady drove back to the office. He would run the wreck story in the issue that would go to press tomorrow night, but there was not enough for a story on Cory Wilde. For that, he would have to dig.

When he walked in, Mrs. Rickenbacker and Ripley were in the middle of one of their weekly fights. For a time, under Kelly's calming influence, they had mended fences, but since she had left for graduate school, the old tensions had flared anew. Now Mrs. R. scampered back to her desk, her face red, as Ripley turned abruptly, ignoring her.

"Now what?" Brady demanded. "Or should I ask?"

Mrs. Rickenbacker puckered her mouth. "Well, he can speak for himself. All I have to say is that as our employer, you're entitled to a certain amount of respect."

"Oh, Jesus!" Ripley threw up his hands. "Mr. Brady, it's not the way it sounds."

"It sounds quite badly enough without your taking the Lord's name," Mrs. Rickenbacker pronounced.

Brady threw up his hands and stifled an oath. "I'll do more than take the Lord's name if you two don't settle down."

"Now you see," the bookkeeper declared virtuously. "You see what it's like being around him all the time."

"Mr. Brady, she's twisting my meaning. We were getting all those calls, the ones about Cory Wilde, and somebody asked if you were crazy, running that threatening ad, and I guess I just lost my temper."

"And?" the long-suffering editor asked.

Ripley shrugged. "I said it was better to be crazy than stupid."

"You see?" Mrs. Rickenbacker said.

"I see we may all be candidates for the couch before this is over with," Brady said. He put a hand on Ripley's shoulder. "In the first place, what Cory gave me was not a threatening ad, though I'm sure that by now it's become a promise to kill everybody in town. Second"—and here he glared at his bookkeeper—"there was no reason for anybody in town to know about the ad except for the people in this office. But, for reasons beyond my ability to fathom, news of it leaked."

Mrs. Rickenbacker turned the color of beets. "Well, I . . ."

46

"And leaks," Brady warned, "are something I cannot and will not tolerate."

Mrs. Rickenbacker's lips moved soundlessly and she suddenly dissolved into tears, head down on her desk.

Brady turned to the younger man. "As for calling me crazy, that may be well founded. But calling the subscribers stupid is a big no-no. Even if it's true."

"Sorry, boss."

"Forgiven. Mrs. Rickenbacker, we have a paper to run. If somebody comes in and sees you like that, they'll think I beat you."

The chagrined bookkeeper dabbed her eyes and blew her nose.

"Now," Brady pronounced, "I think we're about fifteen minutes overdue for our usual Tuesday morning prepub meeting."

By the time they'd finished, at eleven-thirty, Brady had managed to restore a tenuous equilibrium, which was as much as he ever expected. With a good idea of what would appear in the following day's issue, he sent Ripley on his way to school and reassured Mrs. Rickenbacker that her presence was invaluable. Then he took the trial transcript and went home for lunch, where he knew he would not be disturbed.

He made himself a ham and cheese sandwich and then skimmed through the thick record, looking for something, anything, that might strike him as unusual.

He decided to focus on the Jenks testimony, visualizing the courtroom scene as it must have appeared nearly three decades before, as the harried defense attorney circled the man in the witness chair, seeking an opening, any opening at all.

Under intense questioning, Jenks had admitted to being in a saloon called the First Chance, in neighboring LaSalle Parish, but he had denied being drunk. Epstein had used every trick to shake the witness but, despite frequent outbursts and a chorus of warnings from the judge, Boynton Jenks had been firm: He had left the First Chance at nine o'clock, and on his way home, he had seen the Potter girl walking beside the highway; had seen a truck he recognized as Cory Wilde's pull over; had watched the girl get in. He had recognized the truck as Wilde's because of a dented right rear fender. It was an important point, but one on which he stood fast.

Asked why he had waited a week to come forward with his information, Jenks claimed that he had thought the girl would turn up, and that she was merely having a fling. The frustrated defense attorney had then done his best to paint Jenks himself as the murderer, asking him where he had gone after Alice Ann had been picked up, but three family members and a neighbor swore that he had come home by himself, at eleven, and that he was perfectly sober, an assertion that made Brady shake his head.

He went to the defense case. Cory Wilde had taken the stand on his own behalf, but all he could offer was that his wife had been visiting her parents in Winn Parish, thirty miles away, and that he had been by himself on the small farmstead. Anticipating the prosecution, Epstein had asked whether Cory and his wife had an amicable relationship. Cory replied that notwithstanding a brief separation last year, their relationship was now excellent.

He did not know Alice Ann Potter, except by name, and he had been alone on his farm when the crime had occurred. No, he had seen nothing unusual that night and he had no idea how the body came to be buried on his land, although he pointed out that the parcel in question was out of sight of his house and anyone could have turned off onto it from the highway without his knowing.

Next, Cory's wife, Felicia, had been called to the stand. All she could offer, however, was general confirmation of her husband's story. Then, as he was about to close the book, a section of the testimony leapt out at Brady and made him stare down at the paper:

"Mrs. Wilde, was there some particular reason you chose that Saturday to visit your parents?"

Brady could imagine her looking down at the floor, blushing slightly: *"There was something I wanted to tell them."*

"Yes? And what was it?"

"About . . . the baby."

"The baby?" Pretended confusion. *"Would you please explain that?"*

"I just came back from the doctor. He told me I was going to have a baby."

Brady closed the transcript. What had Matt Garitty said? *Cory's wife is dead . . .* He'd said nothing about Cory's *child,* however.

The editor made a note of the exact date and called Emmett Larson.

"Emmett, is it true that Cory Wilde's wife was pregnant when Wilde went to prison?"

"Yes. Now, let me guess the next question: What happened to the child?"

"On the mark."

"But no brass ring. Because I don't know what happened. Soon as Cory went to Angola, his wife moved back to Winn Parish. She died about a year later. Maybe in childbirth. So I don't know if the child survived or not."

"What was her maiden name?"

"Hell, boy, how should I know?"

"Because as soon as you heard Cory might come back you pulled the old issues and started reading everything you could about the trial. I saw some of your cigarette butts on the floor in the morgue room. You have to stop sneaking in there in the middle of the night. Now, I can retrace all that, find some issue that mentions her maiden name, or go to the assessor's office and look at the conveyance records for when she sold the property, but it would be easier if you just told me."

Emmett snorted. "Canby. Her name was Canby. Now, if that's all, I have to rearrange my sock drawer."

Brady thanked him and replaced the phone. *Felicia Canby, from Winn Parish, Louisiana.*

He went back to the office and worked for the next three hours on a series of mundane tasks. At four, Mrs. Rickenbacker made a great stir riffling her desk and packing her purse, and Brady realized with a sigh what was next.

"Mr. Brady," she declared, lower lip trembling as she stood before him clutching her bag with both hands, "it is quite clear that I haven't performed to your expectations. When you came here, I told you I would stay only so long as you needed me and now it is evident from the way you chose to support that boy . . ."

"Resignation accepted." Brady sighed. "Just be here by nine tomorrow morning."

"Mr. Brady, I don't think you're listening to me."

"Mrs. Rickenbacker, you resign every week, usually after a tiff with Ripley."

"He hates me."

"He doesn't hate you."

"He's completely disrespectful."

"That may be, and I'll talk to him."

"That's the way they are over in Winn Parish." She pouted. "The Long influence. Brash to the point of rudeness."

"Winn Parish? Is that where Ripley comes from?"

"His family. Couldn't you tell?"

"Of course. Good night, Mrs. R."

Brady contemplated her departing image. *Winn Parish.*

He ate at a franchise restaurant, garnering some narrow glances, and the waitress had less to say than usual. The steak was rubber, and he began to wonder whether he was getting the treatment, but he put it out of his mind and left his usual tip. He was conscious of eyes on his back as he walked out into the gravel lot.

He drove back to his office and checked the layout for the Thursday edition. He had promised Ripley that as soon as possible, he would buy a computer that justified the columns and produced camera-ready copy, like the ones at most of the other papers throughout the state. The idea had pleased Ripley and frightened Mrs. Rickenbacker, whom the word *computer* sent into fits of shivering. For the present, though, the issue was moot, and likely to remain so until he built up the circulation.

He got up, went back to the morgue files, and opened the drawer for 1959, then shoved it shut. He went back to the phone and called Emmett again.

"I need some information. Where is Cory Wilde's old farm located?"

"Cory Wilde's farm? It's out near New Zion. Why? You don't plan to go there, do you?"

"Just an idea, that's all. Give me directions."

He wrote down what the old publisher told him.

"Do you want me to come with you?" Emmett asked. "I mean, if you're bound and determined to waste your time . . ."

"Thanks, but I just wanted to drive past while it's still light. The place where the girl was found . . ."

"Two tenths after you get there, on the right-hand side.

There's a little gravel road. About five hundred feet down that road, on the right. But there isn't anything to see, and Cory's old place is deserted. The land was too poor for crops. People that bought it sold it to the government, for the national forest, and they leased it to an oil company." Emmett cackled. "No oil, either."

It was a twenty-minute drive, south through the pine hills, where farmhouses shimmered in the late-afternoon sun, their piles of firewood neatly stacked, awaiting winter. Dogs yapped, men looked up from riding mowers, and children threw baseballs in vast yards. Most people waved and Brady reflected wryly that if they had recognized him, they would probably have withheld this instinctive greeting.

The houses and farms died away, replaced by a wall of loblollies. He passed a sign that told him he was entering the National Forest and came to a crossroads. He checked Emmett's instructions. *Right at the crossroads, then a mile and a quarter, to a white wooden voting booth.*

He found the booth easily enough and then, following the directions, turned left onto a gravel track.

The land was higher here, and now and then he could look out over the road, on his left, and see rolling hills in the distance. A forest service sign proclaimed this Eagle's Roost, and Brady smiled to himself at the hyperbole. He checked his odometer. The road curled back to the right, reentering the pines, and he followed for exactly four tenths of a mile and slowed.

The house was just where Emmett had said it would be, in a small clearing on the right. Brady stopped and got out. A thin haze of dust caught the light and played with it, painting the scene gold and then settling back onto the road. Brady walked around the car to the old gate and into the front yard. It was calf-high in weeds and the house itself was half-hidden. A single pine, bent by some past wind, shaded the path that led toward the house, its needles stirring in the faint breeze.

Brady stooped and picked up a handful of dirt. It was poor soil, mostly sand, and living here would have been a struggle. He came to the front door and ran his eyes over the disintegrating structure. A wall of bricks ran waist-high around the outside, and a little pile was stacked to one side, where someone had begun to collect them for some other use and then had thought better of it. The windows gaped like sightless eyes, fragments of glass catching the sun and throwing it blindly back.

Brady went through the open doorway and stood in what had once been the living room. Now all that remained were bare walls of Sheetrock and the slab base. A slight odor of mildew clung to the air and he brushed a spiderweb from his face.

He did not know what he expected to find. Probably nothing. There was a rag on the floor, and when he picked it up, he saw that it was part of an old T-shirt. He dropped it and went into the hallway. A hole gaped in the wallboard and the broken plaster made a chalky pile on the floor. He came to the bathroom and went in, noting the open cabinets and the fallen towel rack. He carefully lifted the cracked top from the commode and turned it over. The date stamped inside was 1955, meaning the house had been built four years before the crime. He went back into the hallway and to the bedroom at the end of the hall. It was evidently what had been the master bedroom, looking out onto a backyard now choked with briars. An old mattress occupied the center of the floor, and a couple of empty rye bottles attested to a sojourn by some interloper within the last few years.

He stared at the decaying room, trying to imagine how it might have been. Cory Wilde and his wife as young marrieds: Had it been a happy union, as the defense had tried to imply, or had it been something else, as other testimony had suggested? That Saturday night three decades ago, Cory Wilde had sat alone in this house, perhaps brooding, and then, if the testimony was to be believed, he had gone out, gotten into his truck, and driven to town, looking for something; and not long after, on the highway, just outside of town, he had found it.

Had he brought her back here? Was that why her body had been found nearby? It made sense. The house was isolated; no one would have heard her screams.

Yes, it all fit, except for one thing, one question that kept returning to haunt him: Who had made the anonymous call about where to find Alice Ann's body? Boy Jenks had denied it in his testimony and the only way he could have known was if he had been the killer himself. However, he had brought forth witnesses to show he was home shortly after seeing the alleged pickup. Of course, his witnesses were family and friends; but the jury had believed him and if the jury was right, that meant there was someone else out there with knowledge of the crime.

Another thing could be assumed: Whoever had called about Alice's body had been male, because it was thought worthwhile to ask Jenks whether he had made it.

But who? Who the hell could it have been? A passerby? An accomplice? A friend to whom Cory had confided while in his cups? After close to thirty years, it seemed unlikely he would ever find out, unless . . .

He went out into the living room and stared out the door at the last slanting rays of sunlight.

Yes. He would have to ask Cory Wilde.

He started out into the yard and the sunlight caught something in the grass, threw a shaft of gold back at him. He reached down, picked the object up, and blinked in surprise.

It was a small golden cat, of the kind worn on charm bracelets. Someone had been here and had dropped it and he knew who it had been, because he had seen the charm before, as part of a bracelet on a person he had interviewed for a special feature.

The bracelet belonged to Penelope Martingale.

7

HE dropped the tiny figure into his pocket and walked back to his car, thoughtful. Penelope. Did he still want to believe that her helping Cory Wilde was just an act of kindness? Or was there more?

He drove the two-tenths of a mile to where a narrow gravel road started into the pines. After two hundred feet, the gravel stopped and the road became a series of ruts. He got out and walked along the side of the trail for another few hundred feet. It was after seven now, and the sun was hovering just over the treetops. Soon the shadows would be merging with the night and visibilty in the woods would be zero. On both sides of the road were walls of brush, composed of high weeds and briars. The land must have been clearer thirty years ago, because no one would have hacked his way through such undergrowth to dispose of a body. Change was a part of the forest, Brady knew. Logging, oil drilling, and reforestation programs all combined to change the vegetation year to year. In any case, it was useless to stay here because, as Emmett had told him, there was nothing to see.

He drove back to town, for once wishing he was still on the *Picayune*. There, he would have had a network of sources, computerized access to a wealth of information, contacts in high places and low, and others to help him with the legwork. Here, he was by himself, and the only story anyone wanted to read was one that would confirm what they knew in the first place.

If he was smart, he told himself, he would just let it go. If he was smart . . . He saw the city-limits sign and turned onto Elm. Time to see Cory Wilde.

Some other people seemed to have the same idea, however. As he slowed, he saw that the street was choked with pickup trucks and cars and a small crowd seemed to be gathered in front of Wilde's house. Brady felt his stomach sinking. What was happening? Or, even worse, had already happened?

He pulled into a space at the end of the block, got out, and went up the sidewalk, hoping the dusk would conceal his features.

As he approached, he saw the crowd was composed of both women and men, and was, in general, orderly, more like a civic meeting than a mob. He recognized some of the faces. They were nervous and most of the talk was in undertones. He edged around the group so that he could get a clear view of the house, and stopped, surprised. On the porch, not forty feet away, in the same rocking chair, was Cory Wilde, moving slowly backward and forward, a thin smile on his face, as if he was completely unaware of what was happening in his front yard. Then, even as Brady watched, a man and woman detached themselves from the crowd and went up the sidewalk to the porch steps and stood like supplicants.

The man, whom Brady recognized as the owner of one of the hardware stores, cleared his throat. "Mr. Wilde," he began, "we came here to talk."

Cory Wilde continued to rock.

"Mr. Wilde, we don't want any trouble . . ."

Cory's smile widened slightly. "You're standing on the monkey grass," he said then, in his soft tones.

The hardware man dropped his eyes to the thick grass along the verge of the walkway and moved aside, as if he had been in quicksand.

"Thank you," Cory said.

"Mr. Wilde . . ." The man cleared his throat. "Why did you come back?"

Cory Wilde looked out over the crowd, then raised his hand and pointed midway back. "Mike Hennessey? Is that you back there? Move up to the front. I haven't seen you in almost thirty years. Not since we went fishing over on Catahoula Lake, must've been fifty-eight, right? You ever marry that little Dennison girl? The one that used to get on you about your drinking?"

A man in the center of the crowd looked away and seemed to shrink as eyes turned toward him.

The hardware man's wife tried to regain control: "Cory Wilde, we don't want you here. Nobody wants you here. You are a murderer and a . . ."

"A scoundrel, a debaucher of young girls," Cory said. "For those of you who don't know the meaning of those words, maybe you ought to spend some time in jail. Gives you a chance to improve your vocabulary. Do a lot of reading, you know."

An angry murmur rose from the group and suddenly a man broke from the others and shouldered his way in front of the original spokesman.

"Wilde, you're going to get the hell out of here if I have to drag you myself," promised Bo Potter, jumping up onto the porch. "And if I have to drag you, it may just as likely be to the tree down in the cemetery, by my sister's grave."

"That's right," a voice from the back yelled. "You killed Boy Jenks, too."

55

"Jenks?" Wilde's brows lifted. "How can that be? I was here at the time Mr. Jenks was killed. I was sitting on my front porch like I am right now and I have a witness to prove it, don't I, Mr. Brady?"

Heads turned toward the editor and he sensed Wilde's mocking smile.

The muttering of the crowd became angrier and a few men stepped toward the publisher.

"Well, folks," Cory Wilde asked over their heads, "what is it? You going to lynch us *both*?"

The crowd surged forward then, only to part as a thin man in a blue uniform stepped through and turned to face them, hands raised.

"All right, folks, that'll be about all. Let me handle this and you people go on home."

"What you going to do, Ned?" demanded Bo Potter, big hands on his hips, "serve him a paper? We've got kids strung out on dope in the high school and all you've ever done is come give a speech on Law Enforcement Day. If we leave this to the city police—"

"Damn it, Bo," cried the police chief, flustered, "you button your lip or I'll lock you up."

"That'll be the day," Potter snorted. "Why don't you lock up this killer instead?" He turned to eye Brady. "And there might be one or two others you could find a place for."

"Now, Bo, I don't want any more talk." The chief was a wizened little man with a long face, whose nervousness was reflected in his darting eyes. "Look, I agree with every one of you here." He jabbed a thumb at the man in the rocker. "I don't want this ex-convict around here any more than anybody else. But the law's the law, and you've got to understand, I can't just throw him out. Besides, do you want a front-page story about mobs in Troy? Mr. Pete Brady here would do it; you all seen what he did in the MacBride business."

"He's right," Cory said. "That would look plumb terrible."

That was when the dam broke. The crowd surged forward, engulfing the police chief and sweeping toward the porch.

A siren blasted the dusk and red lights flashed from the street. Heads turned as car doors opened, and with relief, Brady saw the tall figure of Matt Garitty striding toward them across the lawn, three deputies behind him.

"Somebody giving a speech?" the sheriff asked pleasantly. "I thought all the speech making was over after the last election." He skirted the front of the crowd and, with a single leap, landed atop the porch.

"Back off, Matt," Bo Potter warned. "This is out of your jurisdiction."

Garitty shook his head sadly. "Bo, if I was you, I'd spend more time with the football team. Two and eight is just plain dismal." He looked out over the crowd. "As far as my jurisdiction, this happens to be my town, too. I'm a citizen; I have a duty—as everybody here does—to prevent breaches of the peace, and I smell one brewing. Now why don't you just tell Mr. Wilde here good night and back on down off the porch."

Potter's chest heaved and Brady realized he was half a head taller than the lawman. "I'm not going anywhere, Matt."

Garitty shook his head regretfully. "Yes, you are, Bo. It's just your choice *how* you want to go. But if I have to throw you off the porch, you're liable to land on somebody and hurt 'em."

The crowd backed away instinctively and Potter looked around frantically for support.

"Well?" the sheriff asked.

Potter licked his lips and then, with a muttered curse, turned on his heel and made his way down the steps. Halfway into the crowd, he turned with a raised fist.

"I won't forget this, Garitty. Nobody here will. You just showed what you think of this town. You and that editor friend of yours." He stomped away and the crowd slowly dissolved.

The little man in the blue uniform strode forward, chin outthrust. "Damn it, Garitty, Bo was right. This ain't your business. I had things in hand."

"Sure you did, Ned," the sheriff said easily. "I just thought you might want a little help."

"Well, I didn't." Ned squinted from Brady to the sheriff. "Don't think I don't know what's going on here. I know a setup when I see one. I've known ever since this here publisher went over to you in the election, with that piece on professional law and order, like you was a cut better than the rest of us. I guess

57

there'll be another story on the front page Thursday, about how you took on a mob. Well, why doesn't he ask me? I've got a few things I could say."

"I'm listening, Mr. Triplett," said Brady. "If you have something that belongs in the newspaper, I'll print it."

Triplett spat on the ground. "Yeah? Well, you can start with the stores that've been robbed all over the parish in the last month or so. You can report on how many arrests the parish sheriff has made."

Garitty shook his head again. "Damn, Ned, you've been a police chief for how many years and you still don't know the difference between robbery and burglary?"

Triplett bit down hard on his wad of tobacco and strode away, slamming the door of his police car and leaving tire marks in the street.

"That was kind of hard," Brady said.

"I know," the sheriff admitted in an undertone, "but I couldn't think of any other way to get rid of him. The truth is, I *haven't* made any progress on any of the cases. Well, if he keeps it up, I guess I'll just have to counterattack about young people and drugs in the city."

"Is that true?"

Garitty drew back, offended. "True? Of course it is. But that's *his* jurisdiction, the pissant."

Brady leaned toward the sheriff. "Is there anything on the wreck yet?"

Matt shook his head. "Hell, it'll be all they can do to identify Jenks. We'll send the remains to the state police crime lab in Baton Rouge, of course, but it'll take a while. I just hope the little weasel went to the dentist enough times for there to be records. But those Jenkses are a rowdy lot. He might have got 'em all knocked out before he was twenty."

The sheriff started away, gathering his deputies, and Brady watched. Suddenly, he was aware of a low chuckle in the background. He swiveled, realizing he had forgotten about the man on the porch, the man who was the focus of this entire business.

"Dogs fighting over a bone, Mr. Editor. And I'm the bone."

He laughed harder, until his mirth broke down into wheezing. He coughed into a handkerchief, then folded the handkerchief and replaced it in his pocket. Brady went up onto the porch.

"What sort of game are you playing here, Wilde? What the hell are you *doing?*"

"Me, doing? I'm just rocking on my porch, trying to enjoy the evening. Surely you don't think I had anything to do with that man's death? Or that I *asked* those people to come here, trample all over the flower beds, and threaten me?"

"No, but you're enjoying every bit of it."

Wilde shrugged. "When you get my age, you have to enjoy whatever you can."

Brady stared down at the man in the chair who was obstinately rocking away as if only his motion could keep the universe from doom. He had started out disliking the man intensely, but now the dislike had turned to puzzlement.

"Mr. Wilde, answer a question: Did you kill Alice Ann Potter?"

Wilde turned to look up at the newsman. "Prosecutor said I did. Jury said I did. Judge sentenced me. Isn't that good enough for you?"

"Not necessarily. You claimed innocence at the time."

"But I'd claim innocence regardless, wouldn't I?"

Brady shook his head in perplexity. "Damn it, Wilde, I don't understand. You seem to *want* people to think you're guilty. You seem to want to rub it in."

"You want me to say I'm innocent," Wilde declared. "I already did and nobody believed me. If I did again, would anybody believe me now?"

"I don't know. But if it's the *truth* . . ."

"I told the truth twenty-nine years ago, Mr. Editor. I got down on my knees and told the truth, and it didn't do any good at all. I'm not going to do that again. Guilty or innocent, I served twenty-nine years. I figure that's worth something. It's worth not having to beg them again."

"Can I print that?"

"You can print what you damn please." Wilde coughed again. "But I'd think twice about it if I was you. Might be the newspaper gets a visit from the welcome wagon next time."

"So you don't intend to lift a hand to exonerate yourself?"

"Nope." All at once, the rocking stopped and he cocked his head slightly as he fixed the newsman with a cynical eye. "I figure you'll do that for me."

8

BRADY paced his living room, trying to make sense out of what he had just seen and heard. Could it really be that Cory Wilde was innocent? Brady went back to the transcript, skimming through the testimony of Boy Jenks and then focusing on the presentation of physical evidence by the state-police witness. He stared down at the page and felt his initial excitement disintegrate. There, clearly spelled out in the testimony of the forensic technician, was a fact no one could shove aside: A search of Wilde's truck had turned up a lock of hair matching that of the dead girl.

The publisher let the volume fall onto his desk. Well, that was that. He stared at the pale wall for another few minutes, then, out of a sense of duty, went back to the transcript and read through the cross-examination. The best Epstein had been able to do was elicit an admission that the hair might have gotten there days before, which only made Wilde's problem worse, by implying he and the girl had known each other prior to her death.

Brady turned to the summations. Epstein, obviously alert to the danger of admitting the pair had known each other previously, hinted of incompetence on the part of the state police, asking the jury to consider the possibility that hair samples had become confused in the lab, and pointing out that Wilde's wife, Felicia, was also a honey blonde. When his turn came, DA Honeycutt had hit hard, linking both the testimony of Boy Jenks and the evidence of the hair, and then, oddly, had conceded the possibility that the two might have

60

known each other before, made love, quarreled, and that Alice Ann might have been killed by an enraged Cory. It was, Brady thought, an odd possibility to plant in the minds of the jury.

Whatever the case, though, any possibility of Cory Wilde's innocence seemed to be contradicted by the original evidence. So why was the man here? He had to know he would be watched, his steps dogged. And so far, all he had done was rock peacefully on the front steps of his porch while a man died miles away and then a mob formed in his front yard.

Frustrated, Brady lifted the telephone and dialed Penelope's number. When she answered, it was with the throaty, almost sensual voice of a much younger woman.

"Hello. This is Penelope."

"Pen, this is Peter Brady. I need to talk to you."

"Of course you do. I was in the yard when I got the vibration. That's when I came in, to be close to the phone."

"Penelope, cut out the baloney. This is important."

"I know it is. I can sense your anxiety. It's not good to be that tense, Peter. You should try some breathing exercises. But you *do* sound better. I take it my herbs worked."

"That's another subject I want to take up with you. What the hell did you put in there, mushrooms?"

Penelope chuckled. "The old witch's secret, Peter love. I have to admit, I had some concern afterward that I might have made it a bit strong. But these things are very delicate. With a spirit just slightly out of synchronization with the universal harmonic—"

"Enough, Pen. That's not why I called you. I have something of yours."

"Something of mine? What in the world could it be?"

"Your charm bracelet; the one with little animals."

"My bracelet? But you silly boy, I have it on right now."

"Haven't you noticed anything gone from it? One of the little animals?"

"Animals?" There was a sound of faint jingling and then Penelope spoke again: "Peter, you're right. I'm missing Bast, my cat charm. I wonder what happened? You say you have it?"

"That's why I called."

"But where did you find it? Not at my place."

"No." He took a deep breath. "It was at Cory Wilde's."

There was a short silence. "Cory Wilde's? Well, of course, I must have dropped it when I was showing him the house the other day. How nice of you to call and—"

"Pen, it was at Cory Wilde's old place, the one out near New Zion."

He heard a short gasp. "But that's impossible. I haven't been out that way for *years*. And I've never been to his house. I hear it's abandoned, anyway."

"I found it in the grass by the front door."

"Well, I . . . . Peter, what are you trying to say?"

"Nothing. I was hoping *you*'d have something to say. I don't guess you lend out your jewelry."

"Of course not," she snapped. "And I don't sleepwalk." Her voice softened. "Honestly, Peter, all I can think is that I dropped it somewhere else and someone picked it up and—"

"Maybe so," Brady said. "All right, I'll drop the cat off when I get a chance. In the meantime, if you think of anything, let me know."

"Certainly. I was just going to meditate when you called. Maybe the spirits will have some ideas."

"Right." Brady started to hang up, then caught himself: "By the way, Pen, that medicine you gave me: Is it the same thing you gave Cory Wilde for his throat?"

"Well, yes, basically. Why? Is he having more trouble?"

"Yeah. But not that kind. I was just wondering."

Brady disconnected and then called Ripley Dillon. After exchanging small talk with an unusually stiff Ripley, Sr., the publisher heard his young employee's voice.

"Mr. Brady? What's up? Something hot?"

"I don't know, but it could be. It's on the Cory Wilde thing."

"What else? It's the talk of the town."

"And the family, I imagine."

"You mean Dad? Oh, don't worry about him. What's the plan?"

"You're from Winn Parish, I hear."

"Well, not me, but Dad came from Winnfield, the parish seat. I have a bunch of cousins and aunts and uncles there."

"Cory Wilde's wife came from Winnfield. Her maiden name was Canby. Does that name mean anything to you?"

"I heard of some Canbys in Winn, but I don't know any of them. But, hey, my uncle Milt would. He works in the clerk of court's office."

Brady told him about Felicia Wilde's pregnancy and return to Winnfield. "Can you do some calling and find out when she died and whether the child survived? And if it survived, where is it now?"

"The *child* would be middle-aged by now," Ripley declared.

"Twenty-nine years old, Ripley, is not middle-aged. Do you think you can handle it?"

"Handle it?" Ripley snorted. "What's to handle? I'll do some calling right now and if I have to, I'll drive over there, if you can spare me tomorrow."

"Thanks, Ripley. I knew I could count on you. Oh, one more thing: If I wanted to get a chemical substance analyzed and I wanted it all to be confidential, where could I go? Is there any place without driving to Alexandria?"

"Well . . . you could take it to Sam Berry, at the drugstore. He's got a little lab set up next to the storeroom. You know, ever since that Val-Save discount store opened up out on Eighty-four, he's been struggling to keep from going under. I'm sure if you paid him a little something . . ."

"Thanks, Ripley. That's a good idea."

The next morning, Brady went in early and spent a long time considering the tentative layout of the next day's edition. The lead would be Brady's story on the Jenks accident, followed by a report on the police jury meeting, which Ripley had promised to hand in before the day was out. There would also be a weekly column of local humor by a free-lance named Grady Dibbs and some comments by the mayor on the chances of federal money for a new low-rent project in the black section. The more he looked over what he had, however, the more dissatisfied he was. It was fine for a rural weekly, which was what the *Express* was, but it wasn't what Brady wanted. It was his own story that bothered him, of course: It gave the

63

bare bones but said nothing about the role Jenks had played in the trial of Cory Wilde. It was, he realized, conservative, to the point, and superficial. But what more was there to say? What could he prove? He slammed his hand down on the desk and then did what had been in the back of his mind all week. He lifted the phone and called Judge Honeycutt's chambers.

The judge, he was told, could probably be caught in his private law offices across from the courthouse between nine and eleven, if Brady wanted to drop by. He thanked the secretary and was hanging up just as Ripley walked in.

"I've got some info on that business in Winn Parish, boss," he announced triumphantly. "My uncle says Felicia Canby's been dead for going on twenty-eight years. He remembered about her baby, too. A little girl. It was big talk at the time. But after the mother died, the family sent the baby to some cousins in Baton Rouge to be raised."

"Any idea about the name of these cousins?"

"He's going to talk to some people and get back to me."

"Thanks a lot, Ripley. Good work."

The younger man smiled smugly and then, with a flourish, laid some typed pages on the editor's table. "And here's my story on the police jury. Bunch of boring crap, if you don't mind my saying."

"I don't," Brady assured him. "Now, I have a couple of calls to make. I know you have some morning classes. But . . ."

"You want to know can I stay here until Mrs. Wrecker gets here."

"Ripley, if she ever hears you call her that—"

"She won't, promise. Go on, boss, I'll stay, and then I'll be back after school to help you make up the dummy for the printers."

"You're a good man, Ripley. But please try not to make Mrs. R. cry."

Ripley smiled evilly. "I'll do my best."

Afraid to ask Ripley's meaning, Brady left. He walked home, took the bag of herbal medicine out of his cabinet, and then went back uptown to the pharmacy. There was a HELP WANTED sign in the window, but the only customer was a dark, seedy-looking man in a cheap suit who had been talking to Sam

64

when Brady entered. The editor took a stool at the deserted soda fountain, noticing for the first time the bareness of the shelves. Sam and his visitor mumbled a few final words and then the man left, lugging a battered attaché case with him. Sam watched him go and then came out from behind the counter to shake his hand.

"Trying to explain to the pharmaceutical companies why you don't want to order fifty of everything is like trying to tell the preacher you have doubts about God," Sam complained. "They want you to buy everything in the *PDR* but they want money up front. They think I'm like Val-Save, but I'm not. The only thing I can offer that Val-Save can't is free delivery. Without that, I'm a dead duck."

"I hope not," Brady sympathized.

Sam shrugged and turned to go back behind the counter. "I do, too. But I guess we all have to face facts and changing times. When my father founded this store in 1935, it served a need. There wasn't another one in town. Now, with the big chains discounting their prescriptions, and selling clothes and groceries, the small businessman is up a tree. I add a hardware shelf and they add a whole *department*. It's like trying to beat the house at roulette. Somebody always does, but it's not you." He spread his hands. "Well, what can I do for you besides tell you my problems? Your cold any better?"

"Much," Brady told him. "But that's not why I'm here. I need your help on something. Something, well, confidential."

Sam frowned. "Sounds serious, Mr. B. Of course, I'll help in any way I can. I don't guess it's connected to the Cory Wilde business, is it?"

"I don't think so." He took the paper bag out of his pocket. "I have some *material* here. I'd like it analyzed, with special attention to narcotic content. I realize this is a little irregular and if anybody says anything, I'll take full responsibility."

Sam opened the bag and looked down at the dried herbs and berries. He lifted it to his face, sniffed, and made a face. "Is this some of Penelope's medicine?" he asked, shaking his head. "Never mind. You don't have to tell me. She's going to get into a hell of a mess one of these days. As long as she sticks to using this on herself, that's one thing, but . . ."

"I know. But I'd like to keep it between the two of us. Can you do it?"

"Sure. Might take a couple of days."

"Well, whenever, but as soon as possible, and whatever it costs, let me know."

Sam made a face. "Oh, hell, Mr. B., for you . . ."

"No," Brady replied firmly. "This is business. You set the price and I'll pay." He shrugged. "Besides, it's a business expense I can write off."

"Well . . ." Sam gave him a broad smile. "Okay, but it won't be much. I'll get to it tonight when I finish my deliveries. I'll call you when I have something."

"Thanks a lot, Sam." The two men shook hands and Brady went back out onto the street.

It was just after nine and he sauntered over to the one-story gray brick building beside the barbershop. A sign on the window read, ARDEN HONEYCUTT, ATTORNEY AT LAW AND NOTARY PUBLIC. He pulled open the door and was hit in the face by the aroma of fresh coffee.

"Just pull it hard," the young secretary said easily, putting down the coffeepot. "It sticks."

Brady shut the door and the woman straightened up. She was young, maybe twenty-two, with black curls and a sheath dress that did little for a rather curveless figure, but she had a pleasant face and an ease of manner that made him feel welcome. "You want some coffee?" she asked. "I was just getting ready to carry a cup in to the judge."

"Thank you," Brady said. "I'll fix my own."

"I'll tell him you're here," the girl said, disappearing into the hallway. Brady poured some of the steaming black liquid into a Styrofoam cup and added some sugar and cream. He was stirring when she returned.

"You can go on back," she said.

"Thanks."

Brady went down the hallway toward the office at the end. He had met the judge a couple of times in the year since his own arrival in Troy, but he did not know the man well. Now he wondered how the jurist would react to the questions the younger man had to ask.

The judge rose from behind his desk as Brady entered, and thrust out a hand. He was a thick man in his early seventies, with neatly groomed white hair, worn long in the frontier style, and clear blue eyes. They shook hands and the judge pointed to a padded chair beside the doorway.

"Pull her up and sit down, Pete. I've been expecting you."

"Expecting me?"

The judge winked. "Sure. How long could Cory Wilde stay in town before the editor of the Troy *Express* showed up to get the lowdown on the Alice Ann Potter murder case? I'm just surprised you took so long."

Brady laughed. "Sorry, Judge. I wasn't sure there was a story."

"And now you are."

"Now I think there *might* be."

The judge nodded. "Fair enough." He sipped his coffee, blue eyes on his visitor. "What is it you want to know?"

Brady played with his coffee cup, trying to find the words he wanted. Then he looked up into the judge's eyes and spit it out: "Judge, I want to know why Cory Wilde didn't get the chair."

The lawyer sucked in his cheeks slightly and then blew out. He nodded slowly. "Good question. Cuts to the heart of the matter, doesn't it? If Cory Wilde did what he was accused of doing, and if men were executed for less in those days, how did he get off?"

Brady waited while the judge leaned back in his chair, his eyes on the ceiling. Finally, he looked down at Brady and smiled awkwardly. "Would you print it if I admitted I botched the job?"

"Did you?"

"That's a value judgment, a matter of opinion. I was younger. I hadn't tried but a couple of murder cases and they were easy ones. People make mistakes."

"And you made a mistake in your presentation?"

"Well, I might have underestimated the strength of our evidence." He leaned forward. "You see, Pete, I had to make sure that man was taken off the streets. You wouldn't know from looking at him now, but he was a hothead, had a terrible temper. He was making threats. There were others in his family. You haven't been here long, but this is really different from New Orleans. People take injuries to their families seriously. I was afraid of a full-scale clan feud breaking out. So was Judge Troy. Suppose the only option for the jury had been first-degree murder

67

and the chair? Faced with the possibility, Cory's family might have taken it out on them; one or two of them might have hesitated to convict. It was better to toss in the option of second-degree and have Cory out of circulation. Of course, *nobody* thought he'd be back here, ever. That took us by surprise."

"Why do you think they *did* let him out, Judge?"

The judge smiled cynically. "You know the governor and I aren't exactly on kissing terms. I supported his main opponent in the last election. Sure, I sent a letter to the parole board when Cory came up, but the governor appoints all five members. I have their formal statement, if you're interested." He opened his desk drawer and removed a sheet of paper with the state seal on the letterhead and laid it before Brady.

"As you can see, they claim that Cory Wilde was a perfect prisoner for twenty-nine years; that the federal courts are raising hell with the state about crowded prisons; that Cory is under a strict order not to provoke anyone or to discuss the case; and that they agree with the evaluation of the prison authorities that Cory Wilde has been rehabilitated. And then they cite all those trumped-up figures about how it's younger people that commit all the crimes."

"You don't agree?"

"I figure one murder a lifetime is enough. But I'm not the parole board."

"You're not afraid of him, then?"

"Son, I'm too old to be afraid of anything like that."

"What about Cory's family? Nobody tried to get revenge?"

"Nah. The second-degree conviction kind of took the steam out of that." The judge tugged at an ear. "And most of 'em are gone now."

Brady shifted slightly in his seat. "Have you ever heard of a parolee being released back to the community that convicted him after a crime like this?"

"Rarely," the judge agreed. "I've been calling all over the place and getting the runaround. Best I can make is that Cory Wilde slipped through the chinks. And nobody wants to do anything until the parole board can meet again or the governor comes back from California."

"I see." Brady took a drink of coffee, trying to think which

68

direction to take now. "Judge, I don't guess there's any chance he was innocent."

"Innocent?" The judge snorted. He reached into his lower desk drawer and brought out a heavy volume Brady recognized. "Here. This is the transcript. Read this if you have any doubts."

"I have read it," Brady said quietly. "And I still wonder why Boynton Jenks just happened to be where he was and why he, of all people, was so willing to help the law."

The old judge shrugged. "How do I know? Stranger things've happened. Maybe he didn't like Cory. But don't forget, his testimony was corroborated by the hair sample they found in Cory's truck."

"Couldn't Jenks have put it there?"

"Jenks?" The judge guffawed. "Boy Jenks didn't have enough brains to tie his shoes without help. A hair sample's the last thing he'd have thought of if he was trying to blame somebody. You're talking high technology."

Brady nodded reluctantly. "I guess so. But what about Cory's lack of scratch marks?"

"What about it? He was bigger than Alice Ann. He threatened her if she didn't let him have his way. So how could she fight? There's a copy of the autopsy, if you want to borrow it."

"Thanks," Brady acknowledged, taking the report.

"No," the judge affirmed, "I think the evidence was strong and Cory's lucky still to be alive, not to mention being free. Hell, I figure it was just one of those things. He was probably a little unhinged by the argument with his wife, finding out he was going to have a young one, whether he wanted to stay with his wife or not. She left and he sat there by himself, had a few beers, and then went on the prowl. He picked up an innocent-looking girl but deep down was the feeling she wasn't so innocent, after all." The judge leaned forward, once more the prosecutor in the courtroom: "Deep down, to him, she was just like his wife, a conniving, vicious female who would use her body and his weakness to trap him. Well, this time he wasn't going to be trapped. This time . . ." The judge's voice lowered to a dramatic whisper. "This time he was going to come out ahead. He takes her to his place, he has his way with her, either with her consent or after threatening her. And then, imagining it's really

69

his wife lying there beside him, all the resentment and anger bursts out and he puts his hands on her throat, pressing, like some demon from inside him has suddenly taken control. . . ." The judge strangled an imaginary neck and then sat back in his chair again. "It didn't matter if it was Alice Ann. It could've been any woman or girl he saw. She was just the one that luck threw in his way."

"Quite a summation, Judge."

The older man smiled and put his hands behind his head. "Don't get a chance to do them nowadays. I just have to sit there and try to stay awake."

"Judge, is there anybody else alive who might throw any light on this case? Any of the investigating officers, say, or the state-police personnel?"

"Gawd, Pete, you're talking thirty years. The state-police crew has long since retired and Sheriff Thomas is dead. Nobody on his staff is still around." He thumped the transcript. "I'm afraid that's the best source you'll have."

"I was afraid you'd say that."

"But now you can tell *me* something," Honeycutt said. "Your friend Penelope Martingale . . . what's her stake in all this? Why is she renting him a house when the whole town would just as soon he left on the next bus? Is she just crazy, or is she trying to prove something?"

Brady shook his head. "Judge, when I find out, I'll tell you."

The judge finished his coffee and set the cup down on his blotter. "And another thing: I'd like to know who's supporting the man. You don't think it's that daughter of his?"

"You know about his daughter?" Brady asked, suddenly alert.

"Well, of course, I know he *has* one someplace. But I haven't heard anything of the child since she was born. Hmmm. Guess she's a woman, now."

"I guess so," Brady agreed, rising. "Judge, I appreciate your help."

"Anytime, Peter." Honeycutt shook hands with him and walked back with him to the front door. "If I hear anything, I'll let you know." He squinted at the publisher. "Now, is this going to be a big front-page story?"

"I don't know how big it will be," Brady said. "But I have a feeling it will be, sooner or later."

Honeycutt laid a friendly hand over Brady's shoulder, steering him out the door. "Well, just remember, this is a small town. People can't take a lot of shocks here, like in New Orleans. They're more likely to resent a big hoopla than appreciate the trouble it took you to dig it all up."

Brady stepped out into the sunlight. "Oh, one other question, Judge Honeycutt: Do you have any idea who might have called and reported the location of Alice Ann's body, before Jenks came forward?"

The judge smiled tightly and shook his head. "Sure don't. But it was probably some friend he blabbed to. You can't keep any secrets in a place like this."

The editor nodded. "I hope you're right, Judge."

9

BY the middle of the afternoon, the day's business having been disposed of, Brady settled down again with the dummy for the next day's issue. He had dismissed Mrs. Rickenbacker for an early supper and now considered his options with the lead story.

The judge had been right, of course: People would not appreciate his reopening an old wound any more than they had appreciated his story on the MacBride case last year. And, at this point, what was there to say? There was, he realized, no effective way to link the Jenks accident and the return of Cory Wilde. Regretful, he reverted to his original layout, feeling beaten. He was still staring at the paste-up five minutes later when the phone rang.

"Is this the *Daily Planet*?" asked a voice he recognized.

"Kelly!"

"Who else? I was just sitting down here with a boring assignment and thinking about you all alone up there, with the issue to get out tomorrow."

"And wishing you could be up here to sweat over it with me?"

"Well, the idea of raising a little sweat with you isn't half bad. How's it going?"

"As usual. We'll get it done."

"Sure you will. Anything more on that Cory Wilde business?"

He told her about the incident in front of Cory's house the night before. "Have you got anything on the parole decision?"

"Ah, ha! You expected me to blow it off, didn't you? Well, surprise. I've not only got the transcript of the hearing but I talked to the secretary of the parole board."

"And?"

"I'll tell you about it later," she purred. "You *do* have to go to Alec tonight to deliver the dummy to the printer's?"

"That much hasn't changed," he admitted, dreading the late-night drive to drop off the copy that would serve as the master for printing, and the hour's drive back."

"Well, why don't you just stay over? Take a room at the Bentley?"

"Stay over in Alexandria?"

"I thought you might want to. It's four-thirty now. If I bathed and got a bite to eat, I could be in Alec by seven-thirty and have the covers turned down."

Brady's heart thumped. "But what about classes tomorrow?"

"If I get out by six, I'll be in Baton Rouge by eight. So I miss my first class. Big deal. That's Poirrier's course on the history of the press. I can get the notes from the guy next to me."

"I think you just talked yourself into a sleepless night."

"I hoped so. By the way, shall I register as Mrs. Brady?"

"I like the sound of it."

She made an approving sound in her throat. "See yah."

It was eleven o'clock when Brady at last realized there was nothing further he could do with the issue. He had rearranged a few columns, cut some verbiage from the story on the police-jury meeting, and reassured himself that his own story of the Jenks accident was as much as could be said. He made a final call to Matt Garitty's home to be certain that no late news had come from the crime lab in Baton Rouge, and then dismissed Ripley for the night. Mrs. Rickenbacker had left earlier, which was all right, since there was little she could do on this part of the operation. She would, instead, come in tomorrow at eight to field calls if Brady decided to catch a few extra minutes of sleep. She did not know, of course, that any extra sleep he got would be in Alexandria.

Yes, it was a professional job, Brady told himself, looking back over his work, and yet he knew better than to expect that the blandness of the front page would deceive any of the readers; because there on the third page, with the rest of the notices and advertisements, was the simple box with Cory's announcement. If Brady had gotten calls before, the effect now would be a fire storm.

Well, there was no help for it. He had accepted the notice and he was damned if he'd pull it now.

He locked up the office, his briefcase under his arm, the precious master copy inside, and hurried out to his car. He threw the briefcase on the seat beside him, started the engine, and five minutes later was crossing the tracks just south of town. He opened the window and put on the radio, catching a country-music station. After three selections on the pains of adulterous love, he switched the radio off. The road was almost deserted, except for occasional flatbed trucks loaded with pine logs, and he shot past them, resenting every second Kelly was by herself. It was just before twelve when he made the bypass and a few minutes later he crossed the Red River into Alexandria. He threaded his way through the nearly deserted streets to the printer's, dropped off his dummy, and used the phone to call the hotel.

"Peter?"

His heart jumped at the sound of her voice. "I'll be there in a minute."

"Room three oh seven," she said with a laugh. "The one with the naked lady."

He hung up and sped a few streets over into the heart of the old downtown section, where the Bentley stood like a symbol of past triumphs. He parked, hurried to the elevator, and waited impatiently for the doors to close. The old hotel had been handsomely renovated, with rich carpeting and stately furnishings, but he hardly noticed them, his eyes instead on the brass door numbers. With a throb of excitement, he reached 307 and started to knock. Before his hand reached the wood, however, the door swung open and there she was, all black flowing hair and green eyes, a crimson robe loosely held in place by one hand.

"I thought you'd never come," she whispered, and assumed a mock Mae West pose. She turned suddenly and started inside, letting the robe flow behind her. Brady closed the door, fastened the safety chain, and when he turned back around, she was standing on the other side of the bed, stripes of lamplight across her body. Slowly, with a tantalizing smile, she opened the robe.

It was much later, though how much later neither of them knew. They lay side by side, a soft breath from the air conditioning cooling their glistening bodies.

"Hallelujah," Kelly declared at last, whistling up into the darkness. "Now I can face midterms."

"The best stress experts always recommend vigorous physical exercise," Brady said. "But they never tell how many people the exercise kills."

Kelly turned her head to smile at him. "That only goes for *old* people," she said puckishly. "I haven't thought of you as old since . . ."

"Mmmm," Brady replied, thinking of the first time they had made love—at his house, over a year ago. That had been in the middle of a strange business, too, and the memory of it brought his thoughts back to Cory Wilde. He looked over at her and she frowned.

"Uh, oh. I know that look. Now that he's done his duty, he wants to know where the payoff is."

"No. Just what you found out at the parole board."

"Well, the secretary said they were surprised Matt Garitty was the only one from Troy to come testify against Cory. And they knew Matt hadn't even been sheriff back when it happened. They read the letters the judge and the DA wrote, but personal appearances speak louder than the written word and I think they felt taken for granted just because they'd denied Cory's previous requests and the governor had made a lot of promises about keeping criminals off the streets. But Cory appeared and so did some of the people on the prison staff, and Cory made a good enough impression that the board split two to two and the board chairman voted for Cory."

"I wonder why?" Brady asked.

"Who knows? But I had a funny feeling from the way she answered the questions: I had the impression there was something she didn't want to get into."

"You mean some juice somewhere?"

"*Some*thing. It wouldn't be the first time a parole got sold in this state."

Brady thought for a moment. "No. And that could explain the foul-up over the lack of travel restrictions as a condition of parole. But doesn't it seem funny to you that a paroled convict would have enough money to retire to the country? What do they pay them for work in Angola? Eleven cents an hour?"

"I know what you're saying. I hope you don't want me to find his bankroll."

"No. Just his daughter. They may turn out to be the same."

"His *daughter?*"

Brady sketched his conversation with Ripley. "So, you see, in 1960, after Felicia Canby Wilde died, Cory's daughter was taken to Baton Rouge by cousins. Now, what happened to that child?"

"You look at me like I should know."

"Of course not. I didn't mean that at all. It was a purely rhetorical question. There's no way you could trace a child who was taken from Winnfield to Baton Rouge twenty-nine years ago. I mean, even if I got the name of the family that took her. It would take a private detective, somebody used to investigating. You've got too much to do, and all your experience has been on weeklies, anyway, not as an investigative reporter, and . . ."

She sat upright in bed and reached over to jab his ribs. "Okay, Brady. You made your point. I'll find her. Wherever she is, I'll find where she's hiding."

"I wouldn't dream . . ." He rolled away, but she fell on him, reaching for his ticklish spots.

"Of course not. Because I'm not going to let you. I'm going to keep you awake all night."

This time, the darkness outside was turning gray when they drifted off to sleep in each other's arms.

The sun was just burning off the mist outside as he watched her dress. He wished he could stay here forever, safe from the conflict that he knew was about to explode about him when the paper reached the public. There was nothing he could do about it, so he swung himself out of bed.

"Maybe you can come up on Saturday," he suggested. "Day after tomorrow."

"And bring my homework with me?" she asked, slipping into her blouse. "Or did you just want me to bring the answer to your question about the mystery daughter?"

"That, too," he said. "If you have it. But I don't really expect—"

"Shut up, Brady." She snapped her jeans and went to the mirror, where she seemed to disapprove of what she saw. "I'll do my best, but there're still people *you* could talk to in Troy."

"The ones who were involved are mostly dead, except the judge and your father."

She ran a comb through her hair, regarded the result, and put the comb in her purse. "What about Ernie Hughes? I know he's not dead. I saw him the last time I was up."

"Ernie Hughes? I've heard the name, but—"

"He used to be the district ranger for the Forest Service. He ran that part of the national forest almost single-handed. Stepped down eight or nine years ago. He must be in his seventies by now."

"What's he got to do with the Wilde case?"

She turned around, leaning back against the bureau, and folded her arms. "He was chief deputy sheriff before he took the federal job. He probably knows all about the Potter murder."

Brady nodded, thoughtful. "Makes sense. I wonder why Judge Honeycutt didn't mention him?"

Kelly shrugged. "Who knows? Probably forgot." She picked up her purse. "Anyway, I've given you your lead for the week. The rest is up to you."

She pecked him on the lips and then opened the door into the hallway. "Good hunting, Brady."

He drove back over the river and into the pinewoods, dissatisfaction gnawing away at him. Ernie Hughes. Why hadn't someone mentioned the old man? He vaguely recalled that the Hughes place was a few miles outside of town, with a little pond in front, and he had a vague image of a raw-boned old man in a battered pickup.

However, as he crossed the tracks into Troy, thoughts of Ernie Hughes were crowded from his mind by the sound of sirens. He felt an intimation of dread and went past his office, following the sounds toward the center of town. He arrived in time to see the fire truck stopping in front of the courthouse. My God, was it the building itself, then?

He slipped into a parking lot and saw that the firemen were running in the other direction, toward one of the structures across the street. There was a smell of smoke in the air and even as he watched, Brady saw one of the firemen crash an ax through the window of one of the business establishments.

With a sick feeling, he recognized the place they were entering. It was Sam Berry's pharmacy.

10

TEN minutes after they had entered, the firemen came out. Brady left the small crowd and stepped across a fire hose to talk to their leader, whom he recognized as a salesman at the local Western Auto outlet.

"What's the situation?"

The fireman, a middle-aged man with a clay-dab nose, replaced a small fire extinguisher in its holder.

"Not too bad," he said. "Just the back room. Ain't gonna make Sam very happy, though."

"Any idea what caused it?"

The fireman squinted. "I reckon I'll let Chief Triplett make any statements about that."

As if in answer, the blue-clad form of the police chief materialized from around the fire engine, where evidently he had been talking to some of the other members of the fire crew. When he saw Brady, however, he stopped short.

"What about it, Chief?" the newsman asked. "Was it arson?"

Triplett sucked in his cheeks and gave Brady a narrow look that made it clear that he considered the editor an opponent.

"I'm investigating. I won't have anything to say till I finish."

"Then you won't mind if I talk to Sam Berry," Brady told him, watching the pharmacist get out of his car on the other side of the fire line and hurry forward, face drawn.

"Look here, Mr. Brady . . ." the policeman began, but the publisher was already halfway to the druggist.

"My God," Sam muttered as Brady approached. "What's happened?"

"I don't know," Brady said, "but it sounds like Chief Triplett suspects something."

"What? You mean. . . ?"

Brady shrugged. "I think you should ask him."

Sam nodded and approached the policeman, who seemed to shrink slightly as the pharmacist neared.

"Chief, what the hell's going on?" Sam turned to the fireman. "Harvey, did you say something about arson?"

The policeman looked at the fireman, who licked his lips. "Well, I don't think it's something needs to be in the newspaper."

"For God's sake," Sam protested, his face white. "What do I care about the damn newspaper? I'm asking you about my store. Was it arson or not?"

Harvey gave a shrug. "Maybe. Found the back door stove in."

"You mean somebody broke in and then set it afire?" Sam demanded.

"I'm going to do an investigation," Triplett declared, taking half a step forward.

"Sure," Sam said. He turned away and started for the front door. "Come on, Mr. Brady. You might as well see what happened, too."

Brady followed him through the smashed door and down the aisle. The front of the store, Brady realized, had not suffered much damage, despite the smoke smell. It was only when they crossed behind the counter and went into the rear of the building that the effects of the fire were evident. There, in the back room, the walls were blackened and a white chemical powder from the extinguishers coated the table, beakers, and lab instruments. The shelves were in the worst condition, the cardboard boxes that once had filled them having been reduced to heaps of ashes; and when Brady stepped over to the wall, he smelled the fumes of a strong solvent.

"They were right," he told Sam. "Somebody set the fire."

Sam sighed and raised his hands in frustration. "But *why*? I haven't done anything to anybody." He went to the broken rear door and stared down at the lock. "Do you think it was somebody after drugs?"

"If they were, they didn't do much to burn the evidence," Brady pointed out. "You don't keep any supplies back here, do you?"

"No. They're all up front, behind the counter or in the dispensing area. I keep some of them locked up in a closet, but I noticed on the way in that it doesn't seem to have been touched. Unless . . ." He went over to where one of the wooden shelves had collapsed onto the floor in a charred pile. He reached down and came up with a small fragment of brown paper.

"That's strange."

"What, Sam?"

"The herbs you gave me to analyze: I put them up here, on the shelf with some of the old business records I was getting ready to dump, and it looks like the fire caught them." He stared at the editor. "Mr. Brady, you don't think. . . ?"

Brady bent down and sniffed the burned fragments. When

he straightened up again, his face was set. "Yes, I'm afraid I do. Whoever set the fire poured the starter fluid right here."

The two men were still staring at each other when they heard footsteps and the figure of the police chief came through the doorway, followed by the fireman.

"What's going on here?" Ned Triplett demanded. "Sam, I wouldn't be giving out stories to the paper. I've seen how things get twisted and changed around."

A flicker went through Sam's jaw and suddenly the chalky color of his face went red with blood. "Damn it, Ned, this is my store. This is how I make my living, or I did until this happened. It seems to me that if you were doing your job, we wouldn't be talking about this right now. If I were you, I'd be out there somewhere looking for whoever did this, instead of standing here trying to cover your butt."

The policeman blinked, clearly taken aback. "There's no cause to get your back up. I can't watch everything. City council won't pay for another policeman and that sheriff gets all the free headlines." He scowled at Brady.

The editor folded his arms. "Chief Triplett, if you catch the parties responsible, I can promise you the *Express* will put it on the front page."

Harvey, the fireman, nudged the policeman in the ribs. "Sounds fair to me, Ned. 'Course, if you *don't* catch 'em, he'll probably put *that* on the front page, too."

Triplett shot a venomous look at his colleague. "Seems like the fire department ought to give some help," he muttered. "Or are you just here to run your jaw?"

"I'm here to tell you gents goodbye," Harvey announced. "This is a *volunteer* department, remember? We leave investigations to the professionals." He winked at Brady and sidled out, leaving the chief shifting from one foot to the other.

Triplett licked his lips again and then shrugged. "I'll see what I can do. But it ain't like the whole thing burned down. Hell, that's why folks have insurance." He stomped out leaving Brady and Sam together.

"Well, I guess there's some truth to that much," Brady said, putting a hand on Sam's shoulder. "I'm sure the insurance company will honor the claim."

Sam looked down at the floor and Brady had the impression he was undergoing some inner struggle. He started forward, out of the burned area, and then stopped near the old scale.

"Look at this," he said, touching it fondly. "My father got this scale in the 1940s. It's sort of like the grandfather clock in the song." There was a little catch in his voice and Brady waited. When Sam looked up again, his eyes were moist.

"Mr. Brady, the truth is, I was short of money this last quarter. I needed all I had to keep the place going. I knew the building was old, but it was in good condition."

Brady's stomach sank. "Sam, you aren't telling me that . . ."

Sam nodded. "I guess I am. I was going to renew the insurance policy as soon as business picked up a little. Until then, I thought I could save the premium. I guess I was a fool."

Brady tried to think of something to say but nothing came.

"I reckon over at the Val-Save they're having the last laugh," Sam said. "I was so sure once people realized the little bit more they pay for prescriptions with me meant better service, when they realized that discount store doesn't care about them, about anything but turning a fast buck . . ."

"I'm sure they'll realize it," Brady soothed. "And you'll be on your feet again and open before long."

Sam gave him a bleak smile and shambled out through the doorway, leaving Brady in the smoky room.

When Brady reached the sidewalk, the firemen were gone and the little crowd had already dispersed. He sauntered over to the judge's office and found the old jurist reading the newspaper.

"Little fire over at Sam's?" the judge asked, raising his shaggy white brows. "I saw the fire engine a few minutes ago." He shook his head. "Poor Sam. Nothing's gone right since his father died. And such a nice young man." He put the newspaper aside. "Well, what can I do for you, Peter? Not something else about Cory Wilde?"

"As a matter of fact, Judge, it is." Brady took a seat in the padded chair in front of the big oak desk. "I wanted to ask you about Ernie Hughes. I understand he was chief deputy then."

The judge frowned and tugged at an earlobe. "Ernie Hughes. Of course. I should've remembered him. I plain forgot. Fact is, I don't think of him as a deputy anymore, just as the ranger. He did a damn good job for the Forest Service. Calmed down a lot of people."

"Calmed them? How so?"

The judge smiled and leaned back in his chair. "Son, there's no love lost hereabouts between the Forest Service and the locals. Not the kind of thing city people think about much. National forest, Teddy Roosevelt, conservation, and all that. How could anybody object? Down in the city, folks don't think about where the forest came from. But once upon a time, the people in this parish owned that land. And some of 'em wish they still did. Some of 'em look at the national forest as nothing but a big land grab."

"But the government paid them, didn't it?" the newsman asked.

The old man nodded. "Sure. But how much is the land you love worth? How much is fair market value for land you or your daddy or his daddy cleared with bare hands? And, of course, once the government comes in, it starts making rules and laws about who can use the land and for what. Sticks in the craw of a lot of people that were used to just going out and hunting when they felt like it. Now they have government bureaucrats out there driving green trucks, laying down the law. While I don't condone the practice, I can at least understand why some of 'em set fires."

"You mean to get back at the government?"

"Sometimes that," the judge allowed. "And sometimes because when there's a big enough crew, the government hires on local people to help fight the blaze. Like I say, it's indefensible as a practice, but I can understand their thinking. Of course, it's mainly folks like the Jenkses would do that sort of thing. Most people just hold their resentment in. But it makes it important to have a local man as a ranger, somebody who can smooth things over, talk to people, at least see things from their point of view."

"And that's the way Ernie Hughes was?"

"Absolutely. He could've used that position to build himself a political base, too. It's been done before. But he didn't. Just did his job. When he stepped down, they lost a good man."

"I'd like to talk to him," Brady said.

Honeycutt pursed his lips. "Well, I don't see why he

wouldn't. You want me to call him for you, tell him you're coming?"

"I'd appreciate that."

"You know where he lives?" the old man asked. "Brick house out on Eighty-four, with the wagon wheel in the front yard."

"I know the place," Brady said, rising to shake hands with the judge.

"Good luck," the judge called. "I'll be interested to hear what Ernie has to say."

Brady drove the block to his office, gratified to see that it was open and that Mrs. Rickenbacker was manning the telephones.

"Anything happening?" he asked.

"There was a fire," she reported. "I got a call about it right after I got here. I called your house but . . ."

"That's all right," Brady told her. "I just came from there. It wasn't serious." Except, he thought, to Sam Berry, whom it may have ruined.

"Mr. Brady, I have to go to Natchitoches this afternoon. My sister isn't well at all and I thought I'd leave at noon if that was all right."

Brady, who had been expecting it, nodded. "Ripley should be in then," he said, reflecting that the younger man would be more efficient in dealing with the phone calls about Cory Wilde's ad that would begin as soon as the weekly issue hit the streets. Mrs. Rickenbacker hated controversy and he had no doubt her sister's illness was diplomatically contrived to get her out of the office during a difficult time.

"I'll want to sit down with you soon to look at the cash-flow situation," he said. "But no hurry. Right now, I'm going out to Ernie Hughes's place."

The bookkeeper sucked in her breath and then quickly looked down at her desk.

"Mrs. R., what did I say?"

"Nothing," she said from tight lips. "Nothing at all."

"Mrs. Rickenbacker, I said the name Ernie Hughes and you acted like I'd said Attila the Hun."

"Well, I don't know about *him,* but I know about Ernie Hughes. But that's neither here nor there."

"No? Come on, Mrs. R., talk."

"Well." She firmed her hair with one hand. "Now I'm not one to tell tales . . ."

"Of course not."

"But the man is nothing but a political hack. When he worked for Sheriff Thomas, he was one and when he was district ranger, he was one, too. All those Hugheses were like that. None of them could make a living if it wasn't for political jobs."

"You don't think he did a good job as ranger?"

"A good job?" She gave a bitter little laugh. "How could he? What did he know about being a ranger? No college, no training. My cousin Alvin had a degree in forestry from LSU and they passed him over. You tell me what sense that makes?"

"I don't know, Mrs. R. Why don't you tell *me?*"

"Well, it was connections, that's all. Everybody and his brother called for him. They put pressure so he'd get that job. Grady Epps, the congressman; Senator Foley; Sheriff Thomas; Judge Creswell Troy: They all called and wrote letters. Alvin never had a chance."

"And Arden Honeycutt? Did he write or call?"

"Arden Honeycutt?" She snorted. *"Especially* him. Or so word has it. But he and Ernie were tight. I guess they still are." She shook her head. "It's a pity, a real pity. Alvin would have done a better job."

Brady left her and drove out through the center of town and along the highway, heading west. Ernie Hughes: a man the town powers had pushed into a good job; a man who knew about the Potter murder case; a man whom the judge had forgotten to mention. Did it all mean something, or was it just happenstance? Was it just that Ernie Hughes had been a member of the courthouse crowd and that they had gone to bat for one of their own?

He slowed as he saw the house he wanted, a brick ranch-style dwelling with a wooden wagon wheel imbedded in the earth beside the driveway and a small forest of pines shading the front lawn. A station wagon and a truck were in the drive and as Brady pulled up behind them, a collie ambled out of the garage to in-

spect the visitor. Brady knocked, hearing the distant sound of a
television inside. He had not met Ernie Hughes and for the moment could not recall whether Hughes subscribed to the *Express*.

The door opened and a small bent woman with gray hair
peered out at him. "Yes?"

"My name is Peter Brady, from the *Express*. Judge Honeycutt
called Mr. Hughes about me."

The woman's lip trembled and she shook her head quickly.
"No. I don't know anything about that. My husband isn't here."

"I see. Do you know when he'll be back?"

"No. He's gone for . . . I don't know."

Brady reached into his pocket and took out one of his business cards. "Would you ask him to call me, please? Thank you."

As he walked away, the collie sniffed his heels and he sensed
the woman's eyes on his back. There was no doubt about it: She
was afraid.

11

BRADY drove back, wondering what it was that could have
scared the old man so badly that he would not even talk. He came
to the city limits and saw the new Val-Save on his left, its lot
already starting to fill with cars. The fire at Sam's could hardly
have had anything to do with the Val-Save. They didn't *have* to
start a fire to get rid of Sam Berry. No, the object had been the
herbs he had given Sam to analyze, the herbs that had come from
Penelope Martingale's garden.

He slowed as he approached his office and then forced himself past and turned onto the El road that led to Penelope's. Pen
was eccentric—everyone knew that—but surely she couldn't be
involved. . . ?

This time, she was not waiting for him in the front yard.

Her car was in the drive, though, so he knew she must be home. He went up onto the porch and knocked. There was no sound. He went around to the back and called her name, but still there was no answer. Some sheets waved at him from the clothesline and a hundred feet away, the barn door squeaked in the wind, but there were no other sounds. Maybe, he thought, she was in the barn. He walked over, a few chickens pecking at his tracks as if he might be bringing food. The barn was empty, so he turned and went back to the house.

It was only when he had lifted his hand to knock on the back door that he heard the sound of someone crying.

"Pen?" There was no answer, so he tried the knob. The door opened and he found himself in the kitchen, surrounded by the smells of herbs and spices. A teapot was still on one of the burners and a plate on the counter attested to a breakfast of eggs and toast.

"Penelope?" He started forward, into the hallway, and stopped when it came again: a low moan, followed by something akin to a whimper. It was coming from behind the door on his right. He hesitated and then gently shoved it open.

Penelope Martingale, still dressed in a turquoise nightgown, was facedown on the bed, eyes closed, fingers digging into the sheets.

Brady reached out, grabbed her shoulders, and shook her hard. "Penelope. What's wrong? What's happening?"

She shook her head, as if to deny what was happening, and he tried to turn her over, but she turned her head away. He looked around for something to rouse her. Smelling salts. Maybe she would have some in the bathroom medicine cabinet.

He opened the door opposite the bedroom, but it led into the office, with its computer, modem, printer, and a shelf of software binders. His eyes skimmed over them: D-Base II; Lotus; Dialog; and some business programs. A *Wall Street Journal* lay on the desk and beside it was a framed photograph of a smiling girl in a white prom gown with a grave-looking young man in a dark suit. The girl, Brady realized, was a younger version of Penelope. He set the photo back down, trying to understand what it was that bothered him about the picture. Was it the realization that once Penelope had been like other girls her age, caught up in the cycle of dating, dances, and other school activities? Had she been considered a little odd even back then? he wondered. Or had it all started later on? Then, as he turned, his arm brushed against an envelope and it fell to the floor. He picked it up and replaced it on the desk. It bore the return address of the All-South Corporation and was stamped PROXY MATERIAL ENCLOSED. Brady frowned, trying to recall where he had heard the name All-South. Giving up, he closed the door again and went to the end of the hall, where this time he found the right door.

The smelling salts were in a small bottle on a shelf almost devoid of other medicines. He went back to the bedroom and was halfway to the bed when he realized Penelope was staring at him with a confused expression.

"Peter. What happened? What are you doing here?" she asked drowsily.

"I came to talk to you. You seemed to be in some kind of trouble. I heard you moaning from outside and came in."

She frowned and took a deep breath. "Oh, my God." She turned her face to the wall. "I don't remember a thing."

"Nothing?"

She shivered and closed her eyes, as if trying to rid herself of the memory. When she spoke again, it was in a voice so low, he had trouble hearing:

"A presence. I've felt it ever since . . . for the last week or so. An evil presence, trying to enter, to take control."

"You mean not your Indian guide?"

"Not No-Do-Tah-Wah. He's a benevolent spirit. This one is from one of the other planes." She was crying softly now and Brady patted her shoulder. She turned suddenly, facing him with red-rimmed eyes. "Peter, I'm scared."

Brady thought how easy it would be to tell her there was nothing of which to be afraid, but, damn it, *something* had happened.

"It'll be okay, Pen. I promise. Tell me, who—or what—is this evil spirit? Can you describe it?"

She shook her head. "No. It's just a *presence*."

Then she took a deep breath.

"It'll be all right, Peter. These things sometimes happen to people who are gifted with sensitivity."

87

"Pen, listen. Does it seem odd to you that all this is happening right after Cory Wilde came to town?"

"Cory Wilde? You think he's causing this?" She sat up, dabbing at her eyes with a tissue from the bedside table. "No. It isn't Cory Wilde. I don't have that feeling when I'm around him. He is not an evil presence, no matter what people think."

Suddenly, the picture in Penelope's office sprang into Brady's mind. "Did you know Cory before, Pen? Back before he went to prison?"

"Know him? No. He was fifteen or so years older than I was. I don't think we ever met. What an odd thing to ask."

"Yes. I guess so."

Penelope rolled out of bed, wrapped herself in a crimson robe, and started for the kitchen. "Well, you can at least have some tea while you're here. I don't know about *you,* but I need something soothing."

Brady nodded and accompanied her into the kitchen. She felt the teapot. "Cold. I remember eating. It must have taken me just after that." She started the fire under the kettle and added some herbs to the pot beside it.

Brady lifted her empty cup and sniffed, but the only odor was a faint sweetness.

"Peter, what on earth are you doing?"

"I don't know. I wish I did." He sat down again. "Pen, that medicine you gave me. What the hell's in it?"

"Strong language." Penelope sniffed.

"Strong medicine," the editor countered. "Now 'fess up. I want to know."

"Ordinarily, I don't reveal these things," Penelope said. "But if it's that important . . ."

"It is, believe me."

"All right." She waited for him to take out his pad and pencil. "This won't appear in the paper, for God's sake?"

"No. I don't want to have to visit you in jail."

Penelope shook her head in disgust. "The laws in this country are so archaic. I can't see what possible business it is of the authorities what people grow in their own gardens. But, since it's between friends, and I know you'd *die* before you revealed a confidence, here goes. There was a small amount of spearmint, al-

88

ways good for the digestion, and a specific for any number of flulike ailments. It was from my garden, which is completely devoid of the artificial chemicals that they put in fertilizers today. That's important. There was some dried lemon, which I order specially from a commune in Florida that grows them in special soils. There was some cannabis, which allows an unfolding of spiritual—"

"Cannabis? You mean marijuana?"

"Now don't go getting hyper; your aura is already turning brownish. I have a small plot back in the woods. Then there are some mushrooms that have mind-expanding qualities. I gather them. That's the difficult part, of course, getting the measurements right—"

"Christ," Brady exploded. "And you gave this to Cory Wilde, too? Don't you know he could end up back in jail if they find any of this on him?"

"Philistines," Penelope spat. "In that case, I would be ethically bound to step forward and assume responsibility."

"Which means, the way this town feels, you'd both end up in the same cell."

"Oh, Peter . . ."

"No. Listen to me, Pen. I want you to get rid of that stuff. Now."

"Well, as a matter of fact, I don't have more of the mixture. I gave you the last. As for the marijuana, I find it extremely relaxing, and no one will ever prove that the few little plants back there are mine."

Brady threw up his hands. "I did what I could."

Penelope poured some of the tea into his cup and he tasted it, half-fearful of the result, but this time there seemed to be no cause for concern. He finished his cup and got up.

"I have to go now, Pen. But one thing I wanted to check with you: How did Cory Wilde know you had a house to rent?"

"*Really.* You're some detective, I must say."

"Pen, answer the question."

"It must have been the sign on the front lawn. He came over here and he seemed like a nice man, so we settled on the spot. He paid me a month's rent in advance, in cash, and a two-hundred-dollar damage deposit. He seemed very happy to find something so easily. Any further interrogations?"

"Not just now," Brady said, "but I'm sure I'll think of something later."

Brady was halfway back to the office when he remembered where he had heard of the All-South Corporation. It was the holding company for Val-Save.

12

WHEN he reached the office, Mrs. Rickenbacker had already fled, despite the fact that it was an hour before lunch, but the indomitable Ripley was there, his triumphant smile telling Brady that he had something to report.

"I talked to my uncle last night," Ripley told him. "And the name is Fenstermacher."

"Fenstermacher?" Brady smiled, too. "Are you sure?"

"That's right. Don't I take care of you, boss? It could have been Smith or Jones, but I managed to get you one a blind man could find."

"I don't know what I'd do without you, Ripley," Brady admitted, putting a hand on the younger man's shoulder. "But you didn't run Mrs. R. off, did you?"

"Me? Run her off?" Ripley drew back, pretending to be offended. "I just told her that Cory Wilde was coming in to place another ad."

Brady chuckled and reached for the phone. There was only an outside chance Kelly would be in her apartment, but he had made her agree to buy an answering machine. The line clicked and he heard her recorded voice:

"*Daily Planet*. At the sound of the tone, leave your name and Swiss bank account number."

"Listen. The name is Fenstermacher." He spelled it out for

her. "There can't be more than one or two in the directory. I'll be back in touch."

He disconnected, pondered a moment, and then looked up the judge's number. This time, the secretary seemed confused. "He's not here. Maybe later on. I could give him a message."

"Maybe if I call this afternoon."

"He'll be in court then."

Brady left his own number and hung up. There was no doubt about the hesitation in the woman's voice: The judge was cutting him off. But why? What was it that Judge Arden Honeycutt was afraid Brady might find out? The newsman considered another run out to the Hughes place but decided against it. He had work to do here. Maybe later on he would have a chance, when he had to drive out that way to do a story on a local horse breeder.

For the rest of the morning, he worked on routine projects, took a few calls for coverage of local functions, and sent Ripley out for a sandwich at lunch. Then, as one o'clock approached, he settled in, waiting for the blizzard of protests over Cory's ad.

Oddly, they never came. At three, a woman called to ask whether Cory Wilde was being given free space and when Brady replied that he was not, she seemed somewhat mollified. One person called to cancel his subscription without giving a reason. Otherwise, however, things were normal, and that in itself made Brady uneasy. It was as if people were reading, digesting, and deciding what to do. At three-thirty, he called the judge's chamber and was told the judge was unavailable. He tried the law office and was informed Honeycutt was not in. Finally, he called the jurist's house, but there was no answer.

At four, he left to do the horse breeder story. The breeder, who owned a farm west of town, wanted to give Brady a complete tour. He obviously loved his work and could not imagine that anyone else would not be fascinated. Brady followed him past the stalls, jotting notes as the owner called each horse by name and described it. Then he took the editor outside to the track and explained some of the subtleties of breeding racing stock, while one of his trainers practiced with a year-old mare. Brady asked the obligatory questions, made the right approving noises, and took some photographs, but his mind was still distant. When he was finally able to extricate himself at five-thirty, he drove back past the Hughes home, noticing that both vehicles were still in the drive. He had reached the city-limits sign when he muttered to himself in frustration, turned around, and headed for the little convenience store he had just passed. He went to the pay phone on the outside wall and looked up the Hughes number in the directory. He called and a woman answered.

"Mrs. Hughes, this is Peter Brady of the *Express*. I was there earlier, to see your husband. I was just by and saw his truck was in the driveway. I thought I'd drop by again in a minute. Judge Honeycutt said your husband would talk to me." Then, before she could reply, he thanked her and hung up.

He started back onto the highway and was already slowing for the Hughes house when he saw the pickup backing toward the road. He accelerated past and caught the truck in his rearview mirror; it was turning onto the highway, headed back toward town. He gave it a chance to round the first curve and then made a U-turn and shoved his accelerator to the floor. He caught up with it near the city limits and slowed, letting it stay a few hundred yards ahead of him. He followed it through the heart of town, past his own office, over the railroad tracks, and then south onto the Alexandria highway. The vehicle ahead of him picked up speed, whipping around a log truck and leaving Brady to curse the slow-moving rig as it lumbered up over a hill. When Brady was finally able to pass, the pickup was out of sight. On the roller coaster of hills that followed, Brady forced his speedometer to eighty. The old Ford started to tremble, and he eased off. There was a gravel road ahead, at the top of another hill, and the afternoon sun caught a haze of dust hanging cloudlike over both lanes. He stomped his brake and fought to keep from skidding.

He slid to a stop, a few feet from the summit and slid right, onto the gravel. The dust ahead of him confirmed his hunch. Somebody had turned here, just seconds ago, heading west, toward the lake.

He was in the national forest now, on one of the roads the government had built in the last ten years or so. It was an area he did not know and he wished he had taken the trouble to drop by the district headquarters for a map. As it was, he was getting farther from the highway with each mile, on terrain that was unfamiliar, where even the sheriff did not patrol, and at a time when the Forest Service workers had all quit for the day.

He had driven five miles when he came to a fork. The dust was heavier to the left, so he bore in that direction. Ahead, the trees formed a canopy over the road, like an ancient covered bridge, and the Galaxie bounced as the ruts deepened. It was a beautiful spot and Brady wished he had the time to enjoy it. He sensed that the road was dropping now and he came to several narrow bridges over winding creeks. The pines began to shift to hardwoods and in a few minutes he was in bottomland, with oak and cypress dotting the forest on either side. Even with the air conditioning, there was a smell of rotting vegetation and he knew he was coming to the lake.

Sure enough, ahead of him was a wall of cypress and he glimpsed green water covered by lily pads. The road curved right, following the lip of the lake, and then left again, and when the cypress wall thinned, he caught sight of the pickup coming out of the S-turn. Even as he watched, it slowed and halted, pulling to the edge of the road just the other side of a little bridge that spanned a feeder stream. Brady brought his own car to halt and looked around. There, to the right, was a trail into the swamp, with a pile of garbage off to one side. The surface looked firm enough and he eased his vehicle down off the road and brought it into the cover of the trees, grateful that it had not rained for over a week. He got out, closing his door softly. The garbage stank and he realized that someone had dumped a dead cat amidst the pile of bottles and old diapers. He held his breath and walked up onto the road and looked around. He was hidden from the pickup by trees, but if he kept to the paved surface, he would be seen. He stepped down, away from the road, keeping it between himself and the lake, and started forward through heavy grass. The ground softened and water sloshed into his shoes. He stifled a cough as the road dust settled over him and dodged as the razor-edged brush cut at his face. He was into the bend when he heard the sound of the other vehicle, its motor rising and falling on the warm air, growing near with every second. He increased his pace, oblivious to the mud and the things that slithered away from him in the swamp. He had to get nearer. He had to be able to see what happened.

The engine was close behind him now and he heard the crunch of gravel as the vehicle spun into the curve. He shrank back against the built-up roadbed and caught a blur as the other car passed. He choked and spat out the dust, picking up his pace to a run now. The heavy brown dust cloud was a cover and he broke out of the tall grass, slipping and skidding along the sloping road revetment. The car had stopped and he caught a glimpse of it ahead, a blue Volvo. He let himself slide back down out of sight and crept forward on hands and knees.

The two drivers were talking, in voices too low for him to hear. He edged closer, coming to the concrete bridge sidings. He heard a shout and realized the pair were arguing, but he was still too far away to be able to make out their words. He started across the narrow stream and felt his legs sink into the muck. It was impossible; if he fell, his splashing might be heard by the two men above. He backed out, a thin smelly coat of mud tarring his shoes and ankles. He made his way back under the bridge, to the side facing the lake, and crawled toward the top.

Now he could hear the words more clearly. One man seemed to be doing most of the talking and he was excited.

"I tell you, I don't want to be bothered," he declared.

The other man said something in an undertone as Brady reached the top of the embankment and edged his face around the siding.

The driver of the pickup was standing between the two vehicles, blocking Brady's view of the man in the Volvo. As he watched, however, Brady saw the standing man put out a hand to the window of the Volvo and when he brought it back down, there was something brown in it. The Volvo shot gravel then, lunging away to vanish in the haze. The standing man walked around to the front of the pickup, stopping on the driver's side, and Brady caught a look at his face. It was a face marked by hard living, the red baseball cap shading a long jaw and a nose that had been broken several times. However, what attracted Brady's attention was the envelope in the man's right hand. Even as Brady watched, the man looked into it, as if to reassure himself of what it contained, and then opened the door of his truck and got in. Two seconds later, the truck was moving away. Brady waited and, sure enough, there was a sound of gears clashing and the pickup came back over the bridge, heading in the direction from which it had come. Brady started up the incline, onto the road, and then froze.

The truck had stopped somewhere near the beginning of the turn. Brady waited, but the engine sound neither died nor grew fainter. The truck seemed to be standing still.

Anxiety suddenly flooded through him. What was Hughes doing? Brady started forward once more, his wet shoes crunching the loose road surface. Something was happening, but for God's sake, what?

Then the truck roared into gear and he heard the spatter of gravel being shot from under the wheels. Dust rose in the distance and drifted back toward him like a dirty fog as the engine sound reverberated from the trees and then died away. Brady increased his pace, dread uncoiling like a snake in the pit of his stomach. Ernie Hughes, the man in the pickup, had not stopped just ahead by accident. He had stopped for some reason, and no matter how much Brady tried to convince himself otherwise, deep in his belly the editor knew what that reason was.

He reached the trash dump with its stench of death and forced himself down the incline, along his own fresh tire tracks, to where his car was hidden.

Except that it was not completely hidden. Someone with sharp eyes, driving slowly, someone used to every nuance and change in the forest, would have seen it, if only the glint from the windshield or a difference in the contour of a shadow.

He came to the car and stopped. Everything looked good from the outside and a little flame of hope sprang up inside him. He opened the door, got in, and, taking a deep breath, inserted his key and turned it.

The only sound was a dismal click.

He pulled the hood release, got out, and raised the hood.

His spark plug wires were gone. Hughes had stolen them.

Brady stared at the engine for a long time, then slammed the hood back down, took his flashlight out of the glove compartment, and started back for the road.

He checked his watch. It was six-thirty, two hours until dark. He should make the main highway with the last rays of light, and after that, it was another eight miles back to town. It was going to be a very long night.

His watch told him he had been walking for an hour and three-quarters when a faint light flickered in the distance. He picked up his pace, knowing it was the highway, the flash coming from the headlights of a passing car. His wet socks stuck to his feet and the shoes had worn a blister after the first four miles, but there was nothing to do but flinch and bear the pain.

Darkness closed over him and he switched on his flashlight, its beam dancing like a pale eye ahead of him on the gravel. When he reached the highway, it was just after nine. He sat down to rest for a moment and once more turned the thoughts over in his mind.

Judge Honeycutt had warned off Ernie Hughes and then had made himself hard to find. Hughes had determined to avoid Brady, but maybe what Brady had taken to be fear was something else. Maybe it was simply that Hughes was upping his price for silence.

Brady had not seen the face of the man in the Volvo, but he did not need to see it any more than he needed to see green in the envelope. He had seen the Volvo in front of the judge's office and he had seen it in the reserved parking space in front of the courthouse.

The man who had given Hughes the envelope had been Arden Honeycutt. The judge was being blackmailed.

Brady forced himself up as a pair of headlights approached. He waved his hand, moving the flashlight up and down, but the log truck roared past. He turned to face its retreating taillights and started walking again.

Of what was Honeycutt so afraid? What had happened during the trial of Cory Wilde that could frighten a man into paying for silence almost thirty years later?

A set of headlights broke the darkness behind him and once more he turned to flag it, but the driver only swerved to avoid him and then accelerated.

He reached his house at ten o'clock, feet raw and leg muscles sore. He collapsed onto his sofa, grateful that he did not have a whiskey bottle at hand to tempt him. His whole body ached and he did not want to move. His shirt was ripped by brambles and his pant legs were coated with a crust of smelly mud. Knowing he would fall asleep if he stayed where he was, he forced himself up, shucked off his clothes, and took a hot shower. As he lathered himself, luxuriating in the warm spray, he kept seeing the two vehicles stopped on the country road, and a man peering into a brown envelope. He slipped between the sheets, trying to exorcise the picture from his memory, but it was only replaced by the memory of the long walk back, like an afterimage stamped on his mind.

When he awoke it was seven o'clock and the sun was streaming into the window. He was stiff all over, but he rolled out of bed and sat staring at the clock face.

An hour—the judge went to his office in the mornings around eight, so he had an hour. This time he wasn't going to ask for admission, however.

He dressed and ate, his anger building as he thought of it all again. The sabotaged car and the long walk were an inconvenience, but if a man had spent half of his life in prison because of a conspiracy. . . .

The Honeycutts lived on the northside, in the oldest part of town. It was a section of gentle hills and old homes with steeply sloping dormered roofs. The lawns were neatly cut and the azaleas always well trimmed. In autumn, the lawns were carpeted with pecans and on Christmas, there were cheery wreaths on the doors.

A sober contrast to the prison-camp buildings at Angola, where Cory Wilde had spent the last three decades.

Brady went up the street, across the tracks, to the courthouse. The parking lots were all empty and none of the stores on the square were open yet. The pharmacy was boarded shut and, on a whim, Brady walked over and down the little alley between it and the building next door. The line of structures backed onto a wider alley, where trash containers sat waiting to be dumped. Two buildings down was the judge's law office and, just as he thought, there was a rear door. It would have been easy for the judge to have walked out of his own inner sanctum, down the alley, to the drugstore. But why? That was what made no sense. Why did the judge consider Penelope's herbs a threat?

Brady came back out onto the main street. In a few minutes, he intended to have the answer.

The judge lived on a boulevard where two stone lions guarded the entrance and hickories shaded the median strip. The house itself was in the second block and as Brady approached, he saw the blue Volvo in the steep driveway.

Brady checked his watch. Seven-forty. He waited on the neutral ground, half-concealed by one of the trees. He had been there exactly five minutes when the front door opened and the judge emerged, followed by his wife. The judge was carrying an attaché case, his wife an old-fashioned briefcase and, under the other arm, some books. Her husband said something and she shook her head. The judge spoke again, raising a hand as if in protest, and his wife started away abruptly toward the car, leaving him on the walk. Brady stepped out into the street and started toward them. They reached the car and the judge got in on the driver's side as Brady came across the sidewalk, walking quickly now, to catch them before they could drive away. The engine coughed into life just as Brady placed his hand on the door.

Shock froze the jurist's face as he saw Brady. The editor reached down, opening the door.

"Judge, I think we need to talk."

The old man's face colored. "Peter, I don't know what the meaning of this is, but I insist you let go of the door."

The words were adamant but underneath Brady detected a tremor of fear.

"*Now,* Judge. It won't wait. I saw you and Ernie Hughes yesterday."

The lawyer's mouth opened but no words came. His knuckles whitened on the steering wheel. His wife leaned forward to look at Brady.

"Who is it? What's going on?"

"I . . ." Honeycutt hesitated, then turned to his wife. "It's all right. There's been a misunderstanding. This will only take a minute, Grace."

He reset the parking brake and got out, his hands trembling.

"Peter," he hissed, "this is outrageous. I can explain everything. I . . ."

He never finished. A blinding flash accompanied by a shock wave sent him flying forward. Searing heat scorched the exposed parts of Brady's body and he crashed into the ground like a falling log. He was vaguely aware of bits and pieces of metal flying around him, and a roaring sound in the distance. He tried to get his breath but no air came. His head spun and he tried to cry out, but his lungs refused to function. There was a weight pressing him down and he refused to move.

Then the world fell away and darkness closed around him.

13

THE next few hours were a blur. Brady had garbled memories of an ambulance ride, and of being treated in the tiny emergency room of the Troy hospital before being taken for X rays. Then he was placed in a permanent room on the first floor and a young doctor in a white coat came in, shaking his head.

"Mr. Brady, you're a very lucky man."

The editor raised himself on his elbows and flinched.

"I don't feel like it. What happened?"

"A lot of people would like the answer to that one," the doctor said. His name, Brady remembered, was McIntire, and he had given Brady a story on the problems of practice in small towns. "But, briefly, what happened is that somebody blew up the judge's car. The judge shielded you from most of the blast, or else you'd as likely be in the same shape as he is."

An image flashed into his mind then, of walking up to the car, placing his hand on the door handle; the shock on the judge's face; the old man getting out, starting toward him, a terrible blaze of light. . . .

"How *is* the judge?" Brady asked.

"He's torn up some, but he'll pull through. The blast blew

open the back door and it shielded him from some of the impact. It looks like the bomb was under the car, probably under the gas tank. Everything went up."

"And Mrs. Honeycutt?"

McIntire looked down, embarrassed. "I'm afraid she wasn't able to get out." He sighed. "I haven't told the judge yet. He's still in shock. But he'll have to know. I can't say I'm looking forward to it."

Brady forced himself to the side of the bed. All his bones ached but he noticed with relief that his arms and legs still seemed to function.

"I don't guess there's any reason for me to stay here, then?" he asked.

McIntire held out a hand to steady him. "I'd prefer it if you did, at least for a day. We haven't found any serious problems, but sometimes it takes a while for the effects of a concussion to show up."

"I'll come back if I start seeing double," Brady promised, his feet touching the cold floor. "Where are my clothes?"

"You wouldn't want to be seen wearing them," McIntire said. "And before you take off, there's somebody outside that wants to talk to you."

As if on cue, the door opened again and Ned Triplett stood half in, half out. "Can I have him now, Doc?"

"I guess so," McIntire said. "There doesn't seem to be anything I can do."

He left and the police chief closed the door behind himself. For a long second, he squinted at the man in the hospital gown and then he cleared his throat.

"Mr. Brady, what in the hell is going on?"

Brady sat back onto the bed. "Chief, I wish somebody would tell me."

Triplett eyed the floor as if looking for a place to spit, thought better of it, and swallowed. "Damn it, Brady, you was there. You saw the whole thing. The judge was on top of you, for Christ's sake. Now I want to know what the hell went on."

Brady closed his eyes, trying to clear his head.

"I went to see the judge," Brady said slowly, picking out each memory in sequence. "He and his wife came out of the house and got into the car. I went to the car and asked the judge if I could talk with him. He got out and . . . the car blew up."

"What did you want to talk to him about?"

"A story I was working on."

"*What* story?"

"A story about Cory Wilde."

"You got some new evidence or something?"

"No. I'm just looking at old evidence."

"Well, what was so damn important you showed up outside a man's house before eight in the morning? Answer me that."

"The last few times I called the judge, I had trouble getting ahold of him."

The little man squinted and leaned toward the editor. "Brady, there's something you ain't telling me. I know you're in thick with Garitty and that bunch. Well, I'm here to tell you this crime was committed in my jurisdiction, not his, and you can't hide behind him. If you're holding out on me . . ."

"I know." Brady sighed. "I'm in a heap of trouble."

Triplett snarled, turned on his heel, and walked into Emmett Larson.

"Feisty little bastard," Emmett cracked, shaking his head. "Damn, Pete, this never used to happen when I was the editor here. What did you do, bring the big city with you?"

"Sometimes I wonder," Brady admitted. "Emmett, look, do me a favor and go over to my place and get me some clothes. Then, if you aren't doing anything, I need you to take me somewhere."

"At your service." The old man made a sharp little bow. "Is your key still under the flowerpot?"

Brady nodded. "Thanks, Emmett."

Larson had been gone thirty seconds when Matt Garitty appeared, his concern turning to relief when he saw Brady standing beside the bed.

"Jesus." He exhaled. "When I saw Emmett coming out, I thought they'd called him back to do your obituary."

"Very funny," Brady said. "And a little too close for comfort."

Garitty sat down in the big visitor's chair. "Feel up to telling what happened?"

Brady repeated the story he had told Triplett. "And I have a feeling your friend the chief has me measured for a prison jumper already."

"He would," Garitty admitted. "He needs to close this thing quick, like yesterday. Look, I know you well enough to know you're not telling everything you know. And I know you well enough to realize you're not going to tell until you're damned good and ready. But I think you should know I got the preliminary results of the analysis on Boy Jenks's vehicle back just before I came down here. They found gunpowder on some of the parts we picked up from the road."

"Gunpowder? You mean a bomb?"

"That's right. And enough of a clock to know that's what set it off. They figure it was taped on the underside, or maybe slipped around the exhaust where he wouldn't see it."

"My God. You mean . . ."

The sheriff nodded. "Set to go off at a certain time, like on the long way home. The road has a lot of curves. Pretty good bet it would cause him to lose control and go off the side."

Brady limped over to the other side of the bed. "I don't understand. There're easier ways to get rid of somebody than a bomb. A bomb is risky. It leaves evidence."

"Right," Garitty agreed. "I thought the same thing. Whoever did it was either pretty stupid or pretty smart."

Brady bit a lip, trying to put it all together. "Whoever rigged that bomb wasn't an idiot," he said. "They had to learn it somewhere."

"Any nominees?"

"Well, Cory Wilde had a lot of time in prison and it's a good place to pick up certain skills."

"I thought the same thing," the lawman said. "But the problem is that I've had Cory under surveillance for the last week." He raised a hand. "I know, I know, it's not my jurisdiction, but I did it anyway. And the fact is that Cory hasn't gone anywhere near the judge or his place. Besides his trips to the grocery, all he does is sit on his front porch in that damned rocking chair." Garitty pursed his lips. "Tell you the truth, it's damned spooky."

"I guess he could've hired somebody to do it," Brady suggested.

"Sure. But with what? Best I can make out, the man's broke. Started a small checking account when he came here. There haven't been any large withdrawals so far."

"How did he start the account? Cash?"

"Deposited a cashier's draft on a Baton Rouge bank. Now, this being a small town, I can get Mort Sibley at the bank to let me look at his records without making a federal case out of it, but it would never work in Baton Rouge. And I'm not sure I can get a court order at this point."

"But he could have another account down there."

"Sure. But what does he use for money? And why would anybody give him any?"

"I have an idea on that." Brady explained about Cory's daughter. "She may be fronting him," he concluded.

The sheriff nodded. "Could be. I may call the state police, ask them to look into it."

"I agree. And meanwhile I'll pursue my own leads," Brady said.

Garitty gave his friend an appraising look. "Hmmm. Sounds like you're already a leg up."

"Not really. But Kelly's doing some checking." Brady sat back down on the bed to give his aching legs a rest. "Matt, tell me something. What do you know about Ernie Hughes?"

"Hughes?" Garitty asked, surprised. "What kind of question is that? Damn it, Pete, if you're going to hold out on me again . . ."

"No," Brady smiled, remembering their initial meeting and the murder case that had at first driven them apart and then brought them together as friends. "I know this isn't New Orleans." He told Garitty about his attempts to contact Hughes, and his trip to the lake and the long walk back. "So, you see, there's something Hughes knows that he isn't telling. And it sounds like blackmail to me, if not murder, by now."

The sheriff rose from his chair and uttered an expletive. "Anybody but Ernie, and I could handle it, damn it."

"What does that mean?"

"It means Ernie isn't somebody you drag in and give the third degree. He was district ranger. Back then, that meant somebody with a lot of political pull. He needed it to get the job and once he got it, he used the position to build his base. Of course, it isn't like that anymore. The Forest Service is better run; the district ranger is a civil-service position. But in Ernie's day, he was a law unto himself. And he still has the connections in Baton Rouge and in Washington, for that matter."

"Does that mean you aren't going to do anything?"

Garitty's face flushed. "You know me better than that, goddamn it! I'll go out and I'll drag him in kicking and screaming if I have to. But I can guarantee he'll have a lawyer there inside of an hour and probably some smartass Tulane law graduate, at that. And as soon as he leaves my office, he'll end up in yours, telling you how I browbeat him and used the third degree. And I guess you'll print it, whether it's true or not."

Brady nodded. "I'm running a newspaper."

"Of course. And I'm just the corrupt country sheriff." He turned around and then slammed his fist into the wall. "Oh, hell, Pete, I'm sorry. I didn't mean to sound like that. I guess if I was smart, I'd just leave it to Ned Triplett, let him wallow around and sink himself. But, damn it, this is my parish and my town and people are getting killed. And if I have to take some flak to find out who it is, by God, I will."

"I never expected you to say anything else." Brady smiled. "And if I have to print Hughes's story, you can bet what you just said will be in there, too."

"You sure everybody'll get equal time?" Garitty joked.

"More or less," the editor drawled. "But, like you pointed out, this isn't New Orleans. It's just a country newspaper."

The sheriff put a hand on his friend's shoulder. "You'll do, son, big-time reporter or not." He started for the door, then turned. "Keep an eye on your back, Pete. The results aren't in, but the bomb in the judge's car was too powerful for gunpowder like the first one. My guess is dynamite."

"You mean . . ."

"Yep. Whoever's doing it is raising the stakes."

Brady searched for words but there wasn't anything for him to say. Emmett pushed the door open then, threw some clothes on the bed, and stood by shaking his head as Brady dressed.

"I think you're being a fool," he observed. "You're so stove up, you can't walk."

"I'll manage," the publisher promised. "By the way"—he turned to the sheriff—"is there anything yet on Jenks's body?"

Garitty nodded. "They found a dentist in Alec that the family says treated him once. Let's hope the dentist kept good records."

Brady nodded agreement and limped out. Emmett, grumbling under his breath, drove him to the Western Auto, where Brady picked up some new spark plug wires. The wide-eyed owner, who had evidently heard the entire story by now, handed over the merchandise with a sense of awe, as if dealing with a man who should have been dead, and whispered to his clerk when Brady was gone.

"I think you're becoming a legend," Emmett mumbled as his pickup bounced out onto the highway.

"As long as it's the living kind," Brady said with a smile.

Half an hour later, at Brady's direction, Emmett slowed on the gravel and the younger man pointed to the little dirt track beside the garbage dump.

"You want to tell me what the hell you were doing way back here in the woods?" Emmett demanded. "Some kind of snipe hunt, was it?"

Brady repeated his story and Emmett grunted. "You think he might've come back and planted another bomb?"

A shiver ran through the publisher. "Thanks for warning me," he said laconically. "But I think you're far enough away to be safe."

"Damn straight," Emmett agreed.

But after an inspection of the hood and under the seat, and after feeling under front and rear bumpers and looking under the gas tank, Brady could not find anything out of the ordinary. He attached the new wires, got in, took a deep breath, and turned his key.

The motor roared into life and he exhaled with relief. He put the Ford in gear, wound his way back up onto the gravel, and gave Emmett a wave.

Nevertheless, he was grateful to see the pickup behind him on the highway. He stopped in front of his office and walked over to Emmett's truck. "I'll be okay now. Thanks."

"I have a feeling I ought to stick with you."

Brady laid a fond hand on the older man's arm. "Kelly will never speak to me again if I get you killed, too."

Emmett grunted and put the vehicle in gear. Brady watched him disappear down the street, then limped toward his office.

The vignette that met him took away his breath: Mrs. Rickenbacker sat at her desk with her head pressed against Ripley's shoulder as the young man bent down to soothe her. The sound of the door opening was swallowed by her wails and Ripley's reassurances.

"But he was so nice to me," the bookkeeper was sobbing. "He put up with so much."

Touched, Brady shifted from one foot to the other, wondering how to break the news of his resurrection.

Mrs. Rickenbacker did it for him. She raised her head, glasses askew on her nose, and reached for a tissue, and that was when she saw Brady standing there.

"Oh," she said. "I hope you don't want to pay a bill right now."

Ripley turned his head and his face went white. He swore, shook off the bookkeeper's clinging arm, and, giving a whoop, did a leap into the air.

Mrs. Rickenbacker adjusted her glasses, emitted a low groan, and then sank forward, headfirst, in a faint. Two minutes later, after much fanning and several glasses of water, the two men managed to restore her to her senses.

"Mr. Brady, there was no call . . ." she protested, gasping for air. "We thought you were dead. They wouldn't tell us anything. We heard you were killed. Then, just to come up on us like that . . ."

Brady patted her shoulder with true affection for the first time since he had known her. "I know, it was thoughtless. I hope you'll forgive me."

She dabbed her eyes and nodded primly. "Well. Of course, I mean, you didn't intend . . ."

"Are you okay, boss?" Ripley demanded. "If you're too shook up to write the story, you can tell it to me and—"

"Later," Brady promised. "But, as a matter of fact, I *am* a little shaken up. So I'll leave you two together, since you get along so well now. I have one or two things to do before my muscles stiffen up and I can't move."

He went back out into the parking lot and climbed into his car. His body was still full of adrenaline and he knew it would be impossible to accomplish anything in the office, and besides, there were too many questions.

He drove over to Cory's place, went up onto the porch, where the rocker sat vacant, and banged the door with his fist. One thought hung in his mind: *The man's destroying this town.* But was he the agent or just the catalyst?

The door opened and Cory Wilde peered out. He was dressed in slacks, his shirt open at the neck, and he wore slippers.

"Mr. Newspaper Editor," he said. "Come in. I've been expecting you."

Brady followed him into a bare living room, where an open suitcase lay against one wall and a few books lay against the other. There was something sad about that room, Brady realized, as if it were telling the story of its occupant's life.

"Have a seat," Cory said, pointing to a straight-backed chair. "I was reading." He picked up a book and Brady saw that it was a study of Eisenhower's presidency. "Last President I remember," the old man explained. "Time stopped when I went in the place. Interesting to see what the historians say about him. Great strategist, too." He sat down in another chair and laid the book back down on the bare floorboards. "Never read before I went there. I guess you'd say I was just semi-educated. But in twenty-nine years, I read a lot of things. Learned a hell of a lot."

"Did you learn how to make bombs?" Brady asked quietly.

"Bombs?" Wilde cocked his head to one side. "I don't follow you."

"Could you make a bomb that you could hang under a car's exhaust pipe? Or one that would go off after a car started up?"

Wilde stared and then gave a little nod and sat back in his chair. "Ahh. So it's bombs. I was wondering how they'd do it." He coughed and a vein in his neck bulged. "So who was it this time?" he asked.

"Judge Honeycutt," Brady told him. "He and his wife were leaving their house. There was a bomb in their car."

Wilde's eyes brightened and he leaned forward. "And the judge? He's dead?"

"Not yet," Brady said. "But his wife is."

Wilde straightened slightly and Brady sensed his disappointment. "And they don't know who did it?"

"That's what I came to ask you."

"How would I know?" Wilde asked. "Or did you think I hired it done?"

"Did you?"

Wilde wheezed a cruel little laugh. "'Course not. Didn't have to. I knew if I came back, they'd do it to themselves. And I was right."

"Why?" Brady demanded. "What is it that's such a threat? For God's sake, man, if you have some proof of your innocence, if they set you up—"

"If I had some proof of my innocence, I'd never have gone to jail. Besides, I can't talk about it. Terms of my parole, you know."

"You didn't answer my question," the editor persisted. "Can you make a bomb?"

"Anybody can make a bomb. Simplest thing in the world. Clock, a few wires, some explosive, and a detonator. I knew a fellow in Angola who was illiterate but he was a Ph.D. in bomb-making. He could blow up a carload of nuns and be a thousand miles away when it happened, drinking sangría next to the swimming pool. You see, he used to like to use a timer from an old VCR, the kind that you set for two days, or seven, or fourteen." Again the wheezing laugh. "Now, aren't you going to ask me where I was when it happened? Not, of course, that it proves anything. Like I just said, a good timer takes care of that."

Brady shook his head. "No. I see what you want now. If you were arrested, it would mean reopening the whole thing, regardless of the terms of your parole. So you don't mind setting yourself up. You know this time, with the notoriety, you could attract a first-rate lawyer, somebody from out of state, even. No more pauper's defense."

Wilde smiled. "And I've already got an editor on my side. In spite of the fact he hates my guts."

"Wilde, whether I like you or not is immaterial. I like this town. It may not be the kind of quiet little paradise the welcome

108

sign on Highway Eighty-four claims, but it's a decent town, regardless of a few bad apples, and I don't mean to see you destroy it."

"Good speech," Wilde said, clapping softly. "But you've got it backward. If this town is destroyed, I didn't do it. It did it to itself."

Brady repressed an oath; because, damn it, the man was right.

"What do you know about Ernie Hughes?" Brady asked, changing the subject.

"Ernie Hughes. You mean the chief deputy. Well, I know him very well. Or I used to. Can't say it was exactly friendship."

"He was involved in the investigation?"

"Involved? He ran it. Sheriff Thomas turned him loose like a bulldog. But you know I can't get into that. Happened a long time ago, anyway. I wouldn't want to sound like a man that held a grudge."

"Of course not." He told Wilde about the two men on the bridge. For the first time, a flicker of excitement sparked in the old man's eyes. "I'll be damned. And then the bastard pulled your wires. I knew it, by God, I *knew* it was something like that." He got up, agitated, and began to pace from one side of the room to the other. "So now what do you plan to do?"

"Well, I'd like to talk to your daughter."

The old man froze and his face went a shade whiter. His eyes narrowed and he seemed to be having trouble catching his breath.

"You . . ." He wheezed, taking a halting step forward, his finger pointed at the newsman. *"What did you say?"*

"I said I wanted to speak with your daughter."

Wilde's head shook from side to side, as if he could wish the whole subject away. "No. I don't know what you're talking about. I don't have any daughter."

"Whether you have one now or not, I don't know," Brady said slowly, "but your wife gave birth a few months after you went to prison. The baby was born in Winnfield. It was a little girl. She was taken to Baton Rouge, to live with some cousins named Fenstermacher."

109

"No!" Wilde shouted. "It isn't true. I don't have any daughter!"

"You've been getting money from somewhere."

"It's none of anybody's business. You leave that subject alone, do you understand me?" He stepped forward, his fist raised, his face only inches from Brady's. "You leave that subject alone!"

"I'm sorry, Mr. Wilde, but when it comes to murder, nothing's off limits. You know that if anybody does. Did you think you could use me to make your case and expect to pull the strings? I'm sorry. I can't work with just part of the picture. I'll try not to bring your daughter into it if she isn't involved, but I have to talk with her. If you won't help me, then I'll just have to find her on my own."

"No!" Cory Wilde lurched forward, then wavered. He slumped against the wall, hand to his neck, body racked with a succession of dry coughs.

Brady helped him to the chair and then went into the kitchen and came back with a glass of water.

The old man took it, sipped, and heaved a few deep breaths.

"You get out now," Wilde whispered. "I want you to get out."

Brady nodded. "However you want it," he said, and went to the door. He pulled it open and then, involuntarily, took a step backward.

Facing him on the porch was Ned Triplett, bracketed by two other members of the Troy police force.

"What do you want here, Chief?" Brady asked.

"Well, Mr. Brady, I could ask you the same thing. But there's time for that. Right now, we're here to take Cory Wilde into custody. The charge is murder."

14

"I don't like it," Garitty complained, leaning over his desk. "You and I know Triplett doesn't have a leg to stand on, at least so far. And I'll grant Cory Wilde may be tickled to death for the attention. It *will* get his situation looked into. But the city jail is a damned cracker box."

"You don't expect Cory to escape," Brady asked.

"I'm not afraid of Cory getting *out,*" Garitty said. "It's somebody else getting *in* that bothers me. A lot of folk hereabouts, like Bo Potter, aren't going to care about the niceties of legal procedure. You saw the bunch that was on Cory's front lawn the other night."

"I saw them," Brady admitted, his face grim. "But surely you can call in help, even the state police—"

"Sure. If I have enough time. But if you're right, and Cory really is innocent, then whoever's doing it is smart enough to get around that. It doesn't take a mob to kill a man in a jail. It's been done plenty of times, in better jails than the one across the street. At least if he was upstairs, in the parish lockup, I could have some control, but, damn it, as it is, I don't have any way to get him out of Ned's hands." Garitty paced to the other side of the room. "Everything points to a cover-up, and I don't know if Triplett's part of it or not. But I have a strong feeling whoever it is can pull his strings."

"What about Hughes?" Brady asked. "Have you talked to him yet?"

"He wasn't at home. His wife's playing dumb. I have an

APB out on his truck, but if Ernie wants to disappear, he knows places in that forest we'll never find. Somehow, though, I don't think it's Ernie. If it was, I think he'd stay put and use his political friends to try to take care of him. But something's scared him. Something political henchmen can't take care of."

The phone buzzed and Garitty picked it up. "Yes. Speaking." He eyed Brady and then moved over behind his desk and wrote something on a legal pad. "Thanks. I appreciate the help."

"Something on the case?" Brady asked.

The sheriff nodded solemnly. "I asked the army for some background information on Bo Potter," Garitty said. "That was the answer."

"And?"

"He was in Nam. His specialty was demolitions."

"Are you going to pick him up?"

"I'll talk to him. The evidence in the Jenks case gives me that right, because it took place in the parish, out of Ned's jurisdiction. But if I don't get anywhere, I don't know what to do next. You're always telling me I can't give anybody the third degree. I just hope that message gets over to Ned and his people. He's desperate, and he wants to solve this case. He's not going to let a man everybody already hates get in his way."

"Maybe I can get Cory Wilde a lawyer," Brady suggested.

"Not from around here," his friend said. "I don't think any of the legal eagles in this parish want to ruin their business over somebody they figure hasn't got a wooden nickel."

"Then Baton Rouge," Brady said, making up his mind. "That's where his daughter is, if I can find her. If I can get her to hire a lawyer, I may be able to get him out."

"Or better yet," Garitty suggested, "see if you can get Probations to revoke his parole. Here." He scribbled a name on a piece of paper. "See this man. I'll call him, tell him you're coming. Probations and Parole likely isn't going to want to get into a fight with local law enforcement; after all, once Cory's charged here, the current case takes precedence. But maybe some informal pressure can be brought to bear. If we can get him at least tucked away in a state prison, he may be safe for the time being."

Brady looked down at his watch. It was almost noon, and it

112

would take three hours to reach Baton Rouge. Three o'clock on a Friday afternoon, with the weekend exodus already begun.

"Call your friend," Brady said. "Tell him to stay in his office." He started for the door but Garitty caught his arm.

"Just one thing. Didn't you say Triplett warned you not to go off on your own?"

"The explosion left me deaf," Brady said.

"Go to the girl at the front desk. Tell her I said to fix you a deputy's commission. If anybody asks, you're on official business for me."

Brady smiled, then shook his head. "Thanks, Matt. I appreciate it. But I can't. I'm still a member of the press."

"Sure. You and your ethics. Well, good luck."

"I may need it. Oh, since you're going to call Baton Rouge, there's one more thing I'd like you to do."

"Oh?" Garitty's brows rose.

"Call the state police Bureau of Identification. I'd like them to send you some things."

Brady saw the monolith that was the capitol building when he was still eight miles away. The three o'clock sun was shining off of it, but the smog from the chemical plants north of the city ate the sunlight like it ate everything else it touched, so that the capitol was a dirty blur on the sky.

Huey Long had built the capitol, so maybe, Brady thought, the dirty color was appropriate. The men who had occupied it since hadn't done much to change things. That included the incumbent, who, through his minions on the parole board, had released Cory Wilde for reasons no one could fathom.

Brady slowed for the turnoff, angling off the old four-lane before the honky-tonks of the west side and the old bridge that connected them to the city. Instead, like most of the other cars, he took the two lane that bypassed the riverside town of Port Allen and united with the newer interstate to the south.

The roadside restaurants tempted, but Brady bypassed them. He'd stopped twice for coffee already, once at Lea's in LeCompte, and again at Stelley's in LeBeau. The caffeine had knocked out

113

the sleepiness brought on by adrenaline exhaustion, but now he was wired, his nerves a vibrating matrix. Thoughts chased through his brain like electric trains on a circular track, the same questions, over and over: Who was involved in the conspiracy? Who had set the bombs in two automobiles? Who was Cory Wilde's daughter? What was Penelope Martingale's role in the business?

He swerved to avoid an eighteen-wheeler and realized he had drifted into the wrong lane. He came up under the interstate and turned left, up onto the six-lane, heading for the new bridge. Suddenly, he realized that he had come 160 miles and he did not know the location of the probation office.

He checked his watch for the hundredth time. Three-twenty. If there were no wrecks on the bridge, he would make it.

He squinted up at the steel-girded structure. The traffic flow was heavy but steady. He squeezed the wheel, shoving the pain of his bruised bones into the back of his mind, and felt the road rising under him. Seconds later, he was high above the brown river, with the university to his right, in the distance, and the downtown section off to his left, shrouded in a miasma of chemical fog.

He took the Convention Street exit, crossed over to North Boulevard, and found a parking space in front of the old police station. The police were gone, but a city employee in one of the offices told him that the probation office was on Government, a few blocks away.

He found it easily, a three-story tan brick building on the corner, with pastel tile trim and a sign that could only be called functional. He parked on a side street, went in through the front door, and entered a lobby, where a bored-looking black youth waited with his elbows on his knees. To the rear was a heavy door, and to the left was a window like a cashier's cage, with a bleached-blond woman behind it, working a wad of gum.

Brady went to the window and shoved his business card through. "I have an appointment with Mr. Reynolds."

The woman looked up from a romance novel and regarded his card between chews. "Office at the end," she said and a buzzer sounded. Brady opened the big reinforced door and faced a hallway with offices on each side. He was halfway to the office at the end when the door ahead of him opened and a large black

114

man emerged. He wore a wrinkled checkered coat, and his collar was open under his tie. He thrust a hamlike hand at his visitor.

"Mr. Brady? I'm Wesley Reynolds. Come on back."

Brady followed him into an office crammed with two battered filing cabinets and a desk piled high with manila folders. Reynolds sagged into his chair and pointed to another chair on the other side of his desk. The wall was covered with framed certificates, attesting to completion of various training programs, and there was one certifying fifteen years of loyal service. Reynolds lifted a Coke bottle from the edge of his desk, drained it, and put the empty on the floor.

"Sheriff Garitty says Cory Wilde's managed to get himself in trouble."

Briefly, Brady outlined Wilde's situation. "There's no evidence the man has committed any crime. But his life is definitely in danger."

Reynolds pursed his lips, reached the top folder from the stack on his desk, and opened it in front of him.

"Umhmmm," he intoned, turning the pages slowly. At last, he looked up. "Just checking. He was a hothead his first five years or so, according to this. Fights, rowdiness, even tried a couple of escapes, but then he cooled off and there's nothing in here to show he gave any trouble the rest of the time. Par for the course."

"Oh?"

Reynolds smiled. "You send a young man to prison for a violent crime, he's got a lot of hostility. He's probably going to raise some hell for the first few years he's inside. If he stays very long, though, well, somewhere around his thirties, all the piss and vinegar gets drained out of him. Your older men don't usually give any trouble." He shut the folder and leaned back. "I called his P.O. in Alexandria. Cory's checked in once, and is due again on Monday. Of course, if they have him in jail, he won't make it."

"That's what bothers me. I'm sure Sheriff Garitty explained the dangers. There has to be some way to get him out of jail, even if it means stashing him in a state facility somewhere."

Reynolds nodded. "I understand. But there's not a lot we can do. A parolee commits a crime, the local authorities have jurisdiction. There's no way we can just go in and take him away. I told Sheriff Garitty that." The black man scratched his nose. "You

115

know, it's not every day we get a call from a sheriff about one of our parolees being railroaded. More likely, it's the other way around. Matter of fact, this business is a little strange all the way around. I still haven't figured why Cory Wilde was paroled in the first place."

"I understand it was a three-to-two vote," Brady said.

"That's what it says." Reynolds smiled cynically. "That must mean *something*."

"You're saying Cory Wilde has friends in high places."

"It doesn't say so anywhere in here." Reynolds patted the folder. "But, like they say in poker, the cards speak for themselves."

"Any ideas?"

The big man chuckled. "Plenty. But I work here and I plan to stay on for at least five more years."

Brady exhaled. "What would it take to get Cory Wilde into your custody?"

"You mean revoke his parole? Well, I'm not saying it would work and I can't say I like the idea, because it would mean a hell of a ruckus. But I owe Garitty, so I'll tell you, anyway." He leaned forward and Brady caught a whiff of cologne. "If Cory Wilde violated his parole and was found out by his probation officer, it might give us some claim to jurisdiction. I say *might*. But somebody would have to go to the wall on it and I can't say I'm champing at the bit." He sat back in his chair again. "But what am I talking about? The damn man's already in jail, so how can he do anything else to break his conditions?"

Brady felt an overwhelming sense of helplessness. Then, without even thinking, it came to him and a little flame of excitement flared and then flickered. He was press, damn it. He could not take an active role. He was an observer, not an actor. He was . . . he was the editor of a rural weekly, not the ace reporter of a big-city daily. Wasn't it Matt Garitty who had pointed out the difference to him when they had first met? You didn't play by big-city rules, Matt had said, not if you expected to stay in the town. What were sins in New Orleans, Houston, or Atlanta might be virtues in a town of six thousand, where people were less concerned about professional roles and more interested in a person's social relationships.

116

Besides, he had adhered to his sense of professionalism once, and a man had died.

No, by God, it wasn't going to happen again, not if he could help it. He took a deep breath.

"Suppose you found some narcotics at Cory Wilde's house?"

"Narcotics?" Reynolds frowned, unbelieving. "You mean you know Cory's been using dope?"

"Yes. If you send somebody to look inside his house, you'll find it in a brown paper bag."

"Are you serious? I mean, you've *seen* this?"

"I have a source who admitted supplying Cory Wilde with narcotics."

Reynolds shook his head. "Man. I don't understand. What kind of narcotics?"

"Marijuana. Psychedelics."

"Who's the source?"

"That I can't tell you."

Reynolds sighed and pulled out a piece of paper. "You'll sign an affidavit?"

"Yes."

"Okay. We'll give it our best shot."

Fifteen minutes later, Reynolds looked over the affidavit a final time and then got up. "Okay. No promises, but we'll see if it flies."

Brady stuck out his hand. "Thanks."

"Don't thank me. Just tell Garitty we're even."

The newsman nodded and started back down the hall.

"By the way," Reynolds called, catching up with him, "is there any special reason folks are going to so much trouble for this bird?"

Brady halted at the big door into the waiting room. "I know this will sound funny, but I think he may be innocent."

The probation officer gave a crooked smile. "No, sir, that doesn't sound funny. The people that come through that door?" He pointed. "They're *all* innocent."

Brady headed south, toward the university, trying to dredge up from his protesting brain the location of Kelly's apartment. Had she said off Highland or off Nicholson? He was on Nicholson now, a boulevard that wound lazily from its junky downtown terminus under the freeway, through a zone of shaded houses, all the way to the campus gates. He had been to the campus now and again over the years, to give guest lectures to a journalism class, but he knew nothing of the adjacent areas where students lived.

What was the name of the place? Something French, he knew. Bienville Arms. That was it. And, damn it, it was off *Highland.*

He turned left and went slowly alongside the football stadium and past the tiger cage, then turned left again and curved around the two Indian mounds. He followed the road to Highland and went left at the light and out the campus gates into a commercial area of restaurants and bookstores that had clearly seen better days.

Had she said it was *on* Highland or *off* it? He slowed, slid into the right lane, jerked the wheel back straight, and forged through a yellow light. He shook his head. Now even the caffeine was wearing off. He crept along, faster traffic crowding up behind him, and then, just as he was about to decide he had gone too far, he saw it on the right, a portable sign with some of the key letters missing: IEN ILLE ARMS.

He swerved into the parking lot and drove slowly along the motellike building, looking for numbers. What was hers? Was it 212 or 221?

He parked and forced himself out, his bones sending arrows of pain into him with each step. He went up the steps one at a time, reached the second floor, and tried the door with 212 on it. A small dark woman of obviously foreign origin opened the door and eyed him suspiciously.

"Sorry," he mumbled, and hobbled on, stopping when he got to 221. He knocked and waited, aware that the woman from 212 was still standing in the doorway, watching. There was no answer to his knocking and he rattled the knob; still no answer. He swore under his breath and turned away, giving his watcher his back and heading for the set of stairs at the other end. He managed to negotiate them without falling and limped to his car.

Five o'clock and the sun was still hot enough to send little waves of heat up from the asphalt. He remembered that there were some fast-food places across the street, but he lacked the

118

energy to start the car and drive over. Instead, he rolled his window down, let his head fall back against the seat, and closed his eyes.

He did not know how long he had been asleep when he felt a hand on his shoulder and heard a voice ordering him out of the car. He opened his eyes and saw blue uniforms.

Why the hell hadn't he accepted Matt's offer of a badge?

15

A half-awake Brady felt himself being pulled from the driver's seat and shoved against the side of the car while hands patted him down. What explanations he stammered did not make sense, even to him, and for a moment he thought of jail as a welcome relief, a place he could at least sleep.

Then a voice he recognized intruded upon the policemen's questions—a woman's voice: *Kelly*.

"I know he looks desperate, but I think I can handle him," she was saying. "If he gets out of hand, I'll put him in an arm lock."

The policemen made grudging noises and Brady turned around, blinking in the bright sunlight. Kelly was standing behind the cops, hands on her hips, smiling at him.

"Well, if you need us, call," the younger of the two officers said, obviously taken by Kelly's looks. Brady suppressed a sarcastic remark and waited while the policemen got back into their car.

Kelly waved at them and Brady hobbled toward her, protesting. "Damn it, you don't have to make it sound like auld lang syne."

"Did you want to spend the night downtown?" she asked, giving a final friendly wave. "I have other plans for you. By the way, why the hell didn't you call?"

"What difference would it have made?" Brady asked. "You weren't at home."

"I wasn't at home because I was doing your work for you, ingrate. What's wrong with you, anyway? You look like you've been hit by an atom bomb."

"No atom bomb," Brady said. "Just the run-of-the-mill dynamite kind. Sort of stiffens you up, you know?"

Kelly's jaw dropped. *"What?"*

"Let's go upstairs. I'll tell you about it."

Five minutes later, he lay naked on the bed while Kelly examined with the air of a physician the welts and red marks, turning him onto his back when she had finished the other side. She ran a hand lightly along his belly and smiled at his reaction.

"Well, at least nothing vital is damaged. I couldn't stand that."

"Neither could I," he said, reaching for her, and then groaning as his aching body protested the movement.

"Later," she said, leaning down to kiss his lips. "Right now, you need to rest while I do some more calling."

"Calling?"

"Fenstermacher, remember? I cut classes and spent all damn day running it down in the Louisiana Room at the library. That's where they keep the old phone books, in case you didn't know. And it so happens, there was a family of that name listed from about 1959 through about ten years ago. I guess they even lived here before that, but I didn't check."

"Great," Brady said, fighting the drowsiness, "but where are they now?"

"We don't need *them,* we just need *her,* right?"

"But we don't know if she kept her name or took theirs."

"No, we don't, but I'm betting she took theirs. With a murderer for a father, it makes sense. So I went to the old *Gumbos.*"

"Gumbos?"

"The university yearbook, idiot. And sure enough, starting in 1977, there is a girl named Felicia Fenstermacher. *Felicia,* get it? The same as her mother. Now, two unusual names like that can hardly be a coincidence. She wasn't a sorority girl, which is a pity, because that would make her easier to trace; all the houses keep up with their members. But it fits: As a newcomer from upstate, in a lower-middle-class family, she wouldn't get a rush from the bow-head crowd. But lucky for us she was a good student. She does appear as a member of several honor societies."

"And?"

"And she graduated in 1980. What did you expect, she'd hang around?"

Brady forced himself up onto an elbow. "You didn't go through this song and dance to leave it hanging."

"Well, not exactly. Just as a sort of intro for my plans tonight."

"Your plans?"

"Well, it occurred to me the alumni office might have her address, so I went over to talk to them. And that's where I met Tyler Patin."

"Who?"

"The man with the address lists. A real dyed-in-the-wool nerd. But he has what you want, so I figured you wouldn't mind."

"Wouldn't mind *what*?" Brady asked, exasperated.

"The price was a date." She checked her watch. "Matter of fact, he's picking me up in about half an hour. So I just have time for a shower."

"Kelly . . ."

"I love that jealous streak you have." She laughed, unbuttoning her blouse and draping it over the chair. "Don't worry, I can handle myself. And you *do* want the address, right?"

Brady groaned, and this time it was not from his injuries.

He slept and when he awoke, the room was dark. He turned his head to look at the clock face: ten o'clock. He had slept for nearly five hours. He sat up, wincing as a thousand tiny darts stabbed into him. Fragments of dreams came tumbling back: a blue car, an old man, red-faced and angry, a searing flash.

Except that it wasn't a dream. It had happened. He got up and padded into the bathroom. Her perfume still clung to the air and he fought back resentment at the thought that she had been in here making herself attractive for another man.

He turned on the television in time to catch the ten o'clock news. A serious-faced young anchorwoman was talking about a car bomb explosion in north-central Louisiana. There were photographs of the judge's burned-out Volvo, and an interview with Chief Ned Triplett, who was explaining that an ex-convict named Cory Wilde had been taken into custody. The condition of the judge was said to be improving, while another victim, the editor of the parish weekly, had checked himself out of the hospital, whereabouts unknown.

Brady switched off the tube and went to the telephone. He dialed Garitty's number and got the sheriff on the second ring.

"Matt, I talked to your friend at Probation. Have they done anything yet?"

"Damned right," the lawman said. "Wilde's P.O. came up from Alec two hours ago and I just helped him go through Cory's house. My help was unofficial, of course. He said you swore there was *dope* there, for Christ sakes."

"Wasn't there?"

"We turned the place upside down but Ned's people had already been there. There were some prescription drugs from the prison pharmacy, but that was all. If there was dope, it was gone by then."

"Damn."

"Pete, what in hell's going on? How could you know if Cory Wilde had dope?"

"I'll explain some other time. It was worth a try."

"Pete . . ."

"I'll get back to you as soon as I can," Brady said, hanging up. The dope was gone. What had happened? Did Triplett's men find the little paper bag? Or had Penelope come back for it, afraid it could be traced to her? Damn it, what *was* her role in this?

He was still standing naked in the center of the room when he heard keys jingling outside and the tumblers in the lock started to turn. He stepped back into the bathroom, grabbed up a towel, and opened the door a crack.

Kelly entered, a look of faint disgust on her face. A man in his early thirties crowded in behind her, his expression one Brady had seen on the faces of foxes in nature films.

"Well, Tyler, it's been very nice, and I appreciate your help," Kelly was saying, but Tyler was not listening. He moved toward her, his hands on her shoulders, a cocky little smile on his lips.

122

"Any time, Kel. But the night's not over yet."

Kelly slid away. "Well, I have to be up early tomorrow. I really do."

"Tomorrow's Saturday," Tyler drawled, following her across the room. He had bland good looks, brown hair that must have kept one whole styling shop in business, and a signet ring that gleamed red in the lamplight.

"Tyler, really . . ."

He had her backed into a corner now and Brady decided it was time to make his move.

Towel held in place by one hand, he shoved the door open and uttered an exaggerated yawn. "That you, darling? I thought I heard voices."

Tyler's head shot around and his mouth dropped open. Kelly bit her lips to keep from laughing and Tyler backed away, stumbling into the coffee table.

"I . . ."

"And who is this nice young man?" Brady asked. "Aren't you going to get him a drink?"

All the colors of the American flag passed through Tyler's face in succession and he stammered a good night. The door slammed after him and Kelly broke into a convulsion of giggles.

"You're horrible," she said. "Do you hear me?"

"I was trying to prevent rape," Brady said with mock sternness.

"Were you?" She pressed him back toward the open doorway. "Well, you didn't succeed."

"I can barely move," he told her.

"Then I guess I'll have to do all the work."

She was against him now, tugging mischievously at the towel, and he let it go. She pressed him down onto the bed and he smelled the perfume that he had encountered in the bathroom and was glad it had not really been for Tyler Patin, after all.

"Mmmmm," she said, moving across him. "It's been a long time since I was saved by a naked hero."

"Kel, one thing . . ."

"What?" She pecked his lips.

"The address. Did you get it?"

"Bastard," she cried in make-believe anger. "Of course I got it. But just for that *you*'re going to have to do the hard part."

16

BRADY looked down at the address slip one more time as they arrowed through the swamps on the interstate, heading for New Orleans.

Felicia Fenstermacher. Mrs. Arthur St. Germain. It explained a lot.

"I still say we should have called last night," Kelly said, gunning the Mustang around a car that was doing a tortoiselike sixty-five. "What if nobody's home?"

"It's a risk, I know," Brady agreed, shutting his eyes as she edged to within inches of a tanker truck. "But with my luck lately, a phone call would just give her a chance to be somewhere else."

Kelly blasted her horn and the truck grudgingly moved over.

"I guess it *is* the same Arthur St. Germain," she mused.

"How many are there?" Brady asked. "No, it all makes sense. He was a state senator when I was on the *Picayune.* He's about thirty-five, which would make him five or six years older than his wife. I seem to remember he was married once before, and she died."

"And he'd be able to influence the parole board?"

"As the newly elected attorney general, he wouldn't have any direct influence, but he was elected by a greater margin than the governor. And he endorsed the governor on behalf of the good government forces during the runoff election. The governor owes him. Or he did."

"The attorney general," Kelly said in awe, her eyes hidden by the big sunglasses. "We have the makings of a hell of a story."

Brady said nothing. She was right, of course. But why was it that he did not feel the enthusiasm he should?

It was nine o'clock when they crossed into Orleans Parish, taking the freeway to the Carrollton exit and then dipping down onto Carrollton Avenue and heading for the river.

It brought back memories and Brady's throat went dry. Over there, at the K&B parking lot, he had waited for two hours one day with his window down, until a black man had passed by and dropped in an envelope with the names of twenty policemen involved in a prostitution ring. In the Chinese restaurant on the left, he'd had a meal with a nervous deputy assessor from neighboring Jefferson Parish. The lunch had cost the *Picayune* forty dollars but it had cost the deputy's boss five years in Hunt Correctional.

He had tied on a real one after that story, and everybody had slapped his back and told him it was a hell of a job, and Dockerty had told him to go to Cancun for a couple of weeks. He had, but he could remember very little of the resort because he had spent his vacation in an alcoholic haze. Now, it seemed like something that had happened to someone else, in a television show. It was hard to believe he had ever been that Pete Brady, trapped in the treadmill of deadlines and high-pressure demands. However, like the thirst, it was always there, a tantalizing reminder of a former self, where only liquor could kill the constant adrenaline highs.

The city hadn't changed: still too much traffic, still the smell of exhaust, still the same steam bath outside, even at nine o'clock.

"Daniel Webster," Kelly said, coming to the end of the boulevard and turning left onto another. "Do you know where that is?"

Brady nodded, watching the familiar landmarks on St. Charles flow past. On their left now was Tulane, with its Gothic buildings, and on the right, Audubon Park, where a Saturday soccer game was in progress. A trolley clanged loudly in the median strip and Kelly smiled.

"I always felt like I was missing something for not having lived here," she commented.

"You were," Brady said, his thoughts lingering on the

darker aspects of his past life. They passed Henry Clay and Brady shook himself out of his memories.

"Here," he said, pointing to the next street sign. They turned right, onto a camphor-shaded drive with big houses attesting to the easy affluence of their owners. They were in the heart of the Garden District now, founded by Anglos in the early part of the last century as a bastion against the Creoles who dominated the uptown area. The houses dated from the first years of the present century, but many had passed into new hands since, belonging now to university professors, physicians, bankers, and lawyers.

Brady checked the address slip again. It would be in the next block, on the left.

He pointed to a two-story white house with a broad front porch set off by brick pillars and she nosed the Mustang into the curb. There was a red BMW on the other side, parked behind a Caddie Seville. They went across the street, through the iron-grille gate, and up the walk to the front steps. A dog started barking inside and the door opened. A black maid with a doily apron frowned out at them, her expression indicating that she was prepared to send them on their way.

Before Brady could identify himself, however, Kelly took matters into her own hands.

"Hi. I'm an old friend of Mrs. St. Germain's. We were in the Phi Beta Theta honor society. We promised if we were ever within a thousand miles of each other, we'd look each other up. This year I made Thurston take our vacation in New Orleans so we could see her. Would you tell her Kelly's here, please?"

The maid frowned, then nodded. "Just a minute, please."

Brady gave Kelly a dark look. "Thurston, huh?"

"What's wrong?" Kelly smiled, digging him in the ribs. "You don't like it?"

The maid returned five minutes later, her expression showing nothing.

"Mrs. St. Germain say for you to come in."

She admitted them into a spacious living room where a chandelier gave off muted light. The furniture was antique and the carpet looked like an original from Iran. Through an open doorway on the left, Brady caught a glimpse of a dining table, with the dishes partly cleared away from breakfast. The maid walked ahead of them to another doorway, this one on the right, and pointed for them to enter.

Brady followed Kelly in and stopped.

The room was impeccably appointed, with book-lined polished oak shelves reaching to the ceiling and original oil paintings on one wall. However, what caught Brady's attention was not the room but, rather, the woman in the center of the carpet.

She was in her late twenties, with short blond hair, ocean-blue eyes, and, in the white tennis shorts and cotton pullover, had a figure that pulled no punches. It took a second for Brady to realize that her stance was a pose and that her beauty, as striking as it was, was marred by a slight, spoiled downturn of her lips.

"I'm afraid I don't understand," Felicia St. Germain said. "Am I supposed to know you?"

"Well, actually, no," Kelly said. "But I had to get in and I was afraid you wouldn't see me if I told you who we really were. Here." She fished out one of the business cards Brady had ordered for her last year. Felicia St. Germain looked down at it as if it might be contaminated and then raised her head.

"Ella."

The door opened and the maid appeared.

"Ella, show these *people* out. And next time don't be taken in so easily."

"All right," Kelly said. "I guess we'll have to do the story on your father without you."

The St. Germain woman's jaw tightened and she shot them a murderous look. Then she crumpled the business card in her fist.

"Close the door, Ella." When the maid was gone, the woman in front of them tossed the little card into an ashtray, opened the cigarette box on the coffee table, and lit up. Brady noticed that despite her attempt at poise, her hand was shaking.

"Now what's this about my father?" she demanded coldly. "He's been dead for five years, so . . ."

"You mean Adam Fenstermacher?" Kelly asked, and Brady realized she was talking about the listing in the old telephone books. "No, you don't understand. I mean your *real* father. Cory Wilde."

"I don't know what you're talking about," Felicia said, but her voice was trembling and Brady knew they had struck home.

127

He took a step forward. "Mrs. St. Germain, we're not here to hurt anyone or open old wounds. But your father is in danger. He's been arrested and I'm sure he's innocent. He needs a good lawyer."

Before Felicia St. Germain could answer, the door opened and a man stepped into the room. He was wearing jogging shorts and a T-shirt and exuded an odor of sweat. His dark hair was tousled and a bath towel hung from one hand. He looked from his wife to the two visitors, his expression wary.

"Felicia, what's going . . ." His eyes fixed on Brady and then recognition flashed in his eyes. "Pete Brady." He gave a nervous little laugh. "What in the hell are you doing here? I heard you'd left town to work on some weekly. Wait. It has to be the bombing."

"Oh, my God." His wife's poise crumpled and she sat down heavily on the couch, eyes straight ahead.

"How are you, General?" Brady shook a wet hand. "You seem to be on top of things, as usual."

"Well," St. Germain said, "it's all over the news. That and . . ." He looked over at his wife. "I guess you're here about my wife's father."

"Oh, God, no, Arthur, don't tell them about that!" Felicia cried from the couch, her face ashen.

Her husband shook his head. "Sweetheart, I'm afraid they already know."

"That's right," Brady confirmed. "We know he's not guilty of the crimes they locked him up for."

"You mean the bombing?" the lawyer asked dubiously.

"I mean *any* of it," Brady said. "The bombing, an earlier car wreck, and the murder of Alice Ann Potter."

Felicia buried her face in her hands, her cigarette making lazy question marks in the air. "No," she sobbed. "It can't be."

"What can't be, Mrs. St. Germain?" Brady asked.

She looked up through teary eyes. "That he's not guilty. He was convicted. Sent away. All my life I had to live with that, with the idea of a killer as a father, a man who . . . who picked up and murdered an innocent young girl. You can't come here and tell me all of a sudden it isn't true, that he was innocent."

"I'm afraid I have to," Brady said, and he recounted all that had happened since Cory Wilde's return. "So, you see, he's back to see himself vindicated, and since he can't discuss his case, the best thing he could do was make himself as conspicuous as possible and try to stir up the people that sent him away."

"Jesus." The attorney general blotted his face with the towel and took a seat beside his wife. "I never had any idea he'd do that when I . . ."

"When you intervened with the governor?" Brady asked.

St. Germain nodded wearily. "Yes. You have to understand. It was a personal thing with me. The man is Felicia's *father*."

Felicia frowned at her husband, face unbelieving. "Arthur, what are you saying? You helped him get out?"

The attorney put a hand on his wife's shoulder. "Listen, Felicia, and try to understand," he pleaded gently. "When you told me, years ago, about your background and who your real father was, I thought it was just one of those things. I never told anyone else about it. But I have some contacts in Corrections. When I was a legislator, I made some discreet inquiries. I said your father was the relative of a constituent. I told them I wanted to know if there was anything he needed. I knew he was in for life, but it seemed the decent thing to do. Then, two months ago, when I got the call about his illness, I knew I had to do something."

"His illness?" Kelly asked.

St. Germain nodded. "Throat cancer. They told me it was inoperable. That was when I called the governor."

Felicia dropped her cigarette into the ashtray and shook her head from side to side but no words came.

"Don't you see, Fel? He's your father. He'll be the grandfather of our children. I didn't want to have to tell them he died in prison. It seemed like such a small thing. The governor owed me a big one. And with the election behind him, he could afford to take a little flak. All he had to do was call a couple of members of the parole board."

Felicia stared down at the floor. "Arthur, you should have left it alone," she declared bitterly. "You should have left him where he was."

"*Fel.* He's your father."

She shook her head. "No. My father died five years ago. This is a stranger. Somebody that's done nothing but cause me trouble all my life."

129

"But he's old, sick, dying . . ." her husband protested.

"Yes." She nodded. "And he can cost you your career. Have you thought about that? If it ever came out that you'd helped a murderer?"

"Mrs. St. Germain," Brady said, "What if your father is innocent?"

"Innocent?" Felicia St. Germain looked up then and her eyes were hard. "What difference does that make? *I'm* the one who's innocent. My husband is innocent. Our children will be innocent. And if you open this business up all over again, we'll all be hurt." She got up then, her fists clenched. "My husband was elected as a reform attorney general. He promised to help clean out the crooks and thieves. The last chairman of the pardon board is in jail for selling pardons, for God's sake. Arthur has already started investigations in twenty different parishes. With his record, in four years, or eight, he could go on to governor."

"Felicia!" Arthur St. Germain stared at his wife in disbelief. "My God, do you know what you're saying? This man says your father is innocent, that he was wrongfully convicted. I'm sworn to uphold the rights of the innocent as well as of the guilty. Besides," he said, giving Brady a knowing nod, "these people are reporters. It's already too late."

Brady stared at the tortured man in front of him and made up his mind. "Maybe not," he said.

"What?" The politician turned slowly toward him. "What did you say?"

"I said maybe not. My interest is a twenty-nine-year-old murder and preventing another one. Those are fodder for a big enough story without bringing you in if I don't have to."

St. Germain's head moved slightly to the side, as if he did not quite believe what he was hearing. "All right."

"My God, Arthur," his wife protested. "These are reporters. You remember the election. They'll use anything they can get their hands on."

Her husband shook his head. "Some of them," he agreed. "But I've known Pete Brady for ten years and he's always kept his word." He faced Brady. "I'll call somebody I know, a lawyer in Shreveport. I'll have him in Troy as soon as I can."

"Arthur!" Felicia's shriek sent shivers through Brady and he

saw Kelly grit her teeth. "I told you he was dead. I don't care about him. Once you open this up, there's no going back. I don't *care* what these people say; it's not their lives. Even if he's innocent, there are people who won't believe it. There'll never be any way to really prove it."

"Mrs. St. Germain," Brady began, but she cut him off.

"No. You listen to what I'm saying. I've never seen him and I don't want to now. He's not my father. He abandoned me. In all those years, I never heard a word. He left me to be brought up by people that might as well have been strangers. Now I don't care if he lives or dies. And if you help him any more, Arthur . . ." She moved on her husband, fury distorting her features. "If you do, you can forget we ever met, because I swear to God I'll leave."

Her husband swallowed and looked from his wife to the visitors. "Maybe you'd better go," he suggested, and he followed Brady and Kelly into the next room, shutting the door behind him.

"I'm sorry about this," he said, moving with them toward the front door. "I had no idea she'd react this way. You have to forgive her. She's overwrought. The idea of moving to Baton Rouge next month, leaving all this . . . She's not her usual self."

"No," Brady said, stepping through the door behind Kelly. He turned around. "Tell me. It's you who's providing Cory Wilde with his living expenses, isn't it?"

St. Germain nodded. "Yes. It seemed the decent thing to do."

"Does Cory know where the money comes from?"

"He thinks it's from his daughter. He only agreed to accept it when my banker promised to arrange it so the checks wouldn't be traceable to her. He doesn't want to hurt her."

"And the failure to restrict his travel was your work, too, wasn't it?"

"Guilty as charged. I personally asked the chairman of the parole board not to release anything about his illness. He agreed . . . reluctantly, I might add. And he said they'd let it ride and see if it stirred up too much of a storm. I guess we all know the answer now."

"Yeah," Brady said. "But it occurs to me that a lawyer could be handled the same way, sub rosa."

The attorney general nodded, embarrassed. "Yes. But if Fel ever found out . . . I need some time to quiet her down. You understand."

"Sure," Brady said, taking the attorney general's hand.

"You know, I do appreciate your promise not to involve me," St. Germain said, "There was a time you wouldn't have said that. You've changed."

Brady gave him a wan smile. "Have I? Well, General, so have you."

17

THEY were already back on the interstate before Kelly broke the silence.

"Where does that leave us?" she asked.

Brady stared morosely out the window at the Metairie Cemetery on their left and shuddered. "I honest to God don't know. If it were five years ago, he wouldn't have hesitated." He pounded the dash in frustration.

"She's not going to relent," Kelly said. "She feels abandoned. He may look good on TV, but he won't be able to stand up against her."

"Once . . ." Brady said. "Oh, what the hell."

"So now what's the plan?" Kelly asked.

"Well, we're down to three people: the judge, Ernie Hughes, and Penelope. They'll probably never let me into the hospital to see the judge, and Hughes has disappeared. That leaves Pen. She's a shrewd woman, and a lot of that psychic business is baloney, but not all of it. Some of it's as real to her as her bank account. And that's what I can't figure. I've seen so-called psychics before. Some are phonies and others are just flakes. But with Pen, it's almost as if she's a normal levelheaded person who was

132

forced into a deviation somewhere years ago and yet has learned to make the best of it. I can't shake the feeling that she was normal once and somewhere along the line, when she was young, something happened."

"That's Pen, all right," Kelly agreed. "But what could she know about any of this?"

"That's the sixty-four-thousand-dollar-question, isn't it? Well, if you'll drop me off at my car, I'll drive on back and see what I can do."

"I'll drop you off, but I'll bet I'll be in Troy before you are. You didn't think you were going to ditch me in Baton Rouge, did you? Not in the middle of a story this big."

"Last time, you almost got killed," Brady pointed out.

Kelly nodded. "True. But it made a hell of a story."

Kelly was right. Though Brady pushed his Galaxie to seventy on the straightaways, Kelly was waiting in front of his house when he arrived. He got out stiffly and a blond young man in shirt sleeves came hurrying up from out of nowhere, hand outstretched.

"Mr. Brady? My name is Patrick Gulliver. I'm with the Shreveport *Times*. Everybody's been looking all over for you."

"Everybody?" Brady asked warily.

"The press gang. There's somebody here from the AP, and the *Town Talk*, and the *Morning Advocate*. We took turns staking out your house and I guess I drew the lucky straw."

"Great," Brady said. "Look, it's three o'clock and we haven't eaten. I've been on the road for four and a half hours."

"Oh, that's no problem," Gulliver bubbled. "We have a headquarters set up down at your office. Your man Ripley opened it up for us. We've got sandwiches and coffee and even"—he winked—"a little hair of the dog."

Brady and Kelly exchanged looks and she laughed. "How can you pass up an invitation like that?"

The first thing Brady noticed, aside from the strange cars in his lot, was the hole in his front window. Someone had placed tape over it, but it was an eyesore, nevertheless. He muttered to himself and let the young reporter hold the door open for Kelly and himself.

Four faces looked up from coffee cups, sandwiches, and telephones. The woman from the *Town Talk* he already knew vaguely. The others were strangers to him.

"Gentlemen," Gulliver declared with a flourish. "Mr. Pete Brady, Pulitzer Prize–winner and proprietor."

Four pairs of hands clapped mechanically. One of the men, the fat one wearing the *Morning Advocate* badge, winked at Kelly.

"Hi, beautiful."

Kelly walked over and dropped his half-eaten hamburger back into its paper bag as if it were a dead rat. "You're in my chair, O'Hearn."

The others laughed and at that moment, Ripley backed through the doorway with two barrels of fried chicken under his arms.

"They don't sell liquor in this parish," he was explaining. "But later on I'll—" He turned around, saw Brady, and stopped, motionless.

"What happened to the window?" Brady asked.

"Somebody threw a brick through it last night," a shame-faced Ripley explained. "I swear, if I knew who it was—"

"Right. What's with the chicken?"

"Well, the fellows here were hungry and—"

"The fellows," Brady observed, "never stop eating. Or drinking. But, since you have it here, put it on my desk. Kel, could you go for some fried chicken, courtesy of our *colleagues*?"

Ripley placed the food in front of his employer and backed off. "Boss, a Mr. Dockerty from the *Times-Picayune* has been calling every half hour. He says to tell you he wants you to be their representative and not to forget the time he helped you out with the president pro tem's girlfriend."

Kelly lowered a drumstick and eyed Brady. "That sounds interesting. Did he say more?"

Ripley blushed and the other reporters broke into gales of laughter.

Brady gobbled a chicken breast and appropriated one of the chocolate malts. "So what's happened in the last day?" he asked.

A chorus of howls answered him.

134

"That damned Triplett is guarding the judge like a bull-dog," O'Hearn complained. "We can't get anything out of the bastard. We heard there's a man they're looking for, Hughes is the name, but he's taken off. Word is, *he's* in the forest some-place."

"And Cory Wilde?" Brady asked, almost afraid of the an-swer.

"Still in jail, with a rifle-toting cop out front. Look, Pete, you know more than you're telling. Help us out, will you? You've been someplace for the last day and, knowing you, you were dig-ging up some things." The other heads nodded agreement. Em-boldened by the support, O'Hearn went on: "Now, I say let's be realistic, okay? I mean, we're all colleagues, right? You were an investigative reporter once. You know what it's like to have some-body breathing down your neck. Why you quit and moved up here is your business. The point is, you're not in the game any-more; I mean, not like we are. It's not a matter of urgency with you. So if you have some inside track, some source, you could help us all by pointing us in the right direction."

Brady saw Kelly's face turn red and he cleared his throat quickly to catch her attention. "Well, there may be something I can do. Like you say, we're in a backwater up here. I don't need a front-page story like you guys . . ."

Four heads nodded enthusiastically.

"I think," Brady told them, "that whoever can find this Er-nie Hughes is going to crack the case."

The woman from the *Town Talk* guffawed and tapped her cigarette ash onto the cement floor.

"Come on, Brady, everybody knows that. The question is where *is* the son of a bitch?"

"Well, I have an idea about that, too," Brady told them.

The woman leaned forward and the room went silent.

"Oh yeah?" she asked.

"You see," Brady said, "I have a friend who knows those woods like the back of his hand. If he was willing to take you out there, well, nothing much gets by him. But I don't know if he'd do it."

Gulliver licked his lips and exchanged glances with his col-leagues. "Look, Mr. Brady, I think I can speak for all of us. Our papers will pay a, well, let's say reasonable fee. Now if you can get this old timer . . ."

"He's pretty ornery," Brady said. "But I'll try."

"You want me to *what*?" Emmett demanded, straightening up from his flower bed.

"I told them you were a combination of Davy Crockett and Daniel Boone," Brady explained. "Look, they'll pay and it's only for a day or so."

"You mean nursemaid a bunch of city slickers through the damned national forest?"

"I think it's a great idea," Kelly said. "When I was little, you told me nobody knew the forest like you did, not even Ernie Hughes."

"Well . . ." Emmett rubbed a hand over his head. "Man says a lot of things. Anyway, some of these people know me."

"Does being a publisher mean you can't be an outdoorsman, too? When we were fishing last week you told me—"

"Forget what I told you. Look, this is, well, it's *unethical.*" He took off his gloves. "Those were my colleagues."

"True enough," Brady said. "I guess I ought to be ashamed. After all, they really need the story, and, like they said, all I am is the publisher of a podunk weekly."

"*Who* said?" Emmett demanded.

"Well, you have to see it from their viewpoint," Brady told him.

"Podunk weekly, eh?" He started for the house, his jaw set. "We'll see about that."

"Don't take it so personally, Dad," Kelly said, fighting back a smile.

"Personal? Hell, I'll take 'em so far back in the woods, they'll need *radar* to find their way out. Smart-aleck city kids." He went to the faucet at the side of the house, turned the handle, and raised the plastic hose to his lips.

"Trouble is," he said, rubbing his mouth with a sleeve, "Ernie's still out there someplace, and losing these guys won't find him."

"I know," Brady admitted. "Any ideas?"

Emmett shook his head. "Not really. Man could blend into the woods like a damned Indian. Fact, I heard he had some Choctaw in him. Hell, he's probably out there now, laughing at everybody and chucking down his rye."

"He's a drinker is he?" Brady asked.

"He's been known to bend his elbow."

Brady nodded and stuck out his hand, feigning nonchalance. "Well, thanks a lot, Emmett. Have fun."

The old man snorted and Brady walked back to his car, Kelly at his side.

"Those guys are going to hate you." She giggled. "But they deserve it." She opened the car door and stopped. "Trouble is, it isn't going to help us find Ernie Hughes."

Brady looked over at her and tried to keep his voice even. "It doesn't have to. I think I know where he is."

18

BRADY watched the same farms and pastures pass, saw the same children outside at play, felt the same road climbing upward in a meandering curve.

"Are you sure you know what you're doing?" Kelly asked, turning down the visor to keep the afternoon sun out of her face.

"No," Brady admitted. "But it's the best idea I've had lately."

They entered the national forest and the road became gravel.

"I hope I'm not going to have to walk a long ways," Kelly said. "These sandals aren't made for hiking. Besides, it'll be dark in a few hours."

"Bear with me," Brady said, slowing as they passed the old white voting booth perched beside the road like a warning.

"Wait a minute," Kelly said. "I know where we are. This is the road to New Zion."

Brady nodded and glanced down at his odometer. Two-tenths of a mile past the voting booth, he pulled to the side of the road and opened his door. "Time to walk," he said. "And try not to slam your door."

He locked his side and pointed to the road ahead of them. "It's not far."

Their footsteps crunched in the gravel and he motioned for them to move over to the side of the road. Brady turned and looked back over his shoulder. The dust cloud from his car was already dissipating.

"I know there's a method in your madness," Kelly said.

Brady put a finger to his lips and pointed ahead. They walked on for another five minutes and stopped.

A trio of buzzards was engaged in a meal at the edge of the woods. Brady took two steps down the incline and jumped the ditch to the grassy verge between the road and the forest. Kelly followed, catching his hand as she landed beside him. The birds flapped their wings in warning and then reluctantly took to the air.

Brady steeled himself and looked down at what they had been eating. It was a dead dog.

"Uggg." Kelly turned her face away, but Brady made himself go closer. The dog had not been dead long, a day at the most, and the vultures had destroyed only the body parts. The head was still intact, including the wound that had caused its death.

Brady turned away, leading her by the hand.

"What was that all about?" she whispered.

He pointed ahead of them to the outline of the old house, barely visible through the mask of trees.

"What is it?" she mouthed.

Brady motioned for her to stay and tiptoed to the drive. He looked down and saw tire tracks in the earth, leading from the road into the yard.

Now he knew he was right, and he was unsure what to do. All at once, however, the decision was taken out of his hands.

A shot exploded from the front window of the house, taking a splinter off the wooden gate, inches from his right hand. He dove to his left, landing in the ditch.

"Kelly, down!" he cried. Another shot gouged the earth over his head, sending a river of dirt into his hair.

"Get outta here!" a voice yelled. "This is private property."

Brady crept along the ditch, toward the driveway that bridged it.

"It's too late, Hughes," Brady yelled. "We know where you are. How do you think I found you in the first place? It's all over now. You might as well let us in. We only want to talk."

"No talking," the voice cried. "You just get out. Get out or—"

"Or you'll what? Kill us like you did the dog over there?" He took a deep breath. "Like you did Boy Jenks and the judge's wife?"

"That's a lie!" Hughes screamed. "I shot the dog 'cause it came yapping and howling outside the fence, wouldn't leave me alone. But I never killed no person."

"Then why did you run away? I saw the judge hand you the envelope with the money. You may have thought you were getting rid of me by pulling out my wires, but it didn't work."

There was silence and Brady wondered for an uneasy moment whether the old man was using the time to flank them.

Then the voice came again: "Why are you doing this? Why the hell can't you just leave me alone?"

Brady raised his head cautiously and parted some of the grass with his hands so that he could see the open window and the rifle barrel that rested on the sill.

"A man spent almost thirty years in jail," Brady called. "That's why. People have been murdered. It's all coming unraveled and the best you can do is confess before it's too late. Get on the train before it leaves, Hughes. Don't be the last one waiting at the station. Don't go to the death house for somebody else."

The man in the window gave a yell of rage as a sudden volley of shots spattered into the earth near Brady's head. He dug his face into the ground as the bullets ricocheted past, counting the shots. *Five . . . six . . . seven . . .*

All at once, the shooting stopped, a dying series of echoes thumping down into the valley. A metallic click sounded from the house and Brady rose to his knees.

139

Hughes was out of ammunition. Brady had only seconds to make it to the house before the old man could reload.

He scrambled up the side of the ditch and raced for the yard, oblivious of his aching bones. He ducked through the tall grass, searching for cover, aware that it would take only seconds to load a few rounds, aim the gun, fire point-blank. . . .

He reached the doorway, panting, and crashed through just in time to see the old man shove the final cartridge into the slot in the receiver. Hughes gave an animal growl, raised the weapon, and Brady lunged at him, deflecting the barrel.

The old man swore, but Brady's weight bore him down and the two men crashed to the floor. Brady jerked the rifle away and hurled it into a corner.

He stared down at the figure crouched on the floor. A gray stubble covered the old man's cheeks and his clothes were smudged with mud. His hands trembled and the brown eyes were rimmed with red. He exuded a smell of alcohol and Brady saw a half-full bottle of rye under the window.

Brady went to the door and called. "Kelly, it's okay. You can come in now."

"How did you find me?" Hughes demanded, his voice trembling. "I didn't tell nobody I was coming here."

"Luck," Brady said. "I came out here last week. I saw the rye bottles in the back bedroom. Not too many people around here drink rye. When Emmett Larson told me you were a rye drinker, I figured you must come here sometimes to drown your guilt."

Hughes sucked in air. He put his face in his hands and shook his head from side to side. "Oh, God."

He looked up slowly, his eyes wet. "I just wanted it to go away. I just wanted to pretend it never happened. The judge tried to give me money, but I didn't want his damn money. I just wanted it to all go away."

"It won't go away," Brady said. "It did happen."

Hughes nodded disconsolately. "I used to come here sometimes, when it got too much. I used to come here and drink and think what it must've been like before. . . . Sometimes I thought I really was *him*. I used to walk through the rooms, try to see it the way it was, her in the kitchen, him in the living room, like he was that day we came to arrest him. This house was my own jail."

140

"His was worse," Brady said. "He didn't get to see his children grow up. He didn't get appointed to a federal position. He lost nearly thirty years of his life."

"I'd give it all back," Hughes said. "I swear to God, if I had it to do over again—"

"You don't," Brady said. "All you can do is tell us what happened and hope the courts give you some kind of break."

Hughes sighed and reached for the bottle. He unscrewed the cap and took a long swig.

"I'm too old to go to prison," he whined. "I'm seventy-two years old. I'm too old . . ."

Brady pulled the bottle out of the old man's hand and threw it against the wall. Hughes recoiled into the corner, his shocked eyes following the trickles of brown liquid down the dusty surface of the wall.

"Tell us what happened," Brady ordered. "Unless you want another murder on your conscience."

Hughes started to raise a hand in protest, then let it fall.

"It was all the judge's idea," he said. "He wasn't the judge then, though. Just the DA. Old Creswell Troy was the judge. But he just went along. I don't know how much he really knew, anyhow. It was Sheriff Thomas and Honeycutt that put it all together." He licked his lips. "You got to understand. I just did what they told me."

"And were well taken care of," Brady said with disgust.

"It's not the way you make it sound. I mean, they told me the man was guilty. The rest of it wasn't none of my business. My business was doing what Thomas told me to do."

"What did he tell you to do?"

Hughes faced the wall. "It was a Sunday afternoon. I was in the office when Thomas came in and waved his hand for me to come into his private office. I did. Figured it was something political. That's what he always did when there was politics to discuss. He sat down behind his desk and he said, 'I got a job for you, Ernie. But you're gonna have to keep your mouth shut. You do the job right, there's no telling how far you can go. You don't, and you won't go anyplace at all.' That was the kind of man he was. Laid it right on the line."

"Go on," Brady said.

141

"He told me there was a body out on the El road. 'Young girl. I want you to go out there, but use your private car.'" Hughes shook his head. "I didn't know what to say. My private car? 'And when you get out there, I want you to pick up the body and take it to the place I have marked on this map. It's a logging road near the voting booth at New Zion. It's Cory Wilde's property. I want you to bury the body there.'" Hughes tried to laugh but it came out as a choking sound. "You could've knocked me over with a feather. Hell, I done a lot of things for Sheriff Thomas, but burying a body? I guess he saw what was going through my mind because then he told me that Cory Wilde had done the crime, and that somebody saw him do it, but they didn't want to have to bring that person forward because they didn't have anything to do with it, they was just with Cory and tried to stop him, but if they brought them forward, it would ruin their reputation. 'Cory Wilde's guilty,' he said. 'We just have to see he's convicted.' You got to understand. I believed him."

"So you buried the body and along the way you clipped off some of the hair and put it in Cory's truck."

"It's what Thomas told me to do," Hughes protested.

"And the anonymous phone call about the body's location? I guess that was made up?"

"I let out the story," Hughes said. "But it never happened."

"You got Boy Jenks to swear he saw Cory pick up Alice Ann," Brady stated.

"Yes. Boy was always into something he shouldn't've been. It was easy to get him to testify."

"When did you start to think Cory might be innocent?" Kelly asked then.

"I guess during the trial. We went over his house and truck real good. I was sure we'd find something else, something from her body, more hair, or a bobby pin, or *something*. You don't know how much I wanted to find something to prove we had the right man. But there just *wasn't* anything else. And when I asked the sheriff who it was had really seen Cory do it, and why they'd just stood by, he told me to shut up, that it wasn't any of my business."

"So you shut up."

"What else could I do? By that time, it was my word against

142

his, don't you see? He hadn't dirtied his hands. *I* had. But it was really the jury that did it."

"How many did you have to bribe?"

"Gil Simmons, the foreman. That was the only one I paid. Two thousand dollars."

"But not to convict Cory, right?"

"No. Just to argue with the others for second-degree."

"Oh, my God," Kelly cried. "I think I'm going to be sick."

"They were men of conscience," Brady said sarcastically. "They couldn't stand to see an innocent man go to the chair." He looked down with contempt at the man in the corner. "But why Cory Wilde? There were lots of other people they could've chosen."

"I don't know." Hughes shrugged. "I guess it was because he was available. Him and his old lady, they'd had a fight the day before and we'd been called. She said then that she was going to stay with her folks. The sheriff did some poking around, I guess, found out he didn't have an alibi." Hughes got up shakily. "You got to understand: He had a bad temper. It wasn't the first time he'd beat on her. What kind of man beats his wife?"

"What kind of men send an innocent person to prison?" Brady asked. "All right, come on. You're going to tell your story to the sheriff. Sheriff Garitty, not Sheriff Thomas."

19

MATT Garitty listened impassively as Ernie Hughes told his story. From somewhere beyond his den came the sound of a ball game on television and the smell of fish frying. When Hughes finished, the sheriff nodded curtly, went to the telephone, and dialed from memory.

"Howard? Matt Garitty. I need you down at my office in about five minutes." An outraged buzz protested from the earpiece. "You're still the DA of this parish, aren't you?" Garitty demanded. "Or do you want me to go to the attorney general?"

Garitty put down the phone and addressed Ernie Hughes.

"Mr. Hughes, we're going downtown now. I'm going to drive you into the garage and we're going to take the elevator to the third floor. I'll send word to Howard Blair to meet us up there and you can give your statement."

"But the third floor . . ." Hughes protested feebly.

"The third floor is the jail. I know. But you'll be safer there than anywhere else. Besides, I have a feeling you'd better get used to it."

Brady and Kelly walked outside with the sheriff and his prisoner. Garitty helped Hughes into his unmarked white car and then turned to his two friends. "I hate this like hell," he admitted. "I've known Ernie Hughes all my life. But I have to say, it was a nice piece of work. You don't think Ernie did the actual killings, though, do you?"

"I doubt it," Brady said. "Look, is there any word on Boy Jenks?"

The lawman nodded. "I got a call at two o'clock. One of the technicians at the state police lab agreed to work on his own time, God bless him. Anyway, he's pretty sure they've got a match." He shrugged. "But, then, why shouldn't he? Nobody thought Jenks was still alive, did they?"

"No," Brady admitted. "Not really. But it would've tied things up neatly."

"Right. But as of now, there's still a killer out there."

"Yes." Brady watched the sheriff get into the car. Garitty slammed the door, then rolled down the window.

"Just do me a favor. Don't go hunting for him. He might find you."

Brady and Kelly looked at each other.

"You heard the man," she said.

"He said *him*," Brady pointed out. "I was planning to visit a *her*."

Mrs. Rickenbacker gave a little gasp of surprise when she saw her employer on her doorstep, with her former employer's daughter just behind him.

"Arthur," she called, obviously flustered. "We have company."

Her husband, a squat man with a veined face, got up quickly from his place before the television and shook Brady's hand.

"What did Eleanor do now?" he asked, doubtfully.

"Arthur . . ." His wife protested.

"Nothing," Brady said, following them into a living room with a stuffed bass on one wall and a cheap Winslow Homer print on the other. "I was hoping maybe she could help us, if she has the time."

Mrs. Rickenbacker drew herself up another inch and smiled triumphantly at her husband.

"Well, of course, I'd be happy . . ." Then she caught herself. "Do you mean I have to go back to the office?"

"No, of course not. I just wanted to take advantage of your knowledge of the town," Brady said.

"Hell." Arthur snorted. "What's Eleanor know?"

Mrs. R. gave him a look of scathing disdain.

"Please sit down," she told her guests. "Arthur will get you a Coke."

"Thanks anyway," Brady said. "But what we really need is for you to try to remember something from a long time ago."

"How long?" Mrs. R. asked.

"The time of the Cory Wilde trial," Brady told her.

Arthur guffawed. "You wasn't in school with the dead girl, Eleanor. Don't tell 'em that."

Mrs. Rickenbacker bit her lip. "I never said I was. But I was quite young." She touched her hair self-consciously. "Yes, of course, I remember it. I . . ."

"Hell, she even went to the trial for a couple of days," Arthur put in. "Loved it."

"Everyone went," she defended. "Arthur, these people would like a Coke."

"I thought they said never mind."

"Mrs. Rickenbacker," Brady said, trying to regain the offensive, "I'd like you to forget Cory Wilde for a minute and tell me about some of the other people who lived in the town then. People with good connections, who might have been a little on the wild side. Was there anybody, say, who got in trouble a lot? A

145

town bad boy, for instance? Were there any scandals about people getting out of bad situations because of their political pull?"

"Scandals." Arthur chortled. "You hit her in the weak spot there."

Mrs. Rickenbacker ignored the interruption. "The man is asking about *history*. I do think I've lived in this town long enough to know a little about that subject. As for politics, well, this town has always had that, ever since the days of Huey Long. If you weren't for Huey . . ." She gave a little laugh.

"Eleanor, these people aren't interested in Huey Long. And the answer, Mr. Brady, is that the same politicians always ran things, and some others before them, and if you knew them, or could even claim kin, you could do about anything you pleased, because they'd take care of their own."

"Oh!" Mrs. Rickenbacker gave a little cry and a hand flew to her mouth. "You don't suppose. . . ? I mean, you aren't asking—?"

"What's that, Mrs. R.?" Brady leaned forward, aware that she had hit on something.

"Well, it probably isn't anything, but you were asking, and I just remembered—"

"Yes?" Brady waited, heart thumping.

"Well, I'd hate to speak ill of the dead."

"Oh, come on, Eleanor," scoffed Arthur. "You've never let it stop you before."

It was dusk when they pulled into Penelope's driveway. The smell of fresh hay hung in the evening air and from somewhere down the road came the lazy drone of a chain saw.

"You think Penelope knows something about this?" Kelly asked.

"She's not telling us everything she does know," Brady answered. "That much I'm sure of."

They walked across the grass and up onto the porch, but before they reached the door, it opened and Penelope smiled out at them, the late sun glittering on her jewelry.

"What a nice surprise," she said. "I was out feeding the animals when I had a premonition you were both coming. The spirits take care of me so well." She laughed. "I had time to bathe and change."

Brady followed Kelly into the living room and then faced the older woman.

"Pen, it's no good. We need some answers, not talk about spirits and higher planes."

Penelope laughed nervously. "Well, I don't know what you mean. The spirits can provide answers. My guide—"

Brady grasped her shoulders. "Pen, damn it, people have been killed. Now I have to know what's going on and why."

Penelope's eyes searched the room for a way out. "Peter, what are you trying to say? I haven't done anything. I—"

"Somebody set a fire in the drugstore the other day. Somebody tried to burn up the mixture of herbs you gave me."

"I don't know anything about that."

"You don't own any shares in the corporation that controls Val-Save?"

"Yes. I bought a couple of hundred shares when I heard they were opening up a store here. What's wrong with that?"

Brady grasped her wrist, raising it so that the gold charm bracelet gleamed in the light. "This bracelet: You were wearing it, just like you are right now, when you went to Cory Wilde's old place. It doesn't do any good to lie, Pen, to claim somebody stole it and left one of the figures there. The only logical way for that figure to have gotten where I found it was for you to have dropped it there."

"But I've never been out there. I don't know what you're trying to say. The spirits. . . . The spirits must have done it."

"Not the spirits," Brady insisted, maintaining his hold on her wrist. "You. Penelope Martingale. Now tell me, Pen. *Tell me the truth!*"

"No. Let me go. I don't *know* anything. I don't—" She tried to twist away, her face ashen, but Brady jerked her back to him.

"Talk, Pen. Tell the truth!"

Kelly stepped forward, reaching out to draw them apart. "Brady . . ."

But he ignored her, his eyes never wavering from the tortured face of Penelope. "Talk, Penelope. Tell me what's going

147

on." He shook her, gently at first, and then with increasing vigor. "Tell me what I want to know. I don't care about the spirits. I want to know what *you* did and why. *Talk!*"

"N-o-o-o-o." Penelope gave a little shriek and stumbled back, a fist flying to her mouth. Her eyes searched wildly for escape.

"Pen, damn it, you can't get away with mystical mumbo jumbo this time. This time, you have to face up to it and tell the truth."

"But I can't help it," she sobbed. "It's something I can't control."

"Yes, you can. Now tell me the truth before somebody else dies!"

Penelope's eyes held to his and then suddenly her mouth opened and she screamed, and while the scream still echoed, Brady felt her body going limp.

Brady caught her, lifted her in his arms, and gently laid her on the sofa. He sneaked a glimpse at Kelly, catching an expression of bewilderment and horror. He raised a finger to his lips, then beckoned her over.

He shook Penelope gently, but her head flopped to the side.

"I'll get some water," Kelly whispered.

Brady's hand reached out, caught her before she could get up. He shook his head, leaning close to whisper in her ear.

"Let's wait." He bent over the supine woman. "Penelope, listen. You were upset the other day for some reason. I wondered what it was. I went into your study and I saw a picture there, a picture of you. There's somebody else in the picture with you, Pen. He looked familiar but I couldn't place him. Then I talked to Ernie Hughes about the murder of Alice Ann Potter. He says there was a cover-up, that Cory Wilde was framed. But you knew that all along, didn't you?"

"No." She pressed her face into the cushion.

"I talked to some other folks. They told me who the boy in the picture was. His name was Jason, wasn't it?"

"Oh, God," Penelope sobbed. "Yes, Jason."

"Jason had a reputation for trouble. He'd been in scrapes before, and the whole town knew it, but nobody had ever done anything to him."

"Yes. Or that's what they said. Please, leave me alone. *Please* . . ."

"I can't leave you alone. Cory Wilde served almost thirty years for a crime he didn't commit. You knew the truth and didn't tell."

"No!" She turned around then, her tear-stained face twisted with pain. "I never knew. I just *suspected*. But you can't accuse a person just on suspicion. You can't do anything without proof."

"But you knew Jason better than most people. You were his girlfriend, at least for a while."

"Every girl had a chance with Jason," she said bitterly. "I was never that popular. When he made a play for me, what was I going to do? He was handsome and exciting. That was so important then. You always had the feeling there was danger and mystery associated with him. I knew he went out with other girls, even while he was telling me how much he cared for me, but it didn't matter. I had my chance, and he was looking at me, and I could say I was popular. Oh, God . . ."

Brady waited.

"He was the kind that attracted some girls," she said finally, as if seeing him again. "Romantic, headstrong. And spoiled rotten."

She closed her eyes and dug her nails at them before Brady could catch her hands and draw them back down.

"What happened, Pen? What happened to break the two of you up?"

She stared dully ahead of her, her head moving mechanically from side to side. Tears streamed down her cheeks and she began shaking again.

"Pen, I won't buy any more hogwash about the spirits. You can't get out of it that easily. Now try to remember. It's 1959. Early summer. You've just graduated. You and Jason went to the senior prom. What else happened?"

Penelope raised her face to the ceiling and her body went stiff. Her lips twitched and when she spoke again, it was in a monotone.

"It was a week after graduation. A Saturday night. We drove over to the Chance for a bottle. He had a Corvette. The radio was on. They were playing the *Sea of Love*. I remember

that. Afterward, I kept repeating it over and over in my mind."
She gulped. "He started drinking. He wanted me to have some. I
didn't want any but he insisted. I took some but just a little. It
burned my throat. He took me to the end of the road. The El
road, to a logging trail. People went there to park. It wasn't the
first time, but I'd never let him . . . We'd never . . ." Her voice
trailed off. She kept her eyes on the ceiling, as if seeing it all
played out again. "But that night he wanted . . . He kept putting
his hands on me. He tried to go further than I'd let him before.
He was like somebody I didn't know, a stranger. . . . I pulled
away from him and opened the door but he pulled me back in. I
slapped his face and fought him and finally I made him promise
to take me home."

Brady waited. When she started speaking again, her voice
was a near whisper.

"I went in and didn't tell anybody what had happened. He
called me on Monday, said he wanted to apologize. At first, I
didn't want to talk to him, but after a while, I started to think
maybe he'd just lost control. He promised it wouldn't happen
again. I missed him. Other girls had told me their boyfriends had
acted that way. Some even laughed at me because I was the way I
was, wouldn't go all the way. I agreed to go out with him that
night." Brady leaned forward, trying to catch her words. "He
picked me up at seven-thirty. He was a perfect gentleman. He
said he was sorry, asked what it was I wanted to do, if there was
a movie I wanted to see. He bought me a malt at the shop. He
was changed, almost *too* changed. There was something about
him that made me uncomfortable, almost as if he was mocking
what had happened." Brady waited, afraid to ask a question,
afraid that any noise or movement would break the spell. Penelope went on: "Afterward, he took me for a drive west out
Highway Eighty-four. He pulled off into the woods and I saw it
had all been a game with him. When he turned to me, he was the
person he'd been that Saturday night, his face cruel, his eyes . . .
Oh, God, his *eyes*." She sucked in a lungful of air. Her chest
heaved and then she started talking again. "But he didn't reach
for me. He stayed on his side, behind the wheel, and in a way,
that made it even worse. All I had to do was look at him to know

150

that there was something . . . something terrible he was planning. He was . . . He was . . . *Oh, God!*"

The sudden cry caught them by surprise. Penelope shot backward suddenly, arm guarding her face, and Brady reached out to keep her from tumbling sideways.

"What is it, Pen? Tell us!"

"He said that whatever had happened, I was responsible. That when I refused him, I was responsible for what I drove him to. I didn't know what he was talking about, but he just smiled and said I'd have to live with it. Then he said I was lucky. That I was still alive."

She shivered. "That was when I knew. I knew he was talking about Alice Ann, and I knew she had to be dead. He took me home then, but before he let me out, he just smiled at me, that cruel smile of his, and said, 'If you say anything to anybody about this, I'll call you a liar. Then I'll kill you.'"

"So you didn't say anything," Brady said.

"No. Who would have believed me? What could I say? He hadn't admitted anything. It was just a feeling. . . . After that night, I never saw him again. I told myself he'd just been talking, putting on a show, that Alice Ann would turn up and say she'd been visiting relatives, or something. A few days later, though, they found her body. I can't tell you the horrible feeling that came over me then. And yet, I was still able to tell myself that he hadn't really confessed to anything and that, after all, they found her outside of town, and they had the real killer in jail. I kept telling myself it was just his way of being dramatic. And yet I guess that deep down I knew . . ."

She fixed Brady with a quizzical look. "Odd. It was right after that when I first started communicating with the spirits."

Kelly patted her shoulder and Penelope gave her a wan smile.

"He went off to the army," Penelope said then in a faraway voice. "His parents forced him to enlist. But it didn't do any good. He was killed during training. Nothing was ever said, but the story was that he stole a car and left camp. He was killed in a police chase, they said. And after that, it was easy to pretend none of it was real."

"But it was," Brady said. "Or you wouldn't have made yourself go out to Cory's old house the other day."

"It was the vibrations of the place," she said. "I was hoping I'd feel something that would convince me he was guilty, that I hadn't let him . . ."

Brady sighed. "It's a long time to carry it all, Pen. Maybe it's time to let it go."

"Don't you see?" she begged. "Nobody would have believed me. He was from a good family. They protected him. His father—"

"His father," said Brady. "You mean Judge Honeycutt."

20

BRADY slipped away to Pen's office, leaving Kelly to sit with the older woman. He dialed the sheriff's office and asked for Matt Garitty. After a brief argument with the deputy on duty, he was put through.

"Matt, listen, this is Pete Brady. There's something I have to tell you."

"There's something Ernie Hughes was telling us, too," Garitty said in an undertone. "Is it that important?"

"At least," Brady said. "I want you to send some of your men to the hospital. Make sure Judge Honeycutt doesn't leave. Then call the state police and have Cory Wilde taken out of the city jail if they have to shoot their way in. Meanwhile, I'll do some calling on my own."

There was a brief silence, then Brady heard the sheriff's assent. "Okay, I know you well enough to figure you have a good reason for this. Mind telling me what it is?"

"Honeycutt orchestrated the whole business," Brady told him. "He did it to save his son, Jason."

"Jason? You mean the boy that was killed?"

"That's right. Jason is the murderer. Jason killed Alice Ann Potter. Honeycutt rigged a frame to keep Jason out of jail. Matt, Cory Wilde really *is* innocent."

Garitty whistled. "Jesus. Look, what's your source on this?"

"I have a witness. I'll tell you more about it later."

Brady depressed the telephone button, then consulted a slip of paper. He dialed and heard a voice he recognized as that of the maid who had admitted them that morning.

"This is Peter Brady. I have to talk with General St. Germain. It's urgent."

"Just a minute, please." Brady waited, hearing soft music in the background and the clink of glasses. Someone laughed and then something, presumably a closing door, shut off the noise. After a seeming eternity, the maid returned.

"General St. Germain cannot come to the phone. If you will leave your name and telephone number, he'll call you when he have a chance."

"This is life and death, damn it. Tell him it's Brady, Pete Brady. I visited him this morning. Tell him it's about his father-in-law. Tell him I need his help."

"I'm sorry," the maid said coldly. "I'm telling you what he tell me to say."

"Oh, hell," Brady muttered, and slammed down the telephone.

He hurried back into the living room and took Kelly aside, explaining what had happened.

"You have to go try to do something, then," Kelly declared. "I'll stay here with Pen. She needs somebody."

Brady nodded, acknowledging the logic of her suggestion. He touched her lips with his own. "I'll be back as soon as I can."

The downtown section was normal for a Saturday night, with the usual stream of cars and pickups coming and going at the Dairy Queen and McDonald's. The A&P parking lot was full and the new video store seemed to be doing a good business. Brady jumped the red light in front of the courthouse, drew an angry honk from a car obediently stopped on the other side, and sped

153

past. He turned right at the next corner and saw the lights of the hospital three blocks away. He stopped in the NO PARKING zone in front of the main entrance and dashed through the glass doors, into the lobby, where he collided with an angry Matt Garitty.

"We didn't have any reason to hold him," Ned Triplett was protesting as a distraught-looking nurse and receptionist looked on. "I'm not a damn jailer, Garitty, and you're talking about the judge."

"What happened?" Brady demanded, knowing the question was superfluous.

Triplett turned on him, eyes flashing: "Mister, you better get out of here while the getting's good. This ain't no concern of yours. Your newspaper's already done enough harm and when this is over—"

"When this is over," promised Garitty, his face set, "I'll have your badge. You're in this up to your eyeballs, Triplett, and if you're smart, you'll cut out the bluff and start pulling instead of pushing."

"We'll see about that!" the chief muttered, and then turned on his heel, followed by two ashen-faced patrolmen.

The sheriff sighed and shook his head. "Incompetent bastard," he muttered under his breath. He took Brady by the elbow, guiding him away from the onlookers. "The judge checked himself out an hour ago. Nobody knows where he is. Triplett didn't think to look for him until I came and raised hell, so he could be anywhere. I'm going to try his house, and then a camp he has on the lake. You want to come?"

"No," Brady said. "I have one or two other ideas I want to try first." He caught Garitty's arm. "What about Cory Wilde? Is there any news?"

"He's all right so far," Garitty said. "But Triplett's in a stew now. There's no telling how deep he is in all this and what he may do to get out of it. The man's a weasel."

"What about the state police?"

"I called before I left the office, but they need authorization from their commander before they get involved in a local dispute that could have political fallout. And the commander, needless to say, isn't going to do diddly until he gets an okay from the governor. I tried our state representative, to get him to call the capital, but the useless bastard's at Grand Isle."

"What about the mayor?" Brady demanded. "He could suspend Triplett."

"Could but won't. He'd rather let Triplett take the heat. Politics as usual."

"Well, for God's sake," Brady cried. "There must be somebody. The Distrist Attorney—"

". . . says he'll reopen the case, but that doesn't do anything for Cory."

"Great," Brady," said. "But your men—"

". . . at the city jail right now," Garitty said. "But that's all they can do without me. I'd rather have the judge in tow. Then, if it comes down to it, well . . ."

"I hope it doesn't," Brady said.

"Me, too," Garitty agreed. "I'll be on questionable enough legal ground without one of Triplett's yo-yos starting a war."

Three minutes later, Brady got out of his car in front of the courthouse. The square was quiet, except for a few passing cars. As he raced up the steps toward the door, a deputy stepped out of the shadows.

"Oh, Mr. Brady . . ."

"Has Judge Honeycutt come through here?" the editor asked.

"No, sir. We got a message from the sheriff to stop him. There's a man at the other door, too."

"Is anything happening at the city jail?"

The deputy looked down the street, where a corner lamp lit the old brick building in the next block that was the city police station and jail. "Nothing so far," he said. "We have a car down there keeping an eye on things."

As they watched, something moved in the shadows between the old structure and the street.

"The chief's got his own men down there, too," the deputy said. "Between you and me, Mr. Brady, I'm as glad I'm up here."

155

A sharp crack shattered the night.

The two men stared at each other, perplexed.

"Was that what it sounded like?" Brady asked, wheeling around to scan the shadows.

"Sure sounded like it," the deputy agreed. "Like maybe a twenty-two."

Brady strained to see whether anything was happening up the street, at the jail, but nothing had changed. He looked over at the dark row of buildings across from him, facing the courthouse square.

"Maybe it was a backfire or something," the deputy said, "but I'll call it in."

"Hold up," Brady said. "You people are spread pretty thin. Let me check it first."

The officer nodded reluctantly. "Well, I guess. But if you see anything . . ."

"I'll let you know," Brady promised, and he walked across the dark street to the law offices. The front door was locked but as he squinted through the window, he thought he detected a faint glow of light from the rear.

He went down the sidewalk to the end of the row and then around to the alley. It was dark and he bumped into a garbage can, sending the lid crashing onto the ground with a clatter. He thought of the flashlight in his car, across the street, then abandoned the idea. His eyes were adjusting to the light now and he could make out the square shape of a dumpster ahead of him. He stepped around it, feeling his way along the cold wall until he touched the door. He reached down, found the brass handle, and heard keys jingle. Someone had gone in, leaving them in the door. Someone forgetful, or else agitated. He pulled and the door opened.

Brady stepped from the alley into Judge Honeycutt's inner office. The table lamp was on, casting soft light over the rich furnishings, and Brady was aware of the deer head on the wall, looking down with curious eyes. There was a faint pungent smell in the air and it took a moment for Brady to place it. Gunpowder.

He moved around the big desk and stopped.

The judge was seated in his big chair, his eyes fixed on his visitor. At first, Brady thought he was in shock, and then he real-

156

ized the judge was beyond that. A small black hole blemished the old man's right temple, like a defect on a photograph, and for an instant Brady fought the urge to reach up and wipe it away.

Of course, it would not wipe away, because it had been made by a bullet. The judge was quite dead.

Brady touched the old man's neck, to confirm the impression. The flesh was warm and a tiny thread of blood trickled down from the wound, losing itself in the dark pattern of the dead man's shirt. Honeycutt's right arm hung limply, pointing at the rug, and Brady let his gaze drop. The pistol was a Smith & Wesson .22 revolver, better suited for targets but effective enough at close range. A side drawer of the desk was cracked slightly, and Brady opened it with one finger, bringing it back all the way.

A box of cartridges lay among the papers and pens, as if to indicate a man who was prepared for any contingency, and to one side was a leather holster, safety strap unfastened.

Brady closed the drawer and reappraised the body. For the first time, he noticed the bandage across the judge's head, and the dark black mark under one eye. On the floor beside the desk was a walking cane he had never seen before, all indicating that the judge had only made it here with difficulty.

The editor picked up the walking stick, using a handkerchief to ensure that his prints would not be found on it. It was commonplace enough and told him nothing, so he put it back down. Then he lifted the pistol by the rubber handle, knowing it would not take prints. There was a black smudge on the carpet, under the pistol, and Brady touched it with a finger. His finger came away with a dark smear and he considered it for a moment before wiping it off onto his handkerchief. Definitely not oil. Next he gave his attention to the weapon itself. It had been cleaned recently and a thin film of oil still glistened on the barrel.

Brady replaced the pistol where it had fallen and straightened up. Now he turned to the jurist's desk. He found what he was looking for immediately: two sheets torn from a yellow legal pad and covered with a shaky scrawl.

He took the pages over to the lamp and read:

TO WHOM IT MAY CONCERN:

I, Arden J. Honeycutt, being of sound mind, do hereby make this confession voluntarily and of my own free will, fully cognizant of the consequences.

After the initial statement, the handwriting deteriorated, as if in unconscious resistance to the facts being admitted:

Twenty-nine years ago, in 1959, I conspired with others to obstruct justice in the case of the murder of Alice Ann Potter. I did so because my son, Jason, now deceased, admitted to me the facts in the case when on the morning after the murder I confronted him with incriminating evidence I found in his room. I destroyed this evidence, which consisted of some of the decedent girl's effects, and acted to provide an alibi for my son, who was my only child. I know now that I was wrong and I am prepared to accept the consequences, although no consequences could be worse than what has already happened.

I was District Attorney at the time in question and arranged with certain other people to provide a suspect in the case. This suspect was Cory Wilde. I do not intend to name the others in this conspiracy, and most, in any case, are now dead.

I also made payments to a person on the jury to ensure that the verdict would be second-degree murder and that Cory Wilde would not be sentenced to death.

Brady turned to the second page.

Several months after Cory Wilde's conviction, my son was killed while serving in the armed forces. I thought briefly of admitting the truth of the matter then but realized that to do so would be an admission on my own part of the crimes to which I am now confessing, and would mean my own imprisonment. I therefore kept silent. I did, however, send anonymous sums of money to the family that was caring for

158

Wilde's infant daughter, explaining in my letter that I was a distant relative who wished to remain anonymous. To my knowledge, no one has ever found out about these contributions.

When the child married, I made campaign contributions to her husband in his strivings for various political offices.

I regret the crimes I have committed, and wish to express my apologies to Cory Wilde, who has no particular reason to forgive me. I can only ask any parent who reads this to consider in his or her own heart what he or she would have done in similar circumstances.

The confession ended at the bottom of the page, as if the old man had tired of writing and surrendered to the urge for peace. Brady replaced the papers on the table and walked back over to the door. He stopped once, looking back at the deceptively peaceful scene, and then stepped into the alley.

He thought for a moment, then turned the key in the lock and pocketed the key ring.

He went back down the alley to the street and then up to the corner. Things were still quiet and the bored deputy still leaned against the side of the courthouse.

Brady walked over to where he stood, reaching into his pocket for the keys.

"Find anything?" the deputy asked.

Before Brady could answer, a siren blasted down the street, by the jail, and as the two men stared, they saw a wave of bodies emptying from pickups and cars and flooding into the street.

"Better radio the sheriff," Brady ordered. "Tell him we've got big trouble."

21

BY the time Brady reached the jail, twenty or thirty men were milling around in the street and on the lawn. The blue-clad police guards had shrunk back, two of them now protecting the entrance. Their faces were nervous but Brady was glad to see that they possessed enough discipline to stand their ground.

Suddenly, a rock flew through the air and bounced off the brick wall, over one of the guard's heads.

"We want the murderer," somebody yelled.

Another rock crashed through the front window and one of the policemen unupholstered his gun. The front door opened and Chief Triplett appeared, thumbs hooked in his heavy Sam Browne belt.

"You people are making a hell of a racket," he said.

"Ned, get outta the way," somebody from the back of the mob shouted. "This time we mean to have him. Ain't nothing you can do to change that."

"Why would I want to change that?" Triplett managed a chuckle and Brady felt a coldness creep through him. He shoved his way through the mass until he was beside the chief. Where was Matt, damn it? He had to play for time until Matt came!

"Listen!" Brady cried. "This is all wrong. You're after the wrong man."

A chorus of protests answered him. He raised his hands for silence.

160

"I'm telling you, Cory Wilde is innocent. I *know* who killed Alice Ann Potter!"

Another cacophony of howls, but this time less strident. He looked over the crowd, seeking a face, but the face was not there. He fought the urge to turn around. The face *had* to be out there; it made no sense otherwise.

"Alice Ann was killed by somebody else. Somebody important people in this town covered for. Somebody everybody here knows, or knew."

"Who was it?" somebody screamed. "Jack the Ripper?"

A couple of laughs greeted the joke, but Brady saw a man put his hand on the jokester's arm.

"Let him talk. Tell us who we oughtta go after then, if it ain't Cory Wilde."

Brady took a step toward them. "I'll tell you who killed Alice Ann Potter, but you can't go after him because he's beyond reach of the law or anybody else. He's been dead for almost as long as Alice Ann."

The mob growled in disappointment.

"His name was Jason," Brady told them. "Jason Honeycutt. He was the judge's son."

The mob was suddenly still and Brady knew he had them, but there was still an uneasy feeling in the pit of his belly. The *face*. He still could not find the face.

"The judge and some other people covered up for Jason," Brady explained. "Cory Wilde never had anything at all to do with the killing."

"Prove it," somebody else cried out. "How can you prove it?"

"The judge wrote it all down," Brady said. "A confession."

Men looked at one another in disbelief and some in the front rank shuffled uncertainly.

Then, suddenly, Ned Triplett spoke. "That's poppycock," he exclaimed. "This man is trying to trick you." He came forward a few paces and spat onto the ground. "If what he says is true, then who's been killing the rest of these people? Somebody that's been dead for almost thirty years?"

"No," Brady said. "It's someone else. Somebody with another motive." The *face,* damn it? Where was the *face?*

161

"Who?" a man demanded. "You aren't going to tell us the judge did it? I never thought he was all that smart, but he was smart enough not to put a bomb in his own car."

"It wasn't the judge," Brady said. "It was—"

"It wasn't nobody," Triplett broke in. "Least, nobody this man would claim. We got the right man, don't you ever doubt it. Cory Wilde did it, or had it done, there ain't no doubt at all."

"Then, by God, that's good enough for me," the man shouted. "Get out the way, Ned."

Triplett smiled and then, with a little shrug, stepped aside. "Sure."

"No!" Brady tried to block the door but a wall of bodies knocked him sideways. From the corner of his vision, he saw two of Matt Garitty's deputies racing forward, guns drawn, but the leaders of the mob had already shoved through the doorway of the building and he could hear their feet on the stairs inside.

A knee struck his head and lightning flashed through his vision. He clawed upward, catching a passing body, and got an elbow in the jaw in response. For a fleeting instant, through a gap in the bodies, he saw Ned Triplett's smiling face as the men rushed past him.

Another siren wailed then and a groggy Brady heaved himself to his feet. Two stunned deputies were dusting themselves off and searching for their pistols. Brakes squealed and a grateful Brady saw Matt Garitty's white car slam to a halt in the center of the street, its dashboard light strobing the darkness with red fingers.

Brady staggered toward his friend even as the sheep-faced deputies wavered on the lawn, unsure whether to approach or retreat.

"What's going on?" demanded the steel-faced sheriff.

"They're upstairs," Brady cried. "Matt, for God's sake, you have to do something."

"Too late," taunted a relaxed Triplett from beside the front door. "Too late for the hero to step in and save the day this time."

Garitty strode over to the chief, his eyes flashing sparks.

"By God, Triplett . . ."

"You going to threaten me twice in one night? Back off, Garitty. You're on *my* turf now." He checked his watch again.

"Besides, you think you're the only one with any sense? Maybe even a hick police chief has a trick or two up his sleeve."

"What are you talking about?" Garitty demanded, grabbing the front of Triplett's shirt with one hamlike fist.

Triplett chuckled nervously and shrugged away the other man's grasp. He looked down at his watch. "They been up there about a minute now. That oughtta just about do it."

As if in answer, the glass above his head shattered as someone broke it out from inside and a scream of anger echoed out over the street.

"Better stand aside," Triplett sneered. "They gonna be some hot."

"Damn it, Ned, what the hell are you pulling?" Garitty demanded.

"Wait a minute, Matt." Suddenly, Brady understood; comprehended the meaning of the chief's smile, his strange willingness to let the mob into his jail. "Triplett, are you saying that Cory Wilde . . ."

The chief grinned. "He's smarter than you are, Garitty." He turned to Brady. "Well, Mr. Big City Editor, so happens you're absolutely right. Cory Wilde—"

A pandemonium of bodies thundered from the front doorway then and angry faces surrounded the trio.

"God damn you, Ned!" swore one of the rioters. "The jail's empty. Cory Wilde is gone."

"'Course he's gone," the policeman said. "You think I was gonna let him get snatched outta my own jail, even if he was guilty?"

Brady and the sheriff exchanged looks.

"Where is he, then?" demanded Garitty.

Triplett folded his arms. "He's with my men. They took him out the back while all these good citizens were making a fuss outside. By now, he oughtta be ten miles away." He squinted over at Brady. "Now, I don't expect an apology from you people, but what I want to know is if you're gonna have the guts to publish this in—"

"Chief . . ." One of the policemen appeared at the door, his face haggard. "Chief, it's—"

"Damn it, Lee," snapped Triplett. "Can't you see I'm busy?"

"Chief, it just came over the radio. The car with Cory Wilde in it: They stopped it five miles out of town, on Eighty-four west, before they could even get to the parish line; roughed up Jake and Al, and took Wilde away."

The editor and the sheriff uttered expletives in unison. Ned Triplett wheeled on the radio operator, face livid.

"You damn idiot! How could that happen?"

"Come on," Brady said, heading for the sheriff's car.

Now it all made terrible sense and Brady understood why the face had been missing.

"I always knew Ned Triplett was an idiot," Garitty muttered as they roared west over the dark highway, headlights stabbing the night. "But I'm a bigger idiot for not putting more men there to make sure something like this didn't happen."

"It wasn't your fault," Brady told him, straining his eyes into the darkness as the night streamed past.

"Well, I could've moved faster. From what you tell me about the judge, I have to wonder how much Ned was getting to try to keep Cory in the center of things."

"I don't know," Brady said. "My guess is he just did what the judge told him without knowing why. He probably thought he was being pretty clever to spirit Cory out like this."

"Yeah, well, somebody was cleverer. Damn it, they've probably already lynched Cory by now." Garitty pounded the wheel with a fist. "All they had to do was take him off in the woods somewhere. We might not find him for weeks."

A pair of headlights flashed toward them over a hill and the other car shot past. The editor looked away, at the side of the road. What was the image that kept nagging his mind? A time, a few days before, the mention of a place.

All at once, the memory came clear and Brady put his hand on the sheriff's arm.

"Matt, stop and turn around."

"What?"

"It's just a hunch. But I think I may know where they took him."

"You mean back toward *town?*"

"Yes. Look, humor me." He shrugged. "Anyway, do you have a better idea?"

Garitty nodded grimly and wheeled the Oldsmobile around in a U-turn.

"And I think I'd turn off the flasher," Brady suggested.

The sheriff obeyed. "Any idea where we're going?"

"After that car that just went by," Brady said. "But get ready for a left turn."

"A left turn? There's nothing out here except—"

"The cemetery," Brady said.

Two minutes later, they saw the taillights ahead brighten and a pale stream of light lanced off to the left. The car was turning.

"By God, you're right," Garitty said, shaking his head. "Maybe I'd better get some help."

"No," Brady said. "Too many uniforms and spotlights make people like these nervous. I'd rather we tried talk first."

"Your call," the sheriff said, slowing as a pair of city police cars screamed past, headed in the opposite direction. Garitty waited until they were out of sight and then cut his headlights.

He turned left and slid through the gates of the cemetery. Lights flashed atop the hill and as their tires crackled on the gravel, Brady motioned for his friend to cut the engine and stop.

The sheriff turned down his radio and then carefully opened his door. The two men shut the doors softly and then moved together up the incline, toward the lights, using the gravestones for cover.

Ahead of them, on the other side of the cemetery and out of sight, they heard voices and there was a shatter of glass, followed by an oath.

Garitty pointed to a large obelisk on the crest of the hill and Brady nodded, running forward, hunched over. He reached the white stone and peered around the edge.

Down slope, perhaps a hundred yards away, Brady could make out dim forms huddled around a giant oak, their faces glowing like those of ghosts in the eerie dance of flashlights.

Now and again, a word drifted out over the field of ghostly

165

white stones but it was nothing of which Brady could make sense. He felt the sheriff's hand on his sleeve.

"Stay here," Garitty whispered. "We might be able to take 'em, but I'd rather call for help first."

Brady nodded and heard his friend slip away. He turned his attention back to the little scene below. One of the men cursed, shoved another one, and then he heard the unmistakable sound of a fist hitting flesh.

Damn it, he couldn't just stay here and watch it happen.

He crept around the obelisk, took a deep breath, and then ran forward, hunched over as much as he could, counting on the men below to be too absorbed in what they were doing to notice. He dodged tombstones as he ran, stopping halfway down the hill to crouch for breath behind a thick family slab.

Now he could see more clearly and what he saw sent shivers into his bones.

Three men were gathered in the light of a camper's lantern, sharing a bottle, while another man lay stretched before them on the ground. As their faces passed into and out of the light, he remembered names: Pike, who sold used cars from a lot on the edge of town; Saucier, who farmed a few acres near Yankee Bend; and a man named Ventress, who didn't seem to do much of anything at all.

As for the man on the ground, he did not have to strain to know who it was. It was Cory Wilde.

"Bastard," said the car salesman, rubbing his hand. "I think I busted my knuckles on his lying mouth."

Ventress laughed, but Saucier, the farmer, fidgeted. "Come on, boys, let's do it and get outta here."

Pike looked down at Cory. "You hear that? Man says he wants to get on with it. You in any hurry?"

His laughter blended with Ventress's giggle. Cory got up shakily.

"You haven't got the guts," Cory said.

"What?" The car salesman's face went angry and he grabbed the old man by the shirt, but Saucier pulled him away. "Come on, Pike, let's just do what we came for."

The man called Pike reached up and caught something over his head and brought it down into the light.

166

It was a noose.

Horrified, Brady watched as he looped it around Cory's neck. "Is this what you want?" he asked, pulling it tight. "You been begging for this all night."

Brady glanced back over his shoulder, but there was no sign of the sheriff. He measured the distance to the men below him and considered his alternatives. Something still bothered him: The face was still missing, and yet, by all rights, it ought to be here. Whatever he did would be off balance until he could account for that fact.

But he could not let them hang Cory Wilde.

Then he saw it, a branch, lying twenty feet away on the ground. It wasn't much, but it was something. Something he could use as a weapon, to distract them, perhaps even scatter them if he rushed in yelling. It might give Matt time to get here.

He crawled forward, aware of his exposed position. However, the men below were not watching. Instead, they were busy with the old man in the noose.

"This is something should've been done twenty-nine years ago," Pike snarled.

"Then do it," Cory said, and spat in his face.

Pike cried out in rage and Brady rose from his knees, grabbed the branch, and leapt toward them.

The surprise was total and he almost made it.

At the last second, however, his foot caught on a flower vase and, deprived of balance, he sprawled forward, the branch flying from his hands.

He landed at the edge of the lamplight and then, propelled by gravity, rolled forward into the middle of the gathering.

The three members of the mob jumped back as if someone had thrown in a nest of wasps, and then a cruel laugh sounded from the blackness behind the tree.

A fourth man came out of the darkness, zipping up his pants, and stared down at Brady, shaking his head.

"You want a story that bad, Mr. Big City Reporter? Well, you can have it."

Brady's stomach went weak. He had been right all along, though it was too late to feel satisfaction. The missing face was here after all.

It belonged to Bo Potter.

167

22

"YOU know, you really should've let it be," Bo Potter said. "This ain't no concern of yours. This is private."

"Then why do you need three assistants?" Brady asked, rising to his feet. "Or are they just members of the athletic club?"

"You talk a lot, mister," Potter said, pushing Brady back down with a boot. "But if you want to talk, I'll talk. I'll talk about the little girl that lies over there." He pointed and Brady saw a single slab just to the right of the tree. "That's my sister, the girl this piece of trash murdered. He killed her and they let him out after they promised he'd stay in Angola for the rest of his life. What kind of justice is that? I'll tell you: It's no justice at all. But we're going to make our own justice. We're going to do what they were afraid to do back then. You can write it up in your newspaper as a lynching. I don't give a damn. But it isn't a lynching, it's an execution. It's justice."

"It's not justice," Brady told him, getting to his feet and spitting out dirt. "Cory Wilde is an innocent man."

It was Cory who spoke then: "Look at 'em. You'd think somebody had poured vinegar down their throats. What's wrong with you, Mr. Newspaper Editor? They don't want to hear that. They don't want to hear the truth."

"Truth?" Potter roared and lunged at Cory, but Brady jumped between them, slamming back against Cory, who stumbled, doing a macabre dance to keep his balance with the noose around his neck.

"Listen to me!" Brady cried, grabbing the larger man's arms. "All of you listen! Cory never killed anybody. I have proof. It was all a frame-up, a conspiracy by Judge Honeycutt. Cory was framed to protect the judge's son."

Potter slammed Brady aside with an elbow. "Enough of this crap. Let's get it done," he grunted.

"Wait a minute, Bo." Pike put a hand on the coach's shoulder. "What if what he's saying is true?"

"If it's true, you'll have lynched an innocent man," Brady said.

A wheezing chuckle hacksawed over the clearing and all eyes turned to the man in the noose. "Look at 'em. Like a pack of wild animals. They don't know which way to pull."

Potter screamed a curse and shook free of his friend, ploughing toward the prisoner, but Brady caught his knees and brought him down. The two men rolled in the clearing, the eerie laughter their chorus, and then Potter pinned the editor, his knees on Brady's arms. He pulled back a huge fist, but one of the other men caught him.

"Hold up, Bo, we ain't here to kill *everybody*. I want to hear what this feller has to say. I mean, if Cory ain't guilty . . ."

"Damn it," Potter cried, "can't you see what he's doing? He's got no proof, no proof at all."

"I've got proof," Brady said from the ground. "It's all in a confession Judge Honeycutt wrote before he died." He watched the news of the judge's death hit the others. Even Bo Potter seemed taken aback, getting up from Brady's chest.

"The judge is dead?"

"That's right, with a twenty-two bullet in his brain," Brady told them. "But not before he wrote out everything."

The three men exchanged nervous glances. "And you mean Cory. . . ?" asked the one called Saucier.

Bo Potter kicked the ground. "Aw, hell, can't you see what's happening? He's lying his head off. It's a trick. If nobody else'll take care of this bastard, I'll do it myself."

He moved toward Cory again and there was nothing for Brady to do but use his hole card.

"Just like you did the others?" he asked.

Potter stopped, his face frozen. "What did you say?"

"I said I don't think these men want to be blamed for all your murders."

"What's he talking about, Bo?" demanded Pike.

"Hell, he's just trying to throw everybody off," Potter snapped.

"Am I?" Brady asked, getting back to his feet and fighting down the pain from his bruised ribs. "Who killed Boy Jenks, then? It wasn't an accident. It was an explosive device, just like the bomb in the judge's car. Did you tell them what kind of work you did in the army, Bo? If you didn't, I will." He turned to the others. "He was with demolitions. Rigging a bomb was something he could do with his eyes closed."

The man called Saucier licked his lips and grabbed Ventress's arm. "That's right. He *was* with demolitions. I heard him say it."

"That's crazy," Ventress said. "Why would he be after all those people unless he knew Cory didn't do it? And if he knew Cory didn't do it, then why would he want to get even with him now?"

"Because," Brady said, wishing Garitty would hurry, "he found out somewhere along the line that Cory wasn't guilty. Maybe from Jenks. He realized Jenks and the judge and some others were all part of a gigantic cover-up. So they had to die. But the only way to do it without being caught himself was to blame it on Cory Wilde. If they died, people would figure Cory did it. Using the explosive devices was smart, Bo, I have to give that to you. You knew it would destroy any alibi Cory had . . . a time bomb can be set to go off whenever you want." Before Bo could protest, Brady turned back to the other men: "But don't you see? He couldn't let Cory live after that. There was always a chance Cory could explain his way out, come up with an airtight alibi. So Cory had to be killed. And what easier way than to have some poor slobs do it for him."

Bo swore and took a step toward the newsman, but Pike jumped in front of him. "Shut up, Bo. I want to hear what all he has to say." He faced Brady, swaying slightly. "What's that about having people do it for him?"

"You heard me right," Brady said, wondering where his friend was. "You men were suckers. He used you, can't you see? Do you really think he had any intention of being blamed for the lynching? The man's all bluster. *Look at him.*"

Potter screamed an oath and surged toward Brady, but the other men caught him, held him back. "What did you do? Bribe one of Triplett's men to let you have Cory? Did you ever think about what that man's going to say when he has to explain how his prisoner got away? Is he really supposed to claim he didn't recognize you, because you were wearing masks? That he didn't recognize the car that forced him off the road? I'll bet a dime to a dollar Bo Potter paid that man extra to forget there were four men involved instead of three. Maybe Bo even helped him by staying in the car or pickup when you got Cory away from him."

Saucier looked up at Bo, frowning. "Hey, that's right, Bo. You stayed—"

"Shut up, damn it," Potter cried. "Can't you idiots see what he's doing? It's lies, everything he's saying is lies."

"Is it? Is that what you men really want to do? Take the blame for Bo's private grudge? What's it to you, Mr. Ventress? She wasn't a member of your family, was she? How far out on a limb do you want to go for somebody else's revenge?"

"It ain't that," Ventress protested. "It was that she could've been anybody's sister or daughter. And then they turned around, let the killer loose . . ."

"Except that this man isn't the killer. The killer's dead. So what is there to revenge? Bo killed two people for nothing, nothing at all. Now he wants you men to jump into his sinking boat."

"No!" Bo screamed, but the others were holding him now, faces anguished as the impact of Brady's words sank in.

"He said folks would understand," Saucier whined. "Bo said nobody would testify."

"Maybe," Brady allowed. "If Cory was guilty. But an innocent man? There'll be everything from the state police to the FBI in here. Ever hear of a civil-rights investigation?"

"Hell," Ventress snorted, "that's for niggers."

"It's for anybody who deprives someone else of his civil

rights. It's been used in lynching cases where local justice broke down. So even if you men managed to get past local law enforcement, you'd probably be tried out of parish in federal court, where people don't know you and don't care. Of course, it isn't a capital offense. You probably wouldn't draw but about ten years each and with good behavior—"

"Bo!" Ventress yelled, turning on Potter. "You didn't tell us nothing about that. You said you was in tight with Ned. You said Ned would cover, everybody in town would be behind us."

Something moved in the darkness, on the hill above them, and Brady relaxed slightly.

For an endless second, no one moved and Brady thought he had won. Then, once more, Cory Wilde's ragged laugh came mocking over the clearing like a death rattle. With a sudden exertion, Bo Potter flung away the men holding his arms and rushed like an enraged bull at the prisoner in the noose.

The night exploded with the sound of a shot and Bo seemed to stumble. Then Cory's knees buckled as the athlete's massive arms caught him at the waist and his eyes bulged as the rope bit into his neck. A choking sound bubbled from Cory's swollen lips and Brady had to fight the urge to turn away.

23

THE police had gone, taking their battery-powered lights with them, so that the cemetery had lapsed once more into a gentle darkness broken only by the friendly winking of a thousand fireflies. Down in the creek, frogs croaked and from the hilltop came the fiddles of crickets, free once more to play their music.

Matt Garitty stood under the old tree, his expression mercifully hidden by the night. Brady stood behind him, not speaking, all the tiredness and frustration of the last week congealed in his memory of the last few hours. It was a memory he wished could be wiped from his mind: the figure of Ned Triplett, smoking pistol in hand, standing up slowly from his position on the hillside; the cry of outrage and anguish from Matt Garitty, his big fist raised in frustration; and, most of all, the terrible vision of Cory Wilde swinging limply, knees bent, a dead man's arms clutching his legs like a drowning swimmer grabbing for help.

"I could've done something," the sheriff said finally, his voice cracking. "I could have saved him."

Brady sighed. "You didn't know. It wasn't your fault."

"I should've acted as soon as I saw you down there," Garitty swore bitterly. "But you seemed to have everything under control. You had Bo Potter practically confessing; you had the rest of them singing their hearts out about Bo's deal with Ned. I thought I was getting them all served up to me on a platter."

The editor put a friendly hand on the lawman's shoulder. "Damn it, Matt, Ned was a wild card. Nobody could have seen what he was going to do."

Garitty turned a grieving face to Brady. "I'm *paid* to see things like that. It's why I wear a badge. Instead, I thought how nice it would be to have my main opponent out of the way. All I had to do was stay up there a few minutes longer. I wouldn't have to do a thing."

"You're being too hard on yourself," Brady protested. "There are things nobody can figure." A vision of Ozzie floated into his mind then, floating faceup in the swamp, just off the interstate. How many times had Brady tried to second-guess the past, as Garitty was doing now? How many times had he tried to think of a way it might have turned out differently?

"You know," he said gently, "it was really Cory's call, not yours."

The sheriff gave a little shrug and Brady knew it was an opening.

"Cory wanted to die. Hell, he was going to die no matter what. So he wanted to make sure he got his revenge as part of it. Imagine the scandal of lynching an innocent man. I expect he's steamed right now because he's still alive."

"Well, if revenge is what he wanted, he got it," Garitty declared. "He tore this whole town apart."

"Did he?" Brady asked. "Or was he just the trigger for what was already there?"

"Does it matter? Without Cory, it would've stayed buried."

"You don't mean that. You didn't want a cover-up any more than I did."

"No. It's just . . ."

"I know."

Garitty reached up, took something out of his pocket, and looked down at it. A pale gleam from the rising moon leapt back from the metallic surface and Brady knew instinctively what it was in his friend's hand.

"You know, I thought up to now I'd done a pretty good job. Just goes to show." Garitty put the badge and credential case back into his pocket. "At least I wish Cory had given Bo Potter a chance to clear up all the details."

Brady thought for a second and then made up his mind. "Tell you what: You stop feeling sorry for yourself for a little while and I'll see if I can't fill in the holes."

Garitty shrugged again. "What do you want me to do?"

"Do you remember the call I asked you to make to the state police?"

"Sure. I got the package from them the next day. Why?"

"Because I think it's time to look at some photos."

The next morning, Brady lay in bed long after the alarm sounded. From somewhere near the town square floated the sound of church bells, deceptively joyous, and from the kitchen came the clink of dishes as Kelly prepared breakfast. With a mighty effort, Brady struggled upright and sat on the side of the bed, recalling the events of the night before. They were like a bad dream, but unlike a dream, he knew there was no shoving them back into his unconscious. They had happened and must be dealt with.

Kelly appeared, her enticing form concealed by his bathrobe. She set a plate and a glass of orange juice on the bedside table. Brady looked down at a pair of fried eggs, staring up at him from a fried tortilla. "My version of *huevos rancheros,*" she said. "And you'd better be grateful; I had to go all the way down to the A&P

174

for the frozen tortillas, and I had to tell the manager all about the excitement. People must've stayed up on the phones all night."

"Not every day you lose a judge and gain a major scandal," Brady said wearily.

"No," she agreed. "And it's not the kind of headline people are used to seeing in a parish newspaper. I had the feeling it made ye friendly grocer uncomfortable. He wanted to hear all about it, yet he *didn't,* if you know what I mean."

"I know exactly," Brady said.

The telephone rang and he picked it up.

A torrent of abuse greeted his ear and he held the receiver away until the party on the other end had to come up for breath.

"I don't know what you're talking about," he said sternly. "But if you feel that way, don't give me credit in your story."

He slammed the receiver back onto the cradle. "I think I'm about to be expelled from the news fraternity," he reported. "I wonder where your father took those people?"

He ate, and hoped the food would give him a quick infusion of energy, but when he'd finished, he felt as tired as before. He got up and walked over to the bureau and started to rummage for clothes.

"Why don't you stay in bed?" Kelly asked. "It's Sunday, for God's sake. It's all over except the shouting. Don't be such a workaholic, Brady."

He found a pair of slacks and slipped into them, grimacing as bruised muscles protested. "I have to write the story while it's fresh," he said. "And there's some loose ends to tie up. *And* somebody has to check on Penelope, and also see how Cory Wilde is getting along."

"I checked on Cory while I was at the store," Kelly replied smugly. "The nurse said he was doing fine. And I plan to look in on Penelope later. I already told you she was sleeping like a baby when I left her last night."

Brady grunted and slipped into a short-sleeved shirt.

"I guess old habits are just hard to break."

Five minutes later, his face showing the stubble of a day without the razor, he stumbled out the front door, her protests following.

175

"Well, if that's the way it is," she threatened, "I'm coming with you. I'm sure as hell not staying here to do the dishes!"

"Suit yourself," Brady told her, getting into his car.

He did not go directly to his office, however. He made a lazy loop around the square, as if some kind of inhibition was fighting to keep him from his work. As he drove, he noted the deceptively peaceful storefronts that faced the courthouse. He knew too well that one of them advertised law offices, and nothing betrayed the fact that someone had died inside the night before.

Two minutes later he stopped in the parking lot in front of the *Express* office. The little building looked forlorn with its taped window, and he had the first intimation in many months that he was out of place here, should never have left the city.

Then, feeling Kelly beside him, the premonition fled back to its subconscious lair.

He opened the front door, wrinkling his nose at the stale smell of cigarettes and greasy food. He flopped at his desk and hunted up a yellow legal pad. He searched through his drawers, found the trial transcript Garitty had lent him. Kelly was right, of course: It was too soon afterward. His mind was rebelling against delving back into the tangle of conspiracy and murder, but there was no option. The story had to be written, even if people here ran him out of town.

He considered possible headlines:

INNOCENT MAN FREED, JUDGE CONFESSES CONSPIRACY.

Or, POLICE CHIEF SHOOTS COACH, QUITS UNDER FIRE.

Or, LYNCH LAW IN TROY PARISH.

Not the kind of banner to make him beloved of his readers. Matt was right, of course: People really *would* have preferred for Cory to have served his time and left them alone. Justice wasn't the rights of the individual here; it was public order, the rule of tranquility. An editor who shattered misconceptions had no future on a rural weekly.

He sighed and turned to the transcript. He went over the jury list, then replaced the volume in his drawer and sat back in his chair.

Kelly returned from the refrigerator with a Coke in hand.

"Well, where's the lead paragraph? For all your talk, you should've at least gotten sentence one down by now."

176

"I've got a sore throat again," he said. "Too much dust in here. I'm going to the drugstore. I saw Sam was open. Maybe a good opening will come to me on the way."

"What a crock," Kelly snorted. "You just want to go stand outside the judge's door and pose."

"Believe me," Brady said, "that's the last thing I want to do."

Yet there he was, five minutes later, on the sidewalk outside the law office. He peered through the big front window as if it were a diviner's crystal, morosely wondering about a man who had lived with a lie for three decades, and another man who had been the victim of that lie. Then he wondered about the others, the ones who had profited from the lie.

He fought the urge to reach out for the doorknob. Maybe, he thought, if he turned it, the door would be open and he would go in and find the judge reading the newspaper behind his desk.

Maybe, he thought, the moon is green cheese.

He pulled himself away and went down to the pharmacy. A SALE sign was in the window, below another that said OPEN ON SUNDAY AT 8:00 A.M.

He pushed the door and heard the little bell tinkle above his head. The place appeared empty, but then Sam straightened up from behind one of the shelves, where he had been arranging a display.

"Mr. Brady." He stuck out a hand. "I was worried about you. I heard there was some excitement last night."

"That there was, Sam," said the publisher. "Too much." He took a seat in one of the booths opposite the soda fountain. "So when did you decide to start opening Sundays?"

"The fire did it," Sam said. "I can't make a go of this thing. I decided to sell everything for whatever I could get and move to Memphis. I hear the economy there's a little better. I've got a cousin who's promised to go in with me."

"Too bad," Brady said, shaking his head. "Folks around here will miss you. And this place."

Sam nodded. "It's mutual, but you've got to do what you've got to do. Is there something I can help you with, Mr. Brady?"

"My throat," Brady said. "It seems to be getting sore again."

Sam clucked sympathetically. "Well, we'll nip that in the bud." He reached up and brought down a small box of the same kind of tablets he had sold Brady before. "These should help, if it's a postnasal drip."

Brady got up and reached into his pocket for his wallet as Sam put the purchase into a paper bag.

"It was something else, finding out about Bo Potter," Sam commented, taking Brady's five-dollar bill. "I mean, the man always had a temper, but I can't believe he killed two people . . ."

"No," Brady said, slipping his change into his pocket, "neither can I."

"I guess he did, though," Sam said.

Brady leaned back. "No, not really."

Sam frowned, perplexed. "But the word I got was that you're the one who put it all together."

"Well, you'll say a lot of things when somebody's life is in the balance," Brady explained. "I told Bo's friends that Bo had killed those folks because I *had* to. I was playing for time so help could get there. I had to say *something* to turn them against him, or at least make them stop and listen."

"You mean Bo Potter was *innocent,* then?"

"I guess that depends on what you mean by innocent. He wasn't innocent of plotting revenge against the man he thought killed his sister. He wasn't innocent of conniving with Ned Triplett's men to let him get his hands on Cory Wilde. And he surely wasn't innocent of abducting that man and trying to kill him. But the killings of Boyton Jenks and Mrs. Honeycutt? Old Bo was as pure as the driven snow. He didn't kill them any more than he killed Judge Arden Honeycutt."

Sam's face went white. "Judge Honeycutt? But I heard he . . ."

"Committed suicide? Nah. It was planned to make it look that way. But somebody came in behind him. See, the judge was a little rattled. His whole world had just fallen to pieces and he'd left his keys in his back door. Saved the murderer a lot of trouble. All they had to do was grab the judge around the neck, pull his pistol out of the drawer while the judge was struggling, and shoot him once in the right temple. I figure a wrestler's hold would do it."

"But they have tests . . ."

"To show who fired a gun. Well, you know how lab tests

are. I did a lot of police reporting in my years with the *Picayune*. No test, even the atomic-absorption test for gunpowder residue, is a hundred percent. Interesting thing is, I figure whoever killed the judge knew that, too."

Sam turned around, shaking his head in bewilderment.

"But who in the world?"

"Somebody with a pretty good sense for science, Sam. Somebody who could feel comfortable with the innards of a time bomb. Somebody with access to clocks and chemicals, who could make gunpowder from scratch if he had to. Who had a small hardware shelf in his drugstore."

Brady leaned over the counter, his face inches from that of the other man.

"I figure *you*, Sam."

Sam started to shake his head, then looked away. "Mr. Brady, if that's a joke . . ."

"No joke, Sam." Brady looked down at the floor tiles, smudged from Sam's comings and goings. "By the way, if I were you, I'd mop that floor pretty quickly. The ashes from the back room are getting all over everything. I even found some on the judge's rug, under the gun. Careless, Sam. It places you in the judge's office, behind his desk. It means you must have come in through the rear entrance."

"That's ridiculous," Sam said, his face reddening in anger. "Mr. Brady, if this is the big city way to sell newspapers, then I don't want any of it. I'm going to have to ask you to leave."

"Sure," Brady said. "I *do* have a story to write. But I just wanted to get all the details correct. Let's see, you took the third and fourth pages of the judge's confession, right? The ones that named you? I mean, why else would the judge, legal mind that he was, go to the trouble of writing a document full of lawyer's jargon and then leave it hanging at the end of the second page, no signature? No, the judge just didn't do things that way. Let me see if I can reconstruct a scenario: The judge lay in bed in the hospital, thinking about his crime. His wife was dead. His life was collapsing around him. All he saw left to do was make a clean break, throw himself on the mercy of the court . . . and get the man that killed his wife. After all, if he turned state's evidence against the person who'd killed Jenks and Mrs. Honeycutt,

179

he could hope for some kind of leniency. He checked out, walked home, and then went to the office and wrote his confession. Then he called you. I kept asking myself why he'd do that, what reason he could possibly have for warning you, and I realized it had to be revenge. After all these years, he was ruined, thanks to you, and now he was going to see you sweat. What did he say? Something like, 'I've thought it all over and I'm going across the street to the sheriff's office and tell everything.' You probably asked him where he was, begged him for time to think it over, and somewhere in the conversation you realized he thought you were at home; he didn't realize you'd be working at the drugstore, cleaning things up, getting ready to sell out your inventory. I'll bet if I checked, I'd find you had call forwarding, and the judge's call to your house went through to the phone here."

"Lots of people have call forwarding," Sam protested, licking his lips. "Lots of people call me both places about prescriptions. That doesn't prove anything."

"Then," Brady went on, ignoring the other man's protests, "you went out down the alley, knowing you had an extra five minutes to get to him before he went across the street to the sheriff's. He must've mentioned that he was in his law office and not at home. You found the keys in the door, which made things easy. You slipped an arm around his neck and I figure he managed to open the desk drawer just enough to show there was a gun inside. That ended up helping you, not him. When you came in, you were pretty desperate. But by the time you saw his confession on the desk in front of him, you realized things were a lot better than you could have hoped. But not so good that you still don't have to get out of town."

"This is ridiculous!" Sam thundered. "Brady, if you publish a word of that, I'll sue you for ten million dollars!"

"I don't think so," Brady said. "Because then I'd tell them about the blackmail the judge was paying you."

"You're crazy," Sam muttered, but this time Brady realized the other man's hands had started to shake. "I had nothing to do with any of this. I hardly even saw the judge except to talk to him on the street."

"Or to take a payoff." Brady shook his head sadly. "Come on, Sam, it's no use. Your father was a member of Cory Wilde's jury. I just checked it in the transcript. The foreman was bribed by Judge Honeycutt, the district attorney, to argue for a verdict of second-degree murder. Somewhere along the way, he spilled his guts to your father. Whether your father blackmailed the judge, I don't know. But I'll bet you did all right. Until now. But I have to admit, the fire was a pretty clever idea. It made everybody feel sorry for you, including me. And I was the one who gave you the idea in the first place."

Sam started to protest but this time no words came out. Instead, he turned to the shelf behind him, starting to rearrange bottles and boxes.

"It was Penelope Martingale's herbal concoction. You knew I thought I was onto something and you knew that by destroying it, you could increase my suspicion . . . in the wrong direction."

The pharmacist said nothing and for a few seconds the only sound was the noise of his hands moving the items on the shelf.

"Better yet, you could also throw suspicion on the new store here. By chance, Penelope had some stock in it, though I doubt you knew that. All you knew was that you could send me in two directions at once just by lighting a couple of matches, and at the same time, you could take care of your real problem."

"My real problem?" Sam asked, not bothering to turn around.

"The records, Sam. There was something in your records you didn't want to come out. I was blind, I admit it. It was staring right at me; the fire was set to wipe out your files. The herbs were placed on the shelf right beside the file boxes. Beautiful. I have to give you credit there. What was it in your files, Sam? Wait, let me guess: How about records showing how much money you were taking out of the business for your gambling debts?"

"Gambling?" Sam tried to laugh but his smile froze on his lips.

"Do you remember the day I came in here to get the cold medicine? You told me the only time you ever saw the judge excited was at the racetrack? There aren't any racetracks in this parish. You have to go all the way to Acadian Downs. It's what? A hundred fifty miles? Well, that's no sin. But it seemed interest-

181

ing how on a couple of occasions you made comments about gambling, like how it was trying to beat the house at roulette, and—"

"Brady that's ridiculous."

"Sure. But the tip-off was the man I saw in the store that day. He didn't come from around here. You wanted me to think he was a drug salesman. I've worked the city beat. I've seen his kind before. He had a certain look to him, almost a texture. Guys like him hang around the horse parlors in Jefferson Parish . . . but not to bet. That isn't why they're there. What they do is break the legs of people that don't pay. Well, I could've been wrong, of course, so I asked Matt Garritty to get me some pictures from the state police Bureau of Identification. Known bookies and head-breakers for the juice men in New Orleans, Bossier, and the other cities in the state. I looked at them last night. Want to know whose face came up?"

Sam completed the row of medicine bottles, gave the metal shelf a lick with the dust rag, and then straightened. When he turned around, the dust rag had magically vanished, replaced by a small black revolver.

"I can't let you go out of here, saying that kind of thing," he said tonelessly. "It's a small town. Some people would believe it."

"I think I could find twelve that would," Brady told him, slowly raising his hands. "After all, it's true."

"Yes, damn it, it's true," Sam said. "But why couldn't you have left it alone? I liked you, Brady. I really did, and now I have to kill you just like the others. I'm sorry. I really am."

Brady looked down at the tiles and the black marks from Sam's shoes. "I'm sorry, too, Sam. I guess I was hoping you were telling the truth and I was wrong; that all of it would be my imagination and afterward I'd just feel like a fool."

"That would've been nice," Sam agreed. "But you were right and now you have to die."

He thumbed back the hammer and at that moment the telephone buzzed. His eyes darted over to the irritating instrument, and then back to Brady.

"Better answer it, Sam."

"It can wait."

"No, it really can't."

"What are you talking about?"

"Answer it. I'm not going anywhere. If you don't, people might think it's suspicious."

Sam bit his lip and jerked the receiver up with his left hand. "Hello?"

A voice crackled in Sam's ear and the hand with the receiver came down slowly.

"It was when I raised my hands," Brady said. "One hand was the signal to come ahead. Both hands meant be quick about it. The sheriff's been watching us from his office in the courthouse. Never noticed how his window looks out on your front door? You should have. With a pair of binoculars, he could see us all the while we talked."

Sam replaced the receiver, looked down at the gun as if he was not sure what to do with it now. "But . . ."

"Sure. My body probably blocked the view of the gun, if that's what you're thinking. But you see, I already got what I needed on tape." He lifted a small recorder from his pocket as the bell tinkled and Garitty pushed through the doorway, hand under his coat.

The druggist sighed and placed the pistol on the counter in front of him. "Aw, hell," he said with disgust. "You don't leave a fellow much."

24

BRADY wandered out of the house into his backyard. Kelly and Emmett watched as he slumped into his lawn chair, staring at the red eye of the barbecue pit as smoke drifted lazily upward toward the evening sky.

"Well?" Emmett demanded, setting his empty plate on the ground. "You leave your guests for half an hour for a phone call, it's only fair to say what it was about."

"It was just Matt Garitty," Brady told them. "He wanted to let me know that Sam Berry's signed a full confession."

"And you're upset," Emmett said.

"I guess so," Brady admitted.

Emmett nodded. "Sure. We could all dislike Cory if he'd been guilty. But it's kind of hard to hate a man for tearing up a town that did him wrong."

"Yeah," Brady said, reaching down for his ginger ale. "Anyway, Matt got a wire from the attorney general demanding the investigation be reopened."

"Well, better late than never, I guess," Emmett said, flipping his butt through the grill and into the fire. "What else did Matt have to say?"

"Cough up," Kelly seconded. "I want to know what Sam's game was."

"Well, it was complicated," Brady said. "Sam's father was a juror at Cory Wilde's trial and found out about the bribe Arden Honeycutt gave Gil Simmons, the jury foreman, to arrange a second-degree verdict. Either Simmons paid some of it to Sam's father, for his vote, or felt guilty and confessed it afterward. The two men were friends. Whether Sam's father put the bite on the judge, isn't clear, but I suspect he did, and somewhere along the way Sam found out. Sam's father was content to run a country drugstore and live a comfortable life, and Sam was pretty much like him. But he had a weakness his father didn't have: He loved horses and sporting events. He was into the bookies for a couple of hundred thousand dollars. *That* was the reason his business was folding, not the new store's coming here. By the way, he admitted to Matt that he lied to me about letting the insurance lapse. He was hoping the underwriters would pay off. But that was a hope, a possible extra dividend down the road. Right now, just as for the past few years, he's hurting for money."

"Then he was blackmailing the judge all along?" Emmett asked.

"Yes. But for power, not cash."

"What?"

"The judge had power and a stranglehold on city politics. He pretty well held the strings that made the mayor and the police chief dance. The only man he didn't control was Matt

184

Garitty, but that wasn't too important, because what was going on was in the city, which wasn't Matt's bailiwick."

"Going on?" Emmett asked, exasperated. "*What* was going on?"

"He's just being mysterious," Kelly prodded. "Forget the long face: He's loving it."

"I wish," Brady said. He shifted to face his guests. "What was going on," he explained, "was a pretty good little side business in pills."

"You mean he was selling drugs illegally?" asked Emmett.

"Afraid so, and to high school students."

"What a slimeball," Kelly muttered. "I guess the soda fountain gave him the cover, right?"

"Right," Brady continued. "I'd heard there was a drug problem; it was one of the bones of contention between Ned Triplett and Matt Garitty during the last election. Matt couldn't work on it because it was a city problem, and, of course, Ned was being handcuffed by the judge, thanks to Sam's blackmail. What nobody realized was that the burglaries in the rural parts of the parish, the ones Ned kept throwing up to Matt, were being done by a couple of the students who had to support big habits."

Kelly whistled softly. "So Sam had a habit and he was draining the kids, who had to support their *own* habits."

"You've got it," Brady said.

"And Boy Jenks's new truck didn't have anything to do with the burglaries?" Emmett asked.

"No. He'd been taken care of years before, and after that, there'd been a hands-off attitude by the judge and the old sheriff toward his minor depredations, but he'd never gotten into felonies. When he heard that Cory was applying for parole, though, I suspect he put the screws on the judge for a payoff. The truck was it."

"And Hughes was blackmailing Honeycutt, too," Kelly said. "I almost feel sorry for the judge. Everybody had their hooks into him."

"Well, my pity is a little thin at this point," the publisher replied. "Anyway, the judge wasn't being asked for money. Not by Ernie Hughes. Hughes was satisfied with his payoff as district ranger. He just wanted to be left alone. When I came asking

185

questions, he was scared, not greedy. He called the judge and asked him what to do. The judge arranged a meeting and tried to give him some money to leave town. Ernie took it, but reluctantly. At that point, he just wanted out."

"Christ." Emmett spat. "It sounds like a mess of snakes. About the only innocent person in the whole mess was the judge's wife."

"She was innocent," Brady confirmed, "but she wasn't uninvolved. You see, the bomb *had* to kill her. The judge was immaterial."

"What?" Kelly and Emmett demanded in unison.

"Sam admitted that Grace Honeycutt had caught onto his little scheme. She was the substitute assistant principal at the high school, remember? When I went there to talk to Bo Potter the first time, she was going through records, working on her own time. She'd had some students with drug problems and she was trying to check school disciplinary and health records. She finally narrowed it down to a crowd that seemed to hang out at the drugstore. She talked to one of the girls, broke her down. Then she went to Sam. She gave him an ultimatum: Come forward or she'd tell her husband. In fact, she saw him the same day I gave him the herbs to analyze."

"Wait a minute," Kelly protested. "You mean she didn't know about the judge's involvement, the cover-up?"

"Apparently not. It was strictly a deal among men. No need to bring the women into it. Isn't that how things have worked here traditionally?"

"Still do, even to crime solving," Kelly mumbled. "But if the judge was part and party to the whole business, what harm would it do for the missus to tell him what he already knew?"

Emmett snorted. "Miss Grace was a determined woman. All the judge needed was pressure from home. I can see how Sam would have been in a bad spot." He shook his head at Brady. "So he took the gamble, eh? Ignored the deadline, and Miss Grace told her husband, and told Sam she told him, right?"

"That's what happened," Brady said. "Are you sure you didn't talk to Sam first?"

"Big city reporter isn't the only person around here can think," accused Emmett.

Brady smiled. "Anyway, the judge didn't like being in the middle. He told Sam to back off, leave town, do anything. And that was when Sam acted."

"The bomb," said Kelly.

"Right. If it killed the judge and his wife, who always left home together in the mornings, so much the better. If not, the wife would be enough. Her death would demoralize the old man, even if he survived. It would be an object warning, in case he had any doubt after what happened to Jenks."

"Good God," Kelly said. "You mean Jenks was killed as an example?"

"Yep. The judge was being troublesome, so Sam arranged an accident for Jenks as a warning. It didn't matter if Jenks lived or died; Sam figured the threat would be enough to get the point across to Honeycutt. When it didn't work, he stepped up the violence."

"And the bomb in Jenks's truck?" Kelly asked breathlessly. "Tell us, oh Great One, how that led you to suspect Sam." She winked at her father.

"See if I tell you anything in private again," Brady complained.

"Hell, it ain't any secret," Emmett guffawed. "I already heard the first bomb was gunpowder. I made gunpowder in high school, when the chemistry teacher wasn't looking. Sulphur, saltpeter, and charcoal. A druggist would know how to make it easy. Or he might even take one of those cases of shotgun shells from his hardware section and empty the powder out of them. After that, it's simple to rig a clock and detonator; detonator's easy enough to come by if you burgle a construction shed or two. Hang the whole business on the exhaust and bang!"

Brady glared at Kelly but she only stared back innocently.

"'Course, next bomb would have to be a little more powerful," Emmett went on, "thus the dynamite. Probably stolen from the same place as the detonators. Some kind of electrical contact, I figure, held apart by a little piece of wood or a spring like a mousetrap, and taped under the gas tank. The vibration of the car starting would set it off sooner or later."

"And you figured all this out," Brady said sarcastically.

"Elementary, my dear Pete. Now ask me why Sam wasn't noticed when he set the bombs?"

"You'll tell us," Brady said wearily.

"If you insist. It was a case of the invisible man, like in the Sherlock Holmes story."

"Father Brown," Brady corrected.

"Whatever. Everybody sees the mailman and they ignore him. Well, Sam made home deliveries. I bet Sam took the judge something that night. Or maybe he went to the neighbors. Nobody's think twice about seeing Sam walking across a lawn. All he had to do was stoop down, slap on the tape. Same as with old man Jenks."

Brady crumpled his ginger ale can. "Sam wasn't thinking clearly. All he could think about was getting out of the immediate hole he was in. He never saw that more of the students were bound to talk and that when an investigation was done, the records would catch him up, because there were duplicates with the drug companies."

Kelly nodded slowly. "So the records he got rid of were lists of drug deliveries?"

"Orders from different companies, and prescription files that would have shown that there were no prescriptions covering the quantity that were missing. There were also accounting records that showed just how much he was making and how much he had to be taking out of the business for his gambling."

"Smart," Kelly said. "By the way, what ever happened to the herbs Penelope gave Cory Wilde for his throat? I can't believe Ned's people *and* the probation officers missed them."

"They didn't," Brady said. "Matt asked Cory about it. Cory said he wasn't crazy enough to take that junk, so he threw it all away."

"Simple and elegant, as they say." Kelly nodded.

"What about Bo Potter?" Emmett asked. "I mean, if he was in cahoots with Ned and his people, why the hell did Ned kill him?"

"Bo wasn't in cahoots with Ned," Brady explained. "Bo only claimed that to get his friends to do what he wanted. Bo bought off a couple of Ned's men so he could get Cory away from them. Actually, what Bo did, taking away Cory, enraged Ned and that's why Ned killed him, instead of shooting up in the air or for the legs."

Emmett grunted, then scratched his grizzle. "Makes sense, I guess. What I'm having trouble with, though, is the notion that Penelope Martingale knew who'd killed Alice Ann all along. I mean, I always knew the woman was crazy, but I never thought she had it in her to hide evidence . . ."

"No," Brady corrected. "She's not crazy and never has been. Until her experience with Jason Honeycutt, she was just like all the other girls her age, except maybe for being a little shier. What happened was so painful, she just convinced herself it couldn't be true."

"In other words," Kelly said, "she adjusted."

"Right. Until Cory came back and she had to confront what she'd tried to forget so many years before: the fact of Cory's innocence and Jason Honeycutt's guilt. Once more, it was almost too shattering to deal with. You can imagine the shock of having Cory Wilde turn up at her door one day, and finding she was his only chance to rent a place to live. She was genuinely disturbed the day I found her crying on the bed, but she couldn't let me know why, so she tried to pretend amnesia and pass it off as the work of some presence."

"Well," Kelly declared, "in a sense it was."

Her father snorted, went over to the cooler, and popped another beer can. "She always had a good imagination."

"What do you know?" Kelly retorted.

Emmett cackled and took a gulp of beer. "All in all, Pete, I have to say it was a workmanlike job. One I would have been proud to publish, if I *do* say so. But do you mean to say you fastened on Sam just because of some smudges on the judge's rug and that business about the fire?"

"Don't forget the leg-breaker I saw in his place. Matt sent to the state police for the pictures of known muscle and I recognized him. Why would a man like that be in a drugstore in a small town in central Louisiana? There were too many coincidences like that."

"Like his knowing how to make gunpowder?"

"That and the fact that his father was on the jury," Brady said. "That was what made me think of Sam to begin with.

Though I almost missed it, thanks to your love of obscure words."

"What do you mean?" Emmett demanded, jaw outthrust.

"I didn't pay much attention to the jury list when I read the transcript or I'd have caught it then. But I *did* read your irate editorial about a 'learned jury of gallipots and embalmers, led by a specialist in the tonsorial art.'"

"Ah, yes." Emmett nodded, leaning back. "One of my better turns of phrase."

It was his daughter's turn to snort. "Dad confuses erudition with obfuscation," she sniped.

"Hell," Emmett complained. "It never hurts folks to use a dictionary. I lost six subscriptions over that one; I remember it plain as if it was yesterday, but it was worth every one!"

"And you almost lost me." Brady smiled. "I knew the tonsorial specialist was a barber, Gil Simmons, of course. But *gallipot* as an obsolete name for a druggist? Where did you get that from, a thesaurus?"

"Every good newspaperman should have the tools of his trade," Emmett said smugly.

"God," Kelly intoned, raising her own beer. "It's a wonder I turned out normal."

Emmett eyed her skeptically. "I'd say the jury's still out on that one, young lady. I've been hoping this fellow over here would be a good influence, but I don't know how he can be any damn influence at all with you running off to that university."

"It's not forever," Kelly said.

"Well, I wouldn't blame him if he decided not to wait. There're a lot of other eligible women around here would love to have him marry them."

"Father, *shut up*."

Emmett cackled again at his direct hit. "Well, what about Cory?" he asked at last. "He's the one started all this. Is he planning to stay on, then, until. . . ?"

Brady shook his head. "I don't think so. He's burned out. After almost thirty years, there isn't much left." Brady got up slowly, his muscles protesting. "Hell of a thing. You know what he asked Matt? He wanted to know if he could go back to Angola. It's the only home he has."